HEART OF OUTCASTS

a Wolves of Autumn novel

HEART of OUTCASTS

Nico Silver

WHITE RAVEN PRESS

Copyright © 2023 by Nicole Silver.
All rights reserved. This book or any portion thereof may not be reproduced or used in any manner whatsoever without the express written permission of the publisher except for the use of brief quotations in a book review.

Second Edition, 2024.
ISBN: 978-1-998212-32-3
This book was previously published as by Nicole Silver.

White Raven Press
North Cowichan, British Columbia, Canada

Cover design and digital alterations by Nik Sylvan. No AI was used in any part of the making of this book. We support human creators.

Model stock © Neo-Stock via www.neo-stock.com
Animal stock © Lynn Bystrom via Dreamstime.com
Background stock (moon) © Dary423 via Dreamstime.com
Background stock (cottage) © Shico300 via Dreamstime.com
Fog brushes © Krist A via brusheezy.com
Title typefaces: Eva Antiqua Heavy by Spiece Graphics, and Snell Roundhand by Linotype

Content warning: This book contains material that is not suitable for all audiences. It is recommended for readers 18+. Some content that may be triggering for readers includes explicit sex, violence, and sexual violence.

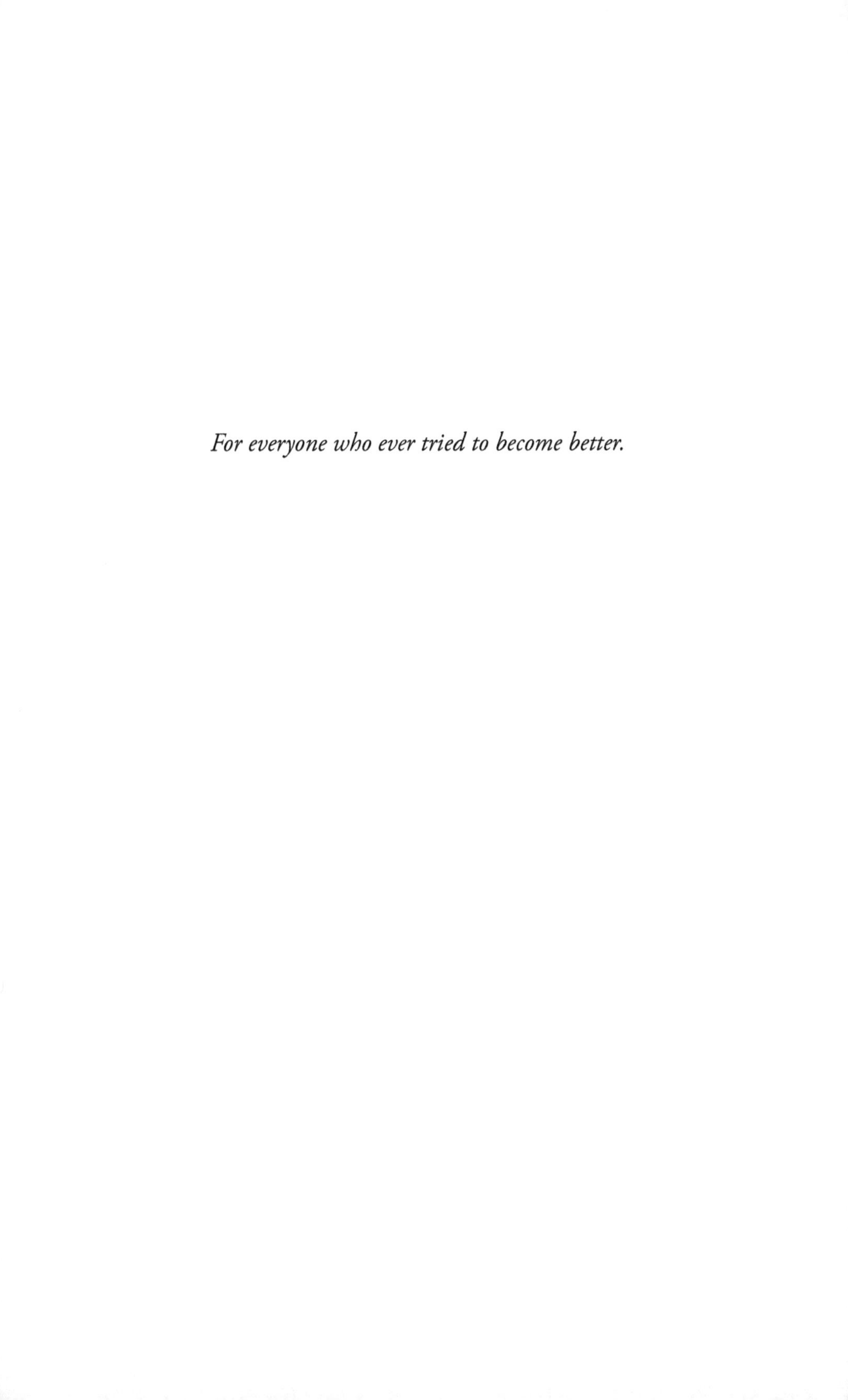

For everyone who ever tried to become better.

Chapter One

IT WAS PROBABLY A MISTAKE, to go for a run in the woods by myself.

I mean, you always hear stories of lone joggers being abducted, or mugged, or otherwise fucked up, but that's usually in urban parks, not out in the middle of nowhere. You know, where it's quiet and out of sight, but there are actually a lot of people nearby. A lot of potential victims to choose from.

And it's usually women who get attacked, not thirty-three-year-old men who look like they know where they're going. Of course, where I was really going was just *away*. And it's not like I'm totally built or anything, but I'm in decent enough shape I usually get left alone. As long as I don't go running somewhere full of frat boys while looking too gay.

And since I seem to have spent my whole life running away, going for a nice long sprint in the woods along the river seemed like a good idea at the time, when everything else in my life was going to shit.

Maybe I should have seen it coming, should have paid more attention when my path took me past a clearing overlooking the river, littered with empty beer cans. Maybe I should have realized something wasn't right when the birds stopped singing and I heard a growl. But there aren't any wolves left in Autumn County, are there?

But no, I ignored it all, just listened to my own pounding feet, my own heavy breaths – getting tired now, time to turn back soon – and tried to forget I have no job to go back to, and probably won't have an apartment much longer, either.

And finally I can't ignore it anymore, because it hits me from behind like a freight train, if trains growl and sweat and have breath that smells like old meat and cheap beer. There's a sharp, searing pain as my ankle twists under me and I fall. And more pain as teeth sink into my neck and claws slash across my back.

I hit the ground yelling, find a rock with one hand, and manage to twist around, to hit back. But my eyes are full of dirt and leaf litter and all I know is that I hit something, something that bleeds all over me and then the weight is gone but I'm still falling. Right into the black inside my head.

"Hey, kid." The voice is deep and smoky, very male, with an undertone I recognize from my own voice, sometimes: self-mocking.

I open my eyes and immediately close them again. The light is too bright, and my head is pounding. Everything hurts, and there's a blank in my memory that I don't want to look at too closely.

"Kid," the voice says again, and now I feel a hand on my shoulder, shaking me gently.

"Go away," I say.

There's a laugh. "Not gonna happen until you sit up and convince me you're okay."

I crack my eyes open again, and it's not bright out at all. In fact, it's not even daylight. There's a big moon overhead, visible between the thick tree branches. Just past full.

And there's a guy crouched next to me, bending over me. A naked guy.

"What the fuck?" I scramble backwards until a tree stops me from going farther.

"Yeah, sorry," he says. "My clothes are about six miles away and you looked hurt."

"Your clothes…" I stop, confused. "What… what happened?" And I don't mean to his clothes. I look at my hands. They're dirty. Filthy, actually, but just normal, human hands. Weren't they…? A flash of memory or hallucination and I see my hands, my fingers curling into claws, my vision going grey, the moon singing to me.

"I was hoping you could tell me," the guy says. He doesn't seem to be the least bit concerned by the fact that he's crouching in front of me completely naked. Like maybe he walks around naked all the time. Is he a nudist?

"I'm Bjarni," he says – like *Barney* but with an extra "y" sound after the "b" that doesn't quite work in English, and pronounced with an accent I can't figure out. "My brother's pack leader in the Bottomlands and the River District."

"He's what?"

He cocks his head at me, sending his dark blond hair sliding across his shoulders. His eyes are pale blue and his skin almost glows in the moonlight. He's the kind of good-looking guy I'd have watched secretly in a bar, but never approached. Too aware of his own good looks. And probably straight anyway.

"You *do* know you're a werewolf?" he says, and I guess I look confused or freaked out, but really I think he's a crazy person, probably escaped from an asylum, running around naked in the woods and howling at the moon. "You *don't* know you're a werewolf," he says. "Fucking hell."

"What do you want?" I push myself more upright, sit against the tree, and glance around for a way out. And I notice my shoes are gone and my bare feet are covered in blood. Dried blood and old cuts, pink and sore, but nearly healed.

I can't breathe right. Another memory or hallucination. Running. But then I'm always running. No shoes and the forest floor feels amazing on my bare feet, even when it hurts. The moon sings to me and I howl back at her. I can't catch my breath.

"Hey, kid. It's okay. You're safe now. Breathe." And the man – Bjarni – is next to me, arm around my shoulders, and how did he move without me seeing? I try not to flinch away, but he must notice my slight movement because he lets go, and instead pushes my head between my drawn-up knees. "Breathe. You're okay."

"What the fuck?" I gasp out.

"Breathe," he says again and there's something almost hypnotic about his voice, something that makes me listen, makes me relax.

When the panic subsides and I can feel air moving in and out of my lungs the way it should, I sit up.

He moves a few steps away and sits down right in a patch of moonlight. He's not super tall, definitely taller than me but then I'm short for a guy at only five seven. But he's totally built. Like every muscle looks sculpted, and it looks like he actually uses them, not like they're just there for show. His torso is sprinkled with freckles, concentrated where the sun would hit him most, and thin pale scars crisscross him like a map. His forearms are covered in tattoos, like some kind of Viking designs, and there are runes across his knuckles. He's got dark blond hair across his chest, thicker down his belly and –

I drag my eyes away from where I was about to look and glance back at his face to find amusement there. He smiles a grin with too many teeth, and fear clutches at my belly. Except the smile creates two dimples, one on each side of his mouth.

"You don't look like a werewolf," I say, because it's the first thing that comes out of my stupid mouth. Because of course he's not a fucking werewolf. I'm not in a horror movie, no matter how shitty I feel.

He laughs. "What does a werewolf look like?"

I shrug and look away, glance down at the holes in the knees of my track pants. I don't remember there being holes. My t-shirt looks even worse, slashed and bloodstained, covered in dirt and who knows what else.

"What the fuck happened to me?" I whisper.

"If I had to guess," Bjarni says. "You went for a run, and someone jumped you. How long have you been out here?"

"I –" I look at my hands, at my wrist. My smartwatch is still there, at least, but it won't turn on when I tap the face. The battery is dead.

"It's Saturday," he says. "When did you go running?"

I think back, try to push past the yawning black that threatens to pull me back in again, into a confusion of running, of hot meat-and-beer breath, of sudden pain. Then I look at him. "It was Wednesday," I say. "Wednesday afternoon."

"Full moon day one," he says. "I think someone decided they wanted to make a new wolf. Thorstein's not going to be fucking happy."

I shake my head. "I was out here three days?" I say. "How? Why don't I remember?"

Bjarni has gotten to his feet and is pacing. He doesn't seem to notice he's barefoot. Or naked. I wonder how it feels to be so confident with your own body. And *I* notice. Or try not to. He's exactly the kind of guy I'd fantasize about, but never go out with. As if a guy that looked like him would even want to go out with me. As if a guy like me would ever have a chance.

"Fuck," he says. Then he turns back to me. "What's your name?"

"I –" It takes me a moment to get my thoughts straight again. "I don't even know you, and you're running around naked in the woods pretending werewolves exist and –"

As I talk, he rolls his eyes, and then suddenly he's *changing.* Like his joints creak and snap and bend wrong and I can only stare as he drops to all fours, sprouts extra hair and a tail, his hands and feet rearrange themselves into paws tipped in dark claws, and his face pushes out into a muzzle full of teeth.

And I fight to keep control of my bladder.

"Let's try this again," he says, words slurring around too many teeth. "My name is Bjarni Thorvaldson, and I'm a werewolf for really, really real. What's your name?"

And the black rushes in to hide the monsters again.

This time I wake up with my head in his lap, and the moon is gone but I don't think we're in the same place. He's human again.

"You're heavier than you look," he says.

I scramble to sit up, trying not to think about the way he smells: musky, warm, wild, very very male. I wish I had something more concealing than track pants on. I'm terrified and turned on at the same time.

He doesn't move, he just watches me with that mocking half-smile on his too-perfect face.

"Where did you park?" he says.

"What?"

"I assume you didn't run all the way from Great Valley, or Riverbend, or wherever you came from."

"Great Valley," I say, without thinking. I clamp my mouth shut.

"Look," he says. "This is all weird and fucked up and your sense of reality has just been seriously shaken. I get that. And I'm sorry. If I could send you back in time to before some shit-stain attacked you, I would."

I stare at him for as long as I can face his intense blue eyes – which turns out to be not very long – then I look down at my hands.

"Justin," I say.

"Come again?"

"My name is Justin. Justin Leyendecker." I look up at him again, and the mocking expression is gone. He looks – almost – kind.

"I came to run out here because… because getting lost in the woods seemed better than facing the complete shit show I've made of my life."

"Getting lost? Were you hoping to die of exposure?" I can't read his voice, but he sounds almost like the idea of just giving up on life isn't entirely foreign.

I shrug. "I don't think I was really thinking at all." I look away again, and realize how dark it is, and how well I can still see.

"I parked by the salmon hatchery," I say.

"Fuck," he says. "There weren't any cars there but mine this afternoon."

I laugh, and it sounds lost and broken, even to my own ears. "So they towed my car," I say. "It was a piece of shit anyway. I'm surprised it stayed running long enough to get me there."

He frowns at me. "You got a place to stay if I drive you back to Great Valley?"

I stare at him. "You don't even have clothes on."

He smirks. "My clothes are in my car. Which is parked by the hatchery, where your car is not. Do you have anywhere to stay?"

I look back at my hands, pick at a loose thread hanging from the shredded knee of my pants. I shake my head. "I imagine my landlord has changed the locks on my apartment by now. He really wants his back rent."

"No family?"

"None that I want anything to do with."

"I get that," he says, and I snap my gaze back up.

"I thought your brother was the, what? Alpha of your pack?"

He snickers. "This isn't a romance novel, sweetheart. He's just the pack leader."

"So *you* have family."

"Some. The worst ones are dead."

"Lucky," I say and he laughs again, but this time it's sharp like broken glass.

"Luck had nothing to do with it," he says, and I shiver at the coldness in his voice.

"Why do you even care?" I say.

"Why do I care about what?" He gets up and starts to walk, and there's not much else I can do but follow him. And try not to stare at the stylized bull tattoo on his back. Or his spectacular naked ass.

"What happens to me?" I say.

He stops and turns and suddenly he's too close, so close I can feel his body heat, the tickle of his breath.

He touches one of the rips in my t-shirt, pushes his finger through until it meets my skin, and I flinch like he's cut me.

"Somebody hurt you," he says. "Somebody made you into a werewolf without asking you, without telling you what it would mean." He stares into my eyes and his are angry, but not at me.

Then as suddenly as he stopped, he's walking again. "I might only be our pack leader's disgraced younger brother, but that shit is *not* okay."

I scramble to catch up, my bare feet seeming to find every broken branch and stone on the forest floor.

"Why can't I remember?" I say. I mean, I really want to keep saying he's crazy and I'm not a werewolf, but I did see him change shape. Unless *I'm* crazy, which would also explain why I hit black whenever I try to think about what happened yesterday, or the day before. Or any time between Wednesday afternoon and an hour ago.

"It's pretty normal," he says. "You'll spend your first few full moons, maybe as long as a year's worth, not remembering much after." He glances back at me. "You'll start to remember more once you develop the beginnings of your wolf shape."

"But I remember… I mean, it's just flashes, but I had claws. Paws. I was running, I was a wolf." I have to trot to catch up again, but the effort helps push back the blackness lurking at the edges of my vision when I think about being a wolf. I'm relieved when we come out of the woods onto a path.

He glances at me again, grins. "Those early months you'll be absolutely convinced you're a full-on wolf," he says. "When you're not busy not forgetting everything."

"So I didn't have claws?"

"Not unless you're a fucking prodigy."

"But you —"

He stops again and I almost walk into him. He steadies me with a hand on each shoulder. "I'm old," he says, then flashes that toothy smile. "Not old in werewolf terms, not really, but I've been a werewolf for eighty-two years, so I've had plenty of time to develop my wolf shape."

"Eighty-two isn't old?" I say. I resist the urge to look him up and down. "You're not that old."

He drops his hands from my shoulders and resumes walking. "I will turn exactly one hundred years old in October," he says. "I've been a werewolf since I was eighteen." He slants a look at me from the corners of his eyes. "Once we become wolves, we also age more slowly."

"So in human terms?"

"Are you sure you want to know all this shit at once? It's a lot to take in."

"How old are you in human terms?" I don't even know why I want to know so badly. It's not like he'd ever go on a date with me.

He shrugs. "Thirty-five. Forty. Something like that. It's not an exact correlation."

"Fuck," I say.

He snorts. We come out of the trees into the parking lot, and sure enough, my car is gone. I mean, I already knew it would be, but actually seeing the parking lot without my shitty little Hyundai in it makes it all more real somehow.

I don't realize I'm falling until Bjarni catches me. He holds me upright, arms strong around me, until I feel steady again.

"When was the last time you ate?" he says, walking me over to lean on the very shiny black Mitsubishi Evo that's the only vehicle in the lot. He fishes under the bumper, comes up with a key fob, then opens the door and starts to put on the clothes waiting on the passenger seat.

I feel oddly sad to see him cover all that beautiful skin and muscle. But wearing clothes, it turns out, doesn't make him any less fine to look at, because his jeans and t-shirt are snug and conform to the shape of his body.

It takes me a while to remember he's asked me a question. "I don't know."

"Here," he says, handing me a granola bar and a bottle of water. "Drink first, then eat. Digesting takes fluids and you don't need to be any more dehydrated than you already are."

Vaguely, I wonder if that's why I didn't piss myself in fear when he turned into a werewolf. Because I didn't have any piss left in me.

He stares at me, one eyebrow raised, until I drink half the bottle of car-warm water and start to peel open the granola bar. Then he points at the passenger door.

"Get in."

"Where are you taking me?" I say, once I'm settled, seat belt strapped across me. And I wonder why I didn't think to ask *before* I got into a stranger's car.

He starts the car, and it gives a well-tuned rumble. He looks over at me. "You really have no one to stay with?"

I shake my head.

He sighs. "Well, Thorstein will want to talk to you, anyway. About whoever attacked you."

"I don't remember who attacked me." I feel cold suddenly, light-headed, and the blackness gathers at the edge of my vision.

And then Bjarni's hand is on the back of my neck, warm and real, and the black fades away.

"It's okay," he says. "You don't have to remember. You just have to tell my brother whatever you can."

I nod. "Is he as scary as you?" I don't know why I say it; it just comes out. I sound like a child, and I definitely don't want to sound like a child in front of Bjarni.

He snorts. "Am I scary?"

I look at the empty granola bar wrapper in my hand so I don't have to look at him. He moves his hand away and my neck feels suddenly cold. Then he puts the car in gear and we're pulling out of the lot.

"A bit," I say. *A lot,* I think.

He bares his teeth at me in a mock snarl and it startles a laugh out of me. "That's better," he says. "And no, Thorstein isn't scary. Most of the time." He shifts gears smoothly and I do *not* look at the muscles sliding across his forearm. "He's a fucking giant, but he's also a marshmallow."

I look back at his face.

"I mean, he *can* be scary," he says. "But mostly he's just too fucking *nice.*"

Chapter Two

WE PULL UP AT A DARK green house, two-story and well-kept. It's surrounded by trees on three sides, hiding most of the farmland that's presumably around it from view. There's a fenced-in meadow in front, complete with grazing goats. It's very idyllic and peaceful in the pinkish light of very early morning.

"I thought you might want to get cleaned up before you meet my brother," Bjarni says. "And anyway, he's probably still sleeping off a late night with his gorgeous girlfriend."

"You don't seem like a farmer," I say.

"More than I seem like a werewolf?" he replies, flashing a smile at me again. He seems to do that a lot, and I can't tell if the grins are genuine or just habit. Or mocking – of me or of himself.

But I smile back anyway. "Fair point," I say. "So this is your brother's house?" I point at the placidly grazing animals. "Very rural, with the goats and all."

He looks at the goats, then back at me. "No, this is my house. And those aren't goats, they're sheep."

I look at the goats. Sheep. They have short brown fur that shades into cream on some of them, and black fur on their bellies. "You're shitting me," I say. "Sheep have wool."

He shakes his head. "Barbados sheep don't have wool. You really are a city boy, aren't you?"

"What are they for, if they don't have wool?"

"Mutton," he says, and I must look blank, because he adds, "Meat."

"Oh." At least I learned something new, even if it made me look stupid.

"Come on." He goes up the steps and into the house, with no need to pause and unlock the door. I guess that's a country thing, not locking your house. Or maybe it's a werewolf thing. Who needs locks when you can rip a burglar's throat out with your teeth?

I follow, reluctantly. I mean, so far he's done nothing but help me, but he still makes me deeply nervous.

"I'm not a boy," I say, as I step inside. Another of those stupid childish things that apparently insist on coming out of my mouth around him.

"Okay," he says, leading me into the house and up a flight of stairs.

"I mean, I'm thirty-three."

"I was speaking… rhetorically? Metaphorically? Whatever. 'City man' doesn't have the same ring." He pauses at the top of the stairs, waiting for me to catch up. "Besides, I've got enough years on you, you might as well be a boy."

"Fine," I say.

"You're kind of prickly, you know?" he says.

"You're kind of an asshole, you know?" I say back, and instantly regret it.

"Not sure I deserved that," he says. "Though you're not wrong."

"Wait, what?"

"I'm an asshole. Been one my whole life, according to my brothers. And pretty much every woman I've ever slept with. You figured me out." I notice he says "slept with" and not "dated," and wonder if that's why they all think of him that way. But he doesn't sound angry, or even annoyed. The tone of self-mockery, though, has shifted from an undertone to a distinct overtone.

"I didn't mean…" But what did I mean? "I'm a total fuck-up," I say. "And apparently so is my mouth."

He slaps my shoulder, but not hard. "You've had a shit couple of days," he says. "Don't worry about it."

He leads me down the hall and points into one of the rooms. "Towels are in that cupboard," he says. "Soap and shampoo on the shelf by the tub. Plumbing's a bit finicky, but once you get the right temperature it'll stay." He gestures at each thing as he mentions it. "I'll see if I can find you something to wear that won't be too huge on you, until we can get your clothes washed. And mended."

I realize I'm staring at him and make myself peer into the bathroom instead. It looks like it was remodeled from a room that's really too big for its new function, and everything is white, like whoever built it figured they'd decide later how to decorate, and then never got around to it.

"Go on," he says. Then, just as I'm passing him to go into the room, he stops me with a hand on my shoulder. "Hang on a sec," he says, and he steps closer, too close, but I can't make myself tell him to back off.

And he bends still closer, his nose so near to my neck and the spot where the werewolf bit me I swear I can feel him even though he's not actually touching me. He inhales, deep.

"What the fuck?" I say, but I'm still afraid to move.

He shifts his hand to my other shoulder. "Just hold still. I'm trying to see if your attacker left any scent on you before you scrub away any evidence."

"You what?" I have to clench all my muscles to keep from trembling, to keep from running into the bathroom and slamming the door. And I don't know if it's because Bjarni is so close, or because memories of my attacker are lurking in the darkness on the edges of my vision.

His face presses between my shoulder blades as he draws in a deep breath. He bends and moves lower, his nose following the line of my spine until he reaches the small of my back.

"He attacked you from behind?" he asks.

"Yeah," I say, and I can't stop the trembling anymore.

"Hey," he says, straightening up and rubbing my back with one hand. "You're safe now."

"Did you… did you smell anything?"

"No, but give me your shirt. Thorstein's got a better nose than me."

"What?"

"Your shirt, Justin." He makes an exasperated noise. "Fine, just don't wash your clothes in the shower or anything weird."

"Why would I do that?" I say.

He chuckles. "People do weird shit when they're scared. Now get cleaned up. Lock the door if it makes you feel better. I'll find some clothes for you and leave them there." He points to a bookcase full of paperbacks just outside the bathroom door. "When you're done, you can eat while we wait for Thorstein."

I do lock the door, though I'm pretty sure he could break it down easily enough if he wanted to, and not even exert much effort. And I shower as fast as I can, feeling useless and vulnerable and weak. When I'm as clean as I'm going to get without a stiff scrub brush and a week-long soak, I wrap a towel around my waist and look at my face in the mirror. And wish I hadn't.

I forgot I chopped my hair brutally short. I'd thought it would make me look tougher, maybe make my family think I looked not-gay enough that they'd stop trying to get me to re-join their church. Over a decade of them trying different tactics was more than enough. But it hadn't worked. It hadn't stopped them from sending me guilt-trip letters and fucking missionaries to whatever shit job I had. And it didn't make me look tough, it just made me look demented.

There are dark circles like bruises under my eyes, and I look half-starved. Like I haven't eaten a proper meal in years. And I look scared.

If I could just get rid of that haunted look, of the fear that makes my eyes too wide, maybe I'd look less… less like a target.

There's almost a week's worth of stubble on my face, and while I'm not a hairy enough guy that it's threatening to become a beard, it still looks unkempt. I barely recognize my own face.

When I open the door to see if Bjarni's found anything I can wear, he's there, leaning in a doorway across the hall.

"Better?" he says.

I rub my jaw. "I was hoping I could shave," I say.

"Can you use a straight razor?" he says, pushing away from the door.

I shake my head.

"That's all I have," he says. "Sorry."

"You actually shave with a straight razor?" I pick up the clothes – jeans and a t-shirt, no socks or underwear – and hold them against my belly.

He shrugs. "I learned to shave a very long time ago. Never saw any reason to switch to a safety razor." He frowns at me, studying my scruffy face. "I'll do it for you."

"You'll do what?" I say, trying and failing to meet his eyes.

"I'll shave you," he says. "Unless you're still afraid of me."

"I'm not," I say, but I am, and I think he knows it. I don't *want* to be and maybe if I pretend not to be, I'll find some courage somewhere.

"Come on," he says, steering me into the bathroom with a hand on my shoulder. I try very hard not to flinch away from his touch.

"Stand here." He moves me in front in the mirror with his hands on my hips and puts the plug in the sink to fill it with hot water. Then he uses a brush and a dish of soap that smells faintly of cedar to work up a lather, which he paints thickly on my face.

"Wouldn't this be easier if I was facing you?" I say, fighting to keep my voice even and steady.

"I shave myself in the mirror," he says. "I'm not sure I can do it the other way around. Now hold still and only move when I tell you to, unless you want me to shave off something you'd prefer to keep."

He stands behind me, reaches around my neck, and flicks open a deadly-looking blade.

I have to remind myself to breathe, to not cower in fear, to stand very very still. Especially when he takes my chin in one hand and tilts my head back, exposing my throat.

The razor across my skin feels smooth, hardly catching at all on my bristles. He draws it slowly over my neck, accumulating foam and stubble on the blade, which he rinses off in the hot water. Each stroke of the razor makes me both more and less afraid, and I want to relax against him. His chest is pressed against my back, and I feel the pull and flex of every muscle as he holds my skin taut with one hand, and wields the razor in the other, as he tilts my head this way and that. It's one of the most intimate, and most terrifying, things another person has ever done to me.

His breath is hot in my ear, his body heat radiating against my back, and I'm glad I have a bundle of clothes to hold in front of me, because I can feel my erection pressing hard against the towel.

"There," he says, giving the blade one final rinse and setting it, open, on a shelf above the sink.

I start to move away, needing desperately to escape his nearness before I say or do something stupid.

"Hang on," he says. "This is best part." And he moves me back into place, hands briefly resting on my hips, two fingers accidentally brushing the bare skin above the edge of the towel.

He runs a facecloth under the tap, water so hot steam rises off it. Then he wrings it out, opens it up, and presses it to my face. The heat is shocking at first, but then it feels wonderful. I can't contain the small moan that escapes from my throat. I can't help but tilt my head back to rest on his shoulder.

"Feels good, doesn't it?" he says. He rinses the cloth again, and presses it to my neck, and for just a brief moment I can relax and pretend I'm cared for.

I want to lean my whole body back against him, to get closer to his body heat, to feel his hard muscles, but instead I hold very still until he takes the cloth away and turns me to face him.

My eyes find his for an instant, but then I have to look away. He wipes the remnants of shaving cream off my face and neck, and then steps back. I feel flushed, head to toe, and then I feel cold.

"Get dressed and come downstairs," he says. "Thorstein will be here soon, but I'll see if I can find you something to eat before he gets here." He turns to go, to leave me alone again. "You like coffee?" he asks as he heads for the stairs.

"I prefer tea," I say.

He frowns. "Don't think I have any."

"That's okay. Water's fine." Then he's gone and there's nothing to do but get dressed. And follow him. Again.

His kitchen is a lot like his bathroom, utilitarian and without much in the way of decor. Like he doesn't spend a lot of time here.

The rising sun is streaming in the window, turning his hair gold, and making his pale eyes seem to glow. I hate to think what it's doing to my ordinary mousy brown hair and hazel eyes. Nothing good, anyway.

"I don't have much food," he says, turning from the counter. "I usually eat at the farmhouse. I hope peanut butter toast is enough to get you through till breakfast."

"That's fine," I say, and almost jump when there's a knock at the door and soft footsteps in the hall.

"Hey Big Bear," Bjarni calls out and a deep male voice – even deeper and smokier than Bjarni's, which I wouldn't have thought possible – answers.

"Morning, Little Bear."

The quietness of the footsteps doesn't prepare me for the man who walks into the room, though maybe the deepness of the voice should have. He's huge, like the tallest guy I've ever seen, and heavy with muscle. Like Bjarni's build but scaled up a foot. His hair is so pale the morning sun turns it to silver and his eyes are even paler than Bjarni's, but with a touch of green where his brother's are like ice. There are braids in his long hair, and he's got a short beard that matches its pale color.

He's the most intimidating person I've ever been up close to, and he makes all five-foot-seven of me feel tiny.

He holds out a hand. "I'm Thorstein," he says.

"Justin," I say, feeling very very small as I hold out my own hand. He doesn't shake; instead, he grips my forearm briefly before letting go.

"How're you feeling?" he asks, and I get the impression that he actually cares.

"I'm okay," I say, and a smile curves his lips. Until that exact moment, I'd have said he didn't look much like his brother, except maybe that they both wear their hair long, but the smile reveals a dimple, and then I can see the family resemblance.

"You can't lie to me, son," he says, and his voice is as kind as his smile. "I'm a werewolf."

Bjarni points to a chair and puts a plate of toast and a steaming mug in front of it, so I sit down. Thorstein sits opposite me.

He tilts his head to one side slightly, like changing the angle he's looking at me from will give him more information.

"You were attacked in the woods?" he says, and it's almost not a question. "Near the hatchery?"

"I found him about six miles upriver," Bjarni says.

"I didn't ask you," Thorstein says, but there's no real reprimand in his voice.

"Hot cider or coffee? Oh, esteemed Alpha," Bjarni says.

Thorstein raises an eyebrow at him. "You been reading Raine's paranormal romance books?" he says. "Alpha." He snorts.

"Oh, it's *Raine's* books now, is it?" There's a weird sort of tension between them, like they aren't used to brotherly banter, which makes no sense, because there's also a closeness that I feel a sudden stab of envy over.

"I'll have cider, if it's the batch you made last fall." Thorstein turns back to me. He doesn't repeat his question, he just waits.

"I went for a run on Wednesday," I say, taking a sip from the mug in front of me. Hot apples, cinnamon, and alcohol. I take a bigger sip, then reluctantly put it down.

"Someone… something jumped me from behind. Knocked me down. He –" I feel the darkness gather. Then Bjarni's hands are on my shoulders, and though I want to push them away, his touch chases the blackness off, and it fades. "He bit me." I touch my neck where I felt the teeth. There's a healed pink wound that I could just see in the mirror. I'll probably have the scar for the rest of my life. "Clawed up my back, my chest."

"Do you think he was trying to kill you?" Thorstein says.

I shake my head. "It felt like it at the time, but… I don't know. I can't remember clearly."

"What happened next?" His voice is soft, like how people talk to frightened animals, and I find myself trusting him.

I rub at the spot the werewolf bit me again and Thorstein's eyes follow the movement.

"Every werewolf bears the scars of their making," he says, voice even softer. "It's a badge of honor. We wear our scars with pride."

I nod, but I don't feel honored or proud. I feel stupid and weak. I take a deep breath, then another. "I couldn't see. When I fell, I got dirt and crap in my eyes. But I found a rock. I guess I hit him hard enough he left me alone."

"Did he bleed on you?"

"Yeah."

"*That* was why he left you alone," he says, and when he sees the slight shake of my head, he adds, "He cut you, weakened you, spilled his own blood on you. He wasn't trying to kill you, he was trying to make you into a werewolf. To what purpose, I can't say." Then he goes quiet.

Bjarni reaches over my shoulder to point at the toast. "Eat, sweetheart," he says, and I can't tell if the word is meant to be kind or mocking. I take a bite, and I'm suddenly ravenous and can't shovel it down fast enough.

"Go easy," says Bjarni. "If you haven't eaten properly in a while, you'll get sick if you eat too fast." I try to slow down, to chew each bite. I had forgotten how good peanut butter is.

Thorstein looks over my head at his brother. "You didn't smell anything on him?"

"Nothing. I think whoever did it was male, but I couldn't tell who."

"Fuck." But the way Thorstein says it, it's less like a swear and more like a simple statement.

"His clothes are upstairs in the bathroom," Bjarni says. "If you want to try."

I finish the last of my toast and gulp down my cider. Thorstein sips at his more slowly.

"Colleen still has some of Magne's old things, I think," he says suddenly, looking back up at Bjarni. "See if you can find him some clothes that fit him better. And some shoes."

"Magne's bigger than *I* am," Bjarni says.

"He wasn't when he was seventeen."

Bjarni chuckles. "True. He was tall, but still skinny."

Thorstein keeps looking at him but doesn't say anything else.

"Oh, you mean now?" Bjarni smirks. "I can take the hint." He pats my shoulder and I see Thorstein notice how I try to hide my flinch. "Don't let him bully you," Bjarni says, then grins. "I'll come back and get you when breakfast is ready."

Thorstein watches me as Bjarni leaves, not speaking. I look at my hands, out the window, at my empty plate. Anywhere but at him.

"How are you really?" he finally asks. "Is Bjarni treating you okay?"

I glance up at him, then back out the window.

"I think I'm going nuts," I say.

"I grew up with a werewolf for a father," he says. "So I can't know what it's like to suddenly find out they exist." He pauses. "But I *do* know what it's like to suddenly learn there are creatures, beings, in the world that you never dreamed could be real."

"Do you like being a werewolf?" I say.

"Very much," he answers. "For a long time, it was the only really good thing in my life."

"I don't have much good in my life," I say. "And I can't blame you if you don't want me in your pack."

"Why wouldn't I want you in my pack?" he says. His voice is so fucking gentle it makes me want to cry. I don't deserve such gentleness.

"Because I'm a fuck up," I say. No point in hiding; I'm going to be rejected, so I want to get it over with as quickly as possible. "I lost my job, got evicted from my apartment. My car was towed, my credit card is maxed out, and my bank account is overdrawn. And I lost all my ID when my car was towed, anyway."

He's quiet a moment, and then he says, "Why were you running alone in the woods?"

"Because I *am* alone. I have nothing, and no one. I've fucked up every relationship I've ever had, driven off every friend. My parents would love for me to go home, but they'd just spend every second they speak to me telling me to repent, or confess my sins, or I'll go to hell."

"You don't believe as they do?"

"They think my existence is a sin."

"Why?"

I look him in the eyes then, daring to challenge him, maybe hoping he'll hit me or walk away in disgust. I'm afraid, but it doesn't matter; I have nothing left to lose. "Because," I say, "I had the audacity to be born gay."

He doesn't react when I say it. Doesn't even blink. "My dad was extremely homophobic, too," he says.

"But you're not gay, so you had nothing to worry about." I can't keep the bitterness and envy out of my voice.

"No," he says. "I'm not gay. I only had to watch as he drove away, persecuted, even killed members of my family for what he called sexual deviance. And he was shitty to me for plenty of other sins."

"Is that what you're going to do to me? Persecute me? Kill me?" I don't even care to run away. Not anymore.

"I am not my father." His voice doesn't change in volume, but the anger in it gives his words a sharp, deadly edge. I look at his eyes and he's not angry at me. He's angry at his father. Angry on my behalf. "You're welcome here, Justin. And you can stay with us on the farm as long as you need to."

"I don't want charity," I say, my voice sulky. I wish I could unsay the words, or at least say them in a less childish way.

"So, I'll put you to work. There's always work on a farm, and I pay my employees a living wage."

I don't know what to say then, so I stare at my hands some more. Then I say, "I was running away."

"Running from what?"

"From my problems. From my parents, from the mess I made of my life." I feel tears threatening and I force them away. I don't want to cry because I know he'll be kind, and then I won't be able to stop.

He reaches across the table and takes my wrist, making my hand look tiny next to his. He turns my arm over. There are scars on the insides of my arms that aren't from being attacked by a werewolf.

"That's how you coped?" he says. "You cut yourself?" He rubs his thumb along one especially long, deep scar.

"I almost escaped that time," I say. I can hear the self-deprecation in my own voice. I hate it, but I can't stop it.

"However bad you fucked up your life," he says. "You can start over. You're a member of this pack now, this family, and we help each other." He lets go of my wrist and I tuck both arms beneath the table.

"I'm not your problem," I say.

He smiles. "I'm your pack leader, which means you *are* my problem. Let me help you."

Then he bites his lip, looks down at his own hands, and seems so uncertain I wonder what could possibly shake a man so solid. He seems to come to a decision.

He pushes both sleeves of his long-sleeved t-shirt up to his elbows, then lays both arms on the table in front of him, palms up.

Deep, jagged scars run up the insides of both his forearms, like someone tried to claw them to the bone, over and over. I can't stop staring. I almost reach out and touch them, but I don't quite dare.

"I know what it's like," he says, "To feel like you have no way out. To feel like the world would be better off without you in it." He makes fists of his hands, and muscles stand out on his arms, and the scars go white, jagged and ugly, but also strangely beautiful.

He looks up and meets my eyes. "It got better for me," he says. "And if you let us help you, it can get better for you, too."

Chapter Three

AT BREAKFAST, I MEET more of Bjarni's family. His stepmother Colleen and his sister Hilde live in a huge white farmhouse not far from Bjarni's and, like his house, it has trees on three sides and a fenced paddock in front, only this time there are horses. Huge blond draft horses like the equine equivalent of Thorstein. The trees behind the house are much farther back, and when Bjarni leads me into the kitchen at the rear of the house, I find out it's because there's a huge garden instead of a back yard.

About all I recognize are tomatoes and lettuce, but there are rows and rows of other plants, all healthy and flourishing. A few tiny chickens peck and scratch among the plants.

"Why are your chickens so small?" I blurt out without thinking.

"I'm going to guess you don't get out much." Bjarni's little sister looks about the same age as me, but if she's a werewolf, too, then who knows how old she is? She looks a lot like a female version of her brother, but much prettier and slim where he's bulky.

"Hilde," her mother says – and she really doesn't look old enough to be her mother, so I'm going to say definitely a werewolf. "They're bantams," she says, standing at the back porch door next to me and looking out. "Bantams are much smaller than most of the chickens you might have seen on television."

"We have this thing called the internet now," says Bjarni, and she swats him with a dishtowel.

"I hope you're hungry," Hilde says. "Mom always cooks enough for six families." She steals a piece of bacon out of a pan on the stove and adds, "It's one of the reasons I still live at home. I hate cooking."

"The other reason is she can't decide which of the seventeen guys she's dating she actually wants to marry."

Now it's Hilde's turn to swat Bjarni, only she uses a spatula from the bacon pan and it connects with his shoulder with a slap that sounds like it stings.

He only grins his toothy smile at her.

"There are only three, and all of them have asked. I'm just not marrying anyone without a symbiont bond."

"What's that?" I say. "A symbiont bond?"

"Well, when two werewolves really, really love each other," Bjarni starts, and Hilde hits him with the spatula again.

"When werewolves fall in love," she says. "If it has the potential to be real and life-long, their symbionts can form a bond. It means they'll always be in love, unless one of them dies." I must look confused, because she adds, "The symbiont is what lives in your bloodstream and makes you a werewolf. You get turned into a wolf by having existing werewolves transfer their symbiont by bleeding on you after you've nearly died." Then she looks sidelong at her brother. "And a symbiont bond is something Bjarni will never experience."

His sticks his tongue out at her. "Just put them out of their misery," he says.

"You should talk," Hilde says. "You never sleep with the same woman twice, let alone go on an actual date."

"Much better that way," Bjarni says. "No decisions required."

"Asshole," mutters Hilde.

"Back atcha," says Bjarni.

"Sit down or I'll call your..." Colleen suddenly trails off, her face going slack. She shakes her head sharply. "I'll call your brother in to sort you out." Was that sorrow on her face? How long ago did Bjarni say his father died? Or *did* he say?

"We're very casual around here, Justin," Colleen says, briskly now, once everyone is seated. "Just reach for whatever you want and help yourself."

The first thing Bjarni reaches for is an enormous teapot in the center of the table. He fills a mug and sets it next to my plate. "You need cream or sugar?" he asks, and I stare at him. "You said you liked tea, right?" There's something a tiny bit uncertain in his voice.

"Oh," I say. "Yeah, thanks. No cream or sugar."

I feel completely out of place, sitting at this table of people talking and teasing each other, passing food, and genuinely enjoying each other's company. But I've sat through enough meals with my own dysfunctional family to pick up on the tension underlying everything like a live electrical wire.

There's something here I'm not understanding, some strangeness, an uneasiness. Like all this family love has been an act they put on and while it's real it's also… rehearsed, maybe? Like I don't think they're pretending to like each other, it's just like they keep expecting someone to suddenly *observe* them, so they're all making sure to get their roles correct.

I wonder if it's anything to do with Bjarni's father being dead, or if it's me, changing their usual dynamic.

After we eat, I try to help with the dishes, but Colleen shoos me out of the room. "You can act like family soon enough," she says. "Today you're a guest."

So I wander down the hall, hands in the pockets of Bjarni's too-big jeans. They're only staying up because I've got a belt cinched tight around my waist – also Bjarni's, and I had to add an extra hole to make it tight enough.

As I pass by a half-open door, I hear a printer spitting out pages and then Bjarni's voice. "Come in here a sec," he says, and at first I'm not sure he's talking to me. But there's no one else here.

I edge around the door and stop. The big room is brightly lit from a window that looks out over the front porch. There are shelves all around, a worktable scattered with papers in the middle of the room, and a desk to one side.

Bjarni takes a stack of pages off a printer and hands them to me.

"What's this?" I say.

"All the forms you need to get your ID re-issued so you can be official again. Fill them out today and Raine can take them into Riverbend tomorrow. Magne knows people who can get everything processed in no time."

I feel my throat go tight, and the air suddenly seems too thin. "I –" I can't make any more words come out and I feel like I'm going to faint.

"Hey, take it easy," Bjarni says, coming around the desk to steer me into a chair. "You're okay."

When I can't stop gasping, he takes the pages, sets them aside, then makes me bend over my lap until my head is almost between my knees.

He rubs my back between my shoulder blades. "Just breathe, sweetheart. You're okay."

I can't get enough breath to tell him that touching me isn't making it better; it's making it worse. Except somehow it does help, the regular stroke of his hand up and down my spine becomes a sort of metronome for my breathing.

"What was it?" he says. He's crouched next to my chair, and when I'm breathing properly again, he tips my face up with one finger under my chin.

"What was what?" I say, not wanting to answer. Hating how weak I am.

He raises an eyebrow at me. "What made you panic like that? Those forms?"

I pull my chin away from his hand so I can look down at the floor. "Money gives me anxiety," I say. "That –" and I nod at the stack of papers "– means I have to face reality again. Real life where I'm going to end up dead begging on a street corner."

"No," he says, and the way he says it makes me look up at him. "You're not fucking alone anymore. And I might be shit about the whole human decency thing, but I'm really goddamn good with money. I'll help you fix it. All of it. No matter how bad you think it is."

"Why?" I say. "I'll just fuck up again."

"No, you won't," he says. "I'll make sure you don't."

I want to ask why again, but it's hard to make words come out past the lump of hopelessness that threatens to cut off my breathing.

"How about this," he says. "I'll fill out the forms. You just give me the answers I don't know and sign where I tell you."

He doesn't wait for an answer but gets up and grabs the papers and seats himself at the desk. It's *his* desk, I realize. *His* office.

"Name," he says. "Justin. You don't spell that weird or anything do you?"

I shake my head.

"Middle name?"

"Charles."

He spells it to himself as he writes it on the first form. "And L-E-Y-E-N-D-E-C-K-E-R?"

"Yeah."

There's a pause as he spreads out all the papers on his desk and fills in my name on all of them. I sit hunched in the chair, arms wrapped around my stomach, as if by holding in my guts I can keep panic from overwhelming me again.

We go through my birthdate, social security number, and so on. Then I sign and he taps the pages into a neat pile and slides them into an envelope.

"Who's Raine?" I say.

"Thorstein's girlfriend, why?"

"You said she was going to take the forms into Riverbend. To… your other brother?"

"Right. She's going in to pick up more of her stuff from her apartment. You want to go along? She'd probably be happy for the company."

I look down at myself, the too-big clothes that make me look even skinnier than I am, my bare feet looking pale and grimy.

"Shit, I was supposed to be finding you more clothes, wasn't I?"

"It's okay."

"Nope," he says. "Wait here." He vanishes out the door and I can hear him somewhere farther in the house, talking. Colleen's voice answers, but I can't make out the words. Then footsteps, heading upstairs, I think. More stairs, a weird creaking. I stop listening when I realize I don't know what

I'm listening to.

So I look around. The shelves hold file boxes and books on farming with titles like, *Modern Regenerative Agriculture* and *Mixed Farming Strategies*. Really riveting stuff.

The worktable looks more interesting, so I get up and walk over. There's a big map on top, under a layer of heavy glass, and someone has used colored markers to make notes on it.

There's a house labelled "farmhouse" and another marked "small house" with "Bjarni's" added under it. And a third one says "Granddad's," but that's crossed out and "Thorstein's" written in. Those labels are directly on the map, and they look like they've been there a long time. It's the Thorvaldson farm, obviously, and it's way bigger than I thought, bigger than it seemed driving in, because of all the trees and hedges breaking up the landscape. Each of the fields and areas has a name, and most have crops or livestock labelled on top of the glass where they can be easily changed.

"Like my map?" says Bjarni. "That's how I figure out what goes where every year. Or every week, as the case may be."

He's holding a big cardboard box with "Magne's clothes" written in the side in black marker. "Move those papers," he says, "so I can put this down."

I gather up the random pages that litter the top of the table and move them to the desk and he plops the box down on top of the map.

"Magne's your younger brother?" I ask.

"Yeah. He's Colleen's son. Hilde's full brother. The baby of the family."

"He lives in Riverbend?"

"Mmm." He opens the flaps of the box, reaches in, and pulls out a pair of black Levi's jeans. "These should fit you better," he says. "Though we're going to have to chop the legs off shorter." He holds them up and the legs look like they belong to a giraffe.

"I take it your baby brother is tall and skinny."

"*Was* tall and skinny," he says. "Now tall and beefy." He grins. "The funny thing is, he was a tiny kid. Runt of the litter, Dad used to say." Something unpleasant crosses his face. "Then he hit puberty and didn't stop growing until he was six foot four. After he left home, he started filling out, bulking up. So, he's never going to wear any of this shit again."

I take the jeans he hands me, hold them up to myself.

"Those'll fit. You'll look decent enough for going into town tomorrow."

"I don't need to go to town," I say. "Do I?"

"You need boots if you're going to work on the farm. Toothbrush. A razor you can use by yourself."

He grins and shows both teeth and dimples.

By the time Thorstein's girlfriend Raine shows up to collect me to go into Riverbend the next day, I still haven't figured out how I'm going to pay for new boots, or even a toothbrush. I don't have any credit left, or money in the bank, even if I still had my cards and the other contents of my wallet, which I don't.

So I figure I'll just tag along, and when we get there I'll tell Raine I don't need anything after all. I can manage with Magne's castoffs until I get another job. There were even a few pairs of runners in the bottom of the box, and one of them fits well enough. I don't like not having boxers or socks, but I can deal.

But as I'm about to get into the passenger side of a really nice 1990s midnight blue BMW, Bjarni appears in the farmhouse door and comes down the stairs.

"You almost forgot this," he says, handing me a thick envelope with my name on the front.

I take it automatically. "What is it?"

One of Bjarni's dimples appears, like he's trying to hide a smile. "Advance on your pay. Thorstein's assuming you'll take him up on his offer of a part-time job." He flicks the edge of the envelope. "Or full-time, if you want."

I open the envelope like there might be something inside that will bite me. There is, in a manner of speaking. It's a thick stack of twenties. I try to hand it back.

"I can't take this," I say.

Bjarni shrugs and doesn't take the money "You don't have much choice," he says.

I frown and his look softens.

"Thorstein's going to make you work it off," he says. "And you need some stuff in the meantime. I figured cash would be better than a check or a transfer, until you have a new debit card." He puts a hand on my shoulder in what might be sympathy and I almost manage not to jerk away. "You need boots, and don't get cheap ones. You don't want a cow stepping on your foot in anything you bought at the discount store."

He leans over to look in the car door at Raine, who's watching with an amused look on her face. "Don't let him cheap out," he says.

"Don't be a bully," she replies, then smiles and winks and flips her long dark brown hair back over her shoulder. "I promise I'll make sure he gets farm-appropriate footwear."

"I'll set up another phone on the farm's account, so don't worry about that."

"Okee-dokee Mr Farm Manager, sir."

"Fuck off," he says, but he's smiling when he says it. I'm pretty sure they're actually friends, but it's hard to tell.

"You, too," she replies.

He steps back to let me get in the car. "You want me to text a list? He can use my soap and shit, but he'll need a toothbrush, socks, that kind of thing."

"I think we can manage," Raine says.

I say, "And a razor I can use by myself?" I can't help the smile that curls my lips. On one hand, I just want to abandon the envelope of money and go hide somewhere, but on the other hand it feels really good to have people care enough to lend it to me.

"Unless you want me to teach you how to use a straight razor. I think we have a few extras kicking around."

"Would you?" I say, both terrified at the thought, and filled with sensory memories of him shaving me and how turned on I was.

One shoulder lifts and drops. "If you want."

I shut the door and Raine puts the car in gear to pull away but pauses as Bjarni taps on the window. I fumble to find the right button to lower the glass.

"And get something fun," he says. "You're allowed to relax, you know."

"Sure," I say.

He leans down again and raises an eyebrow at Raine.

"I know what your idea of fun is," she says. "I'm not taking him trolling for a one-night stand."

"I meant a videogame, or a book, or a case of beer, you harridan," he says. "I've got all the game systems, so get anything."

"I don't play videogames," I say.

"Well," he says. "We'll fix that." Then he steps away and Raine carefully navigates the car down the gravel driveway.

I stare at the envelope in my hands. I don't dare count it.

"Thank you for letting Thorstein help you," Raine says, as she waits for a car to pass before pulling out onto the road.

"What?" I say. Yeah, fucking intelligent, that's me.

"It helps him, to be able to help other people. He takes his role as protector of the pack very seriously. It helps him… make amends for his father."

"Why does he need to do that? He's not responsible for what his father did."

"No," says Raine, smoothly switching gears and sending the car flying along the road. It's sure a contrast to the shitbox I was driving. "But his father used him to control the pack, so he *feels* responsible."

"Used him how?"

"It's not really my story to tell," she says. "But I guess you're going to hear it from somebody eventually." She sighs. "He's a berserker. Thorstein. He controls it well, except when he was made a werewolf it would take him over at the full moon. Mostly his dad kept him locked up and just used the *threat* of him, of his mindless violence, to make other werewolves do what he wanted. But sometimes, he'd make good on those threats. And Thorstein would come back to his right mind after the moon waned, to find somebody else's blood all over him, with no memory of what he'd done."

"Shit," I say. That explains… well, I guess that explains a lot. Thorstein's gentleness, his sadness, the terrible scars on his wrists. "Is that why he tried to kill himself?"

"He told you?" she says softly, and I can almost feel her glance at the scars on my own arms.

"He showed me," I answer, resisting the urge to hide my shame.

She smiles. "Yeah, I guess he would. He doesn't like people to know, but you… I think he felt you're a bit of a kindred spirit."

I shake my head. "I had a shit childhood, but nothing like that."

"But you've felt worthless, haven't you?" she says. "Like no one would care if you were gone, and the world might be a better place without you?"

"Yeah." The word is almost inaudible, even to me.

"You're not useless. And fucked up as he was, and as broken as he still is, Thors is an excellent judge of character."

"He might have made a mistake with me," I mutter.

"He didn't," she says. "And I know because I am also an excellent judge of character, and I've decided we're going to be friends, so don't try to resist." She glances over at me and grins, and it lights up her already beautiful face.

I can't help but smile back. "Is that how you won over Thorstein?" I dare to tease. "You just told him he was your boyfriend now and don't bother fighting it?"

She laughs, a sound that makes my heart lighter, and I swear the sun even gets brighter. "I like you," she says. "You keep up those little barbs and you'll fit in perfectly. Hell, you'll even make Bjarni respect you." She shakes her head, still smiling. "And for the record, that pretty much *is* how Thorstein and I ended up together."

Chapter Four

I HAVEN'T BEEN IN A BOOKSTORE with money to spend for so long, I don't even know where to start. I want everything.

I tried to convince Raine that we didn't need to come here, that I could just buy the absolute necessities, but she wasn't having it.

"I need to pick up a book I ordered, anyway," she said. And that was that.

I stand just inside the doorway of the shop while Raine heads straight for the counter, and I just look around, take it all in, breathe in the atmosphere, the comfort. And then I read the section signs. Horror, fantasy, literary fiction, biography, travel. The one that jumps out is poetry. I head for it like I'm in a daze.

The store is brightly lit, but it's not a glaring brightness, it's an easy-to-read-in brightness. I reach out and trail my fingers across the spines of the books as I pass them, calculate how much is left in the envelope – because Raine at least agreed to buy necessities first before coming here – and how much I can safely spend on books. None of it, really. So, I decide to allow myself one book, one treasure. And today, poetry feels like the right choice.

And face out, on the top shelf, sits *Swann Song: The Reconstructed Poetry of Frank Swann*. I'm intrigued by what "reconstructed poetry" might mean, and the cover features a beautiful illustration of a man standing on what looks like a church spire, with a swan in flight behind him, or maybe manifesting from him. The style is all soft colors, except for a fiery sunset, or maybe sunrise, behind the spire.

I've heard of Frank Swann. He was known for writing the most beautiful poems, reciting them once – never allowing a recording – and then burning the only copy in front of his audience. I think I remember some scandal about the manner of his death years ago. Twenty years? Maybe more. I wasn't that old at the time and had just started sneaking into the poetry stacks at the library to read what my parents called "degenerate fairy trash." That may have been when I first started to realize I was gay.

I pick up the book. It's not thin, like most poetry books, but I guess it's what you'd expect from a lifetime's worth of writing, and to my surprise I find it's illustrated in a variety of styles by artists who were inspired by him and contains pages and pages of tribute poems and essays by other writers, plus a biography and a few photographs.

I read the first line of one poem, "reconstructed" from the memory of another writer who heard it recited. Then I read a line of another, and another, and I know this is the book I'll be taking home. I don't even look at the price. I know it's going to be high – the book is hardcover and well-made – but now that I've found it, I can't bear to put it back.

I shake myself out of the trance I've fallen into and make my way up to the counter.

"Found something?" Raine says. She's waiting while the guy at the till slides a hardcover with wolves and a half-dressed guy on the cover into a paper bag.

"Paranormal romance?" I say. "Or urban fantasy?"

She raises an eyebrow. "You going to make fun of my taste in reading?"

I shake my head. "I wouldn't do that."

She smiles. "Good, because I read total trash."

That startles a smile out of me and hers grows bigger.

"Hey, I'd like you to meet my friend Elias," she says. "He's the ass man here, and he can get you any book you're looking for."

"He's the what?" I say, feeling a flush creep up my neck. I look at the attractive Black man holding out his hand for me. I take his hand, shake, and let go quickly.

"She *means*," says Elias. "That I'm the assistant manager." He looks sidelong at Raine and adds, "And also that I'm very gay."

"Oh," I say.

"Justin's the quiet type," Raine says.

"Quiet men are hot," says Elias, taking the book from me to scan it. "Good choice," he says, as he slips it into a paper bag. He smirks at Raine again and says, "Isn't that right, girl?"

"It is a good choice," she says. "And since I'm madly in love with the quietest man in the universe, I have to agree with your first point, too."

I'm blushing even more now, and I'm pretty sure my face has gone beet red. "I'm not *that* quiet," I say.

Raine laughs and touches my shoulder, briefly enough that I don't feel the need to pull away. Then she points at Elias and says, "One, don't be mean to the new boy, and two, you are not taking him out. I know you, I used to be *like* you, and you're not going to start breaking my friends' hearts with your one-night stands."

"Oof," Elias says. "Message received. I shall be friend and provider of books only."

"I'm not actually a child," I say. "I can manage my own life." But obviously I can't, or I wouldn't be in this situation, and the words come out more petulant than I meant them to. And apparently that's my theme these days, but nobody seems to notice.

"Obviously," says Raine. "But I know *this* guy, and I can tell from the look on his face that he thinks you're a tasty morsel."

Elias sticks his tongue out at Raine. "Speaking of off-limits tasty treats," he says. "There's a book here for one Bjarni Thorvaldson, brother of your most true love ever. Did you want to take it? If you're heading back to the farm today?"

"I'll take it," I say, impulsively. "You can put it on my bill. Raine's already paid."

She looks at me, head tilted slightly to one side. "You sure?" she says, and I nod. So Elias adds a thick paperback with some kind of airplane on the cover to my bag, and my bill, and I pay without thinking too carefully about the total.

"Also speaking of tasty treats who are not to be touched or even flirted with, and also also speaking of Thorvaldson brothers, here comes the younger, darker-haired version." The door chimes and we all turn to look.

For a moment my heart seems to stop. He looks so much like Bjarni, it's uncanny. But when the moment has passed, I realize he has shorter, dark brown hair and dark eyes, and the way he moves is much less self-conscious, less cocky than Bjarni. Also, he's like five inches taller and I can't even guess how many pounds heavier with muscle.

He's fucking beautiful, but he isn't Bjarni.

When he reaches the counter, he pulls Raine into a hug and reaches out to shake Elias's hand.

"Hey, little brother-almost," Raine says.

"What, he hasn't married you yet?" His voice is deep and smoky like Bjarni's too, or maybe more like Thorstein's.

Then he turns to me, and I can see a hundred little ways he isn't like his brother. "You must be the new guy," he says, holding out his hand. "I'm Magne. Thorstein, Bjarni, and Hilde's brother."

"Justin," I say, holding out my hand. Instead of shaking it, he grips my forearm, which I guess is maybe a werewolf thing. I grasp his in return and mercifully it's a brief contact and I don't feel the urge to jerk away.

"Nothing came in for you this week," says Elias. "Sorry."

"No worries. I'm actually here to meet these two." He turns back to Raine. "Lunch? Or did you just want to hand over the paperwork you need processed?"

The paperwork. *My* paperwork. I feel my guts clench and suddenly regret spending money on a book I don't need.

"We still need to stop in at the gallery to see Katie," Raine says. "I was kind of hoping Justin would fall madly in love with the place and agree to a part-time job working for us, so I can spend more time making my own art."

"And so you can go into quarantine for a few months?" says Magne as we leave the book store and turn down the sidewalk. I trail behind and try to resist checking out Magne's butt. I fail. It's very nice.

"That, too," says Raine. She glances back at me. "Did Bjarni tell you about that yet?" she asks, and I shake my head.

"It's a bit of a long story," says Magne. "I think you should let me buy you lunch while you tell it. Then you can go see Katie." He ends the debate before it can begin by opening the door to a cafe we happen to be passing and waiting for us to go inside.

We take a table near the door, and I try to order the cheapest thing on the menu. Before I can even get "I'll just have a green salad" out of my mouth, Magne turns the page on my menu to the burgers and says, "I recommend the mushroom bacon burger." Then he stares at me.

"I'm not really that hungry," I say, which is naturally exactly when my stomach rumbles. Loud.

He raises an eyebrow. "If you don't order exactly what you want instead of what's least expensive, I will be very insulted." I'm pretty sure he's joking, but he's a werewolf and does poker face extremely well.

"Well, *I'm* having the mushroom bacon burger," Raine says. "With sweet potato fries and a chocolate shake."

"Me, too," says Magne. "But I'll have coffee instead of a shake."

"Okay," I say. "I'll have that, too."

"Coffee or shake?" says the server, holding her pen poised over her notepad.

I try not to look up at Magne, try not to seem like I'm asking permission, but I do.

"Shake?" he asks, gently, and I nod.

"Vanilla, please," I say. I feel small and stupid, and way younger than I am. "Sorry," I whisper, when the server has gone. Magne puts a hand over mine and I almost hide the flinch. He holds my hand firmly until I relax, and then he lets go.

"Somebody really hurt you," he says. It's not a question. "And I don't mean the asswipe who turned you into a wolf without asking."

I shrug.

"I know what getting kicked around your whole life does to you," he says. "I got out when I was eighteen, but I saw what it did to both of my brothers."

I look up from where my hands are clenched in my lap and meet his eyes. They're dark brown and kind, and there's no judgement in them. No pity, either, just understanding.

"You're safe now," he says, and in that moment he sounds so much like his brothers I want to cry. I want to crawl into his lap and be protected. But of course I don't. I can't.

"Thanks," I say, and carefully let out my breath.

"I'm just glad that whoever did this to you waited until Dad was dead."

That startles me. He says it with almost no emotion in his voice, his face neutral.

"Was he that bad?" I say.

Raine leans over to bump my shoulder with hers. "Worse," she says. "And I only met him twice."

"Worse," Magne agrees.

"Magne used to help queer werewolves escape their pack," Raine says. "Now Thorstein's making it safe for them to come back."

"If any of them want to," Magne says. "Can't blame them if they don't." He pauses when the server brings our drinks. The milkshakes come in tall glasses and include extra in malt cups on the side.

I take a sip and stare into my glass and I say, "You know I'm gay, right?"

"I guessed," Magne says. "But I didn't want to assume." He sips his coffee, adds a tiny amount of honey, stirs, then sips again. "Is it safe to assume you had a shit childhood?"

"Yeah," I say, still talking to my glass. "My parents belong to an evangelical cult. I came out to them when I was fourteen and suddenly I was homeschooled and going to conversion camp every summer."

"Shit," Magne says. "I'm sorry."

I shrug. "I finally got my head together enough to leave when I was twenty. It was much better until they found out where I was and started sending their missionary friends to visit me at work, at school, at the places I used to hang out." I clench my hands on the glass, then force them to relax. "I lost a lot of jobs, and a lot of friends, that way."

"They can *try* to visit the farm," Magne says and when I look up, he's smiling with a lot of teeth.

I try a laugh, and it actually feels pretty good.

After the server brings our burgers, which make my stomach rumble again when I catch the delicious smell, I venture to ask, "What did you mean about quarantining?"

"Oof," says Raine. "That is a bit of a tale."

"Thorstein's a *berserkr*," Magne says.

"Like a Viking? Raine mentioned that," I say and he nods.

"He's always been kind, gentle, you know? So suddenly being uncontrollably violent must have freaked him out. I wasn't born yet, not till a long time later, but you can ask Bjarni about it." Magne takes a bite of his burger, so Raine takes over.

"He managed the fits, the rage, pretty well," she says. "Taught himself ways to stay calm, because if he didn't let the anger take over, he didn't lose control of himself. Then his dad decided it was a good idea to make him a werewolf."

"He likes being a werewolf," I say, pausing with a fry halfway to my mouth.

"He *loves* being a werewolf," Raine says.

"Anyway," Magne says. "Suddenly, full moon meant uncontrollable werewolf *and berserkr* nature. Thorstein would... basically become unaware of who he was. He was dangerous and unpredictable, so Dad locked him up. And then he figured out how to control Thorstein, to use him to make the rest of the pack do what he wanted."

"But last month," Raine says.

"Two months ago," says Magne around a mouthful of fries.

"Right. Two months ago, we found a way to put Thors back in control of himself. But in the process –" She pulls her t-shirt sleeve up to reveal three recent scars, like deep scratches across her upper arm. "He accidentally clawed me."

"Which wouldn't have been a big deal," says Magne. "Even with how slow human healing is."

"Except Bjarni needed to get my attention and grabbed my arm, and his hands were covered in blood. His or Thorstein's, we don't know."

"The blood got in Raine's cuts and infected her with werewolf symbiont."

They both go back to eating and I'm left looking from one to the other. "And?" I say. "You're a werewolf now?"

"Sort of," says Raine.

"Yes, but," says Magne.

I look at them both again. Finally, Magne wipes his fingers on a napkin and says, "It's supposed to be a quick process. The wolf to be bleeds a lot, till they're nearly dead. Then they get bled *on* a lot – traditionally from wounds they inflicted on their attackers – and lots of symbiont gets transferred. Developing a wolf shape takes time, but becoming a werewolf is fast."

"Except," says Raine, holding a fry up like an exclamation point, "for me. I was infected, but with so little symbiont my human immune system should have cured me of it, keeping me entirely human. But it didn't, so instead it's going to take more time for it to actually make me a werewolf." She pops the fry into her mouth. "But in the meantime," she continues. "It weakens my immune system, so I'm likely to catch any sickness I run into. Thorstein thinks I should avoid the city for a while, until the symbiont does its work, and my body recovers so I don't get sick with something I maybe *won't* recover from." She eats another fry, then pushes her plate away.

"He's right, you know," says Magne.

"I know," Raine replies. "And he didn't try to tell me what to do, he just recommended what he thought was best. Which is why we haven't had a giant fight over it."

"I can't imagine you having a giant fight over anything," I say. "Or even a small fight."

Raine laughs. "We probably wouldn't, really, because he'd never try to order me around in the first place. Though he wasn't very happy about me coming into town today."

"Because you could get sick?"

"Exactly."

"I wondered why you waited outside when I went into the department store."

"That and I figured you didn't need supervision to buy boxer shorts and a toothbrush." She grins and bumps her shoulder against mine again and it feels nice. I smile back at her.

"I am able to manage that much," I say.

Magne leans his head on his hand and says, "You know, if you're going to keep spending time with my family, you're going to have to get used to people trying to take care of you. They don't care how old you are, they're still going to treat you like a kid. Hell, my mom treats Thorstein like a little boy and he's a fair bit older than her."

"I'm trying not to be a dick about it," I say. "I guess I'm not used to people caring about me."

Magne snorts. "You've just fallen into a family with three very dominant werewolf brothers, all equipped with an overblown protective instinct. You have no hope but to be cared for." His smile curls wider and both dimples appear.

"Just wait until you meet Katie," Raine says. "She's probably going to want to take you shopping and dress you up like a Ken doll." She grins a wicked grin.

"Admit it," says Magne. "You want to do that yourself."

She pokes his arm. "Maybe a little," she says. "He is awfully pretty."

When I meet Katie, and Raine tells her I might be interested in working for them part time so she can take some medical leave, she looks me up and down and says, "He's decorative enough, but does he have a brain?"

I blush fiercely at being called decorative, especially since I know what I look like in the mirror and it's not all that.

I say, "I do have functional ears," and she laughs.

"And a spine," she says. "What do you know about art?"

"Mostly Old Masters," I answer. "I didn't study anything contemporary at uni."

"You have a degree?"

"No, just six years of random courses." I look at my feet.

"If you apologize for that, I'll smack you," says Raine.

"What?"

"Thorstein used to apologize for absolutely fucking everything." She puts her hands on her hips and pretends to glare.

"If you're willing to do some reading in your spare time, I'm willing to let you try out the job for a couple of weeks. Our older lady clients will love you," Katie says.

"They will enjoy having a good-looking young man help them," Raine adds.

"So, part time, right?" I say. "I told Thorstein I'd work a few days a week on the farm, too."

"How does Thursday and Friday sound to start?" says Katie. "Ten to five?"

I nod. "I'll have to figure out transportation," I say. I look back at the floor. "My car got towed."

"Just let me know when you can start," Katie says. "And if you're sick of shopping with Ms Flowy Linen and Other Natural Fabrics, I can take you out to find gallery-appropriate clothes."

"We've done okay so far," I say, noting her probably not inexpensive, put-together retro look, and thinking with dismay of the shrinking pile of twenties in my pocket.

"Coward," she says, but smiles kindly. Then, to Raine, she says, "Take him to Charles's. Tell him I sent you and he'll give you a killer discount."

As we leave, I ask, "Who's Charles?"

"He owns the swankiest men's consignment shop in Riverbend," Raine says. "But don't worry. A couple of nice pairs of pants and a few dress shirts will do for now. And a good pair of shoes."

She touches my arm briefly, taking her hand away before I can feel uneasy. It's like she knows how it makes me feel. Like Magne and Thorstein seemed to know, though they handled it differently.

"It's like Magne said, you're part of the family. That's really what a werewolf pack is, you know. A family. I mean, a lot of the pack is literally related. Cousins and shit, but even those who aren't are still family. And we look after each other. If you run out of cash, I'll lend you some."

I start to open my mouth, to object, but she looks at me with her eyebrows raised and I close it again.

"I don't suppose you want to sub-let my apartment?" she says, out of nowhere.

I just manage *not* to stammer out, "What?" like an idiot, but then just end up staring at her.

"Not right away," she says. "But keep it in mind. It'll save you from having to drive back and forth all the time." She looks at me sidelong and stops to open the door into a very stylish-looking shop with male mannequins in the window. "You can always stay with Bjarni the rest of the week."

I don't have an answer for that, and she's stepped into the shop before I can come up with one. At least she can't see the blush that creeps up my neck to make my whole face feel like it's on fire.

Chapter Five

WHEN RAINE PULLS UP in front of Bjarni's house to drop me off, my piece of shit Hyundai is sitting in the driveway next to his Mitsubishi, the hood up.

He ducks out from under the hood when I get out, waves to Raine as she turns around and drives away, and directs his toothiest grin at me.

"Look what I found," he says.

"How?"

"I know a guy," he says, and shrugs. "It really is a piece of crap."

"It's probably not even worth whatever you paid to get it back," I say, holding my shopping bags in front of me, like they can somehow shield me from his presence. Because he keeps getting closer.

"Didn't cost me anything," he says. "Like I said, I know a guy."

"Like I said," I say, feeling a smile curl the corners of my mouth despite myself. "Probably not worth what you paid."

He grins. "It can be fixed."

"What's wrong with it?" I step around him, move past to peer under the hood, as if I know what I'm looking at.

He stands next to me, looking down at the grimy engine. "What *isn't* wrong with it?" he says. "Did you ever take it in for maintenance?"

"I could never afford to. I just hoped it would keep working."

"Well, we'll get it running so you'll have a way to get to your fancy new job." He looks at me, trying to keep a straight face. "Assuming you decided you want to work at an art gallery and frame shop. With the dazzling and foul-mouthed Katie Hemmingway."

"Thursdays and Fridays," I say.

"Starting when?"

"Whenever I have a way to get there."

"I can drive you if you want to start right away," he says. "Otherwise, it'll be a few weeks. I need to get some parts."

"Will it cost a lot?" I don't want to think about money, but I can't seem to avoid it. I just try to keep breathing normally.

He shrugs. "I'm not going to put top-quality parts in that thing. We'll start by replacing plugs and wires. Serpentine belt. Brake pads. See if we can find you some decent used tires. New oil. Check the rest of the fluids. That might be all it needs."

"That sounds like a lot," I say. My stomach hurts and I hold my shopping bags tighter. He puts a hand on my shoulder and squeezes. I only twitch a little.

"Hey," he says. "I'm pretty sure I can get it running well enough to be safe. If not, I'll ask Magne to look at it." He looks at me closely, and I can't meet his eyes. "You want to learn how to fix it?"

"I don't know anything about cars," I say.

He smacks the shoulder his hand was resting on. "That much is obvious," he says. "But do you want to learn?"

I think about how helpless I feel, about everything it seems. How useless. I nod. "Yeah, I would like to learn."

"Okay," he says. "Put your stuff in the kitchen and I'll show you how to check the oil."

Yeah, I'm so useless I don't even know how to check the oil in my own car. It's a wonder I even know how to put gas in it.

So I drop all the bags in the kitchen and go back outside. Bjarni's leaning under the hood, his back to me, and for a moment I let myself have a good look at his ass, and the muscles in his back that show where his t-shirt stretches across them. Later, I can berate myself for fantasizing about someone who will never be interested in me, but right now I can enjoy the view.

When I stop beside him, he turns his head then puts his hand on a wire-like handle sticking up from the engine.

"You want to look for the one that says 'oil'," he says, dimple appearing as he smiles.

"I figured out that much," I say, and lean over next to him. The smell of gasoline creeps up my nose and hits the back of my throat, and at first I think something must be very wrong with the car, because suddenly it's all I can smell, and surely it shouldn't be so strong. But then I realize it's something wrong with *me*, like I'm overcome by more than just that smell. It brings a memory with it. Running, falling, pain, a rag over my nose and in my mouth and it stinks like gasoline and I can't breathe and he's *hurting* me and he's –

And Bjarni's arms are around me and I'm fighting against him, trying to get away, thrashing, desperate. "Leave me alone!" I say, I yell, and I don't know who I'm talking to, because it wasn't Bjarni who hurt me. But it *is* Bjarni who won't let me go, who holds my arms pinned to my sides, who presses me against an unyielding surface with his body weight.

"I'm not going to hurt you," he says, voice gentle, low, soft. "Justin, you're safe. Stop fighting me."

But I can't. Part of my brain is trying to tell me that everything is okay, that here I'm safe, with Bjarni I'm safe. But the other part of my brain only knows I can't get away and I'm terrified and weak.

He moves one hand to the back of my head, presses my face against his shoulder and tells me to breathe. I try to listen. I try to breathe, and slowly the stench of oil and gas is replaced by warm skin, laundry detergent, male musk, cedar-scented soap.

I stop thrashing, but I can't stop the sobs that come out instead.

"Hey, sweetheart," he says. His voice is quiet, more soothing than I would have thought possible. "You're safe, *kjaereste*, I promise." He moves the hand that was pinning my arms to stroke my back instead, pulling me away from the hard surface I now recognize as his car to rest snugly against his chest. His other hand cups the back of my head and his voice rumbles directly into my ear. I feel his breath on my neck.

"Ssh," he says. "I'm here. You're okay."

"I think I got snot all over your shirt," I say. My voice sounds raw and my shoulders tremble.

"My shirt is washable," he says. He lets go of my head, looks at the front of his shirt, damp with my tears and shiny with my mucous. He reaches over his head, grabs the t-shirt behind his neck, and hauls it off in one smooth motion. Then he uses it to wipe my face. I start to step away, find the car still behind me, and he moves with me, keeping me pressed against him. Now I'm desperate to get away for an entirely different reason. Because I can feel myself responding to his nearness, feel my jeans getting too tight, and I don't want him to know.

But he puts his hand on my face, strokes my cheek with his thumb, and makes me look into his eyes.

"What was that?" he says. "What made you panic like that?"

My throat goes tight thinking about it. "I smelled oil and gas," I say, realizing how stupid it sounds. I was bending over a car engine, of course I smelled oil and gas.

"Did it make you remember something?" he says. "From when you were attacked?" He has both hands on my face now, dropping his shirt to the ground, keeping me pressed back against the car with his body. He *has* to be able to feel how I want him now. How could he not?

But if he's noticed, he doesn't say anything. He just keeps stroking my face, keeps his eyes on mine, and instead of feeling like a threat, his gaze is calming, mesmerizing.

I nod. "After he bit me," I say, my voice breaking on the words. "And I hit him… I thought I got away. That he left. But I ran and he knocked me down again."

"It's okay," Bjarni says. "Take your time, *kjaereste*."

I swallow, keep staring into his pale blue eyes, finding his direct look like a lifeline now and not something to be afraid of. And mercifully, the fear has made my erection subside and even the comfort of his eyes doesn't bring it back.

"He… clawed me again." I go to touch my chest where his claws tore into me and realize I have both hands clenched around Bjarni's belt. I'm holding him against me as much as he's pressing me to the car.

I force my hands open, press my palms back against the warm metal of the Mitsu. "And he shoved a greasy rag in my mouth when I screamed." I shake my head. "That's all I remember."

"You didn't see him?"

I shake my head. "He smelled like sweat and beer and raw meat."

"And oil and gasoline?"

"Yeah."

"Okay," he says, stepping away from me and moving his hands from my face to my shoulders. I twitch, just stopping myself from jerking away.

"You don't like it when I touch you," he says, voice so soft I barely hear it.

"I don't mind," I say. I want very badly for him to touch me. "It's just… it scares me, at first."

"You're scared of me," he says, and he's not asking. "I don't want you to be scared of me. I want you to know you're *safe* with me. You're safe *here*, on the farm."

"I know," I say. "I know that. I just can't…"

"You can't help it," he says, touching my face again. I don't flinch, but I have to close my eyes to manage it.

"I'm sorry," I say, and I'm startled by how angry he is when he replies.

"No," he says. "You have nothing to apologize for. And whoever made you think that you do deserves to rot in whichever hell his religion thinks is worst."

That startles me enough that I open my eyes. He smiles. I try to smile back, and I might even succeed.

"I have something for you," he says. "That might help you feel a little more safe."

"What?"

He heads for the house. "Come on." So I follow him to the kitchen where I dropped my shopping bags. I see the one from the bookstore.

"I have something for you, too," I say.

He opens a drawer, looks inside and says, "Shit. I left it upstairs."

I pick up my bags and follow him upstairs, where I put my purchases on the guest room bed – my bed for now, I guess – and get the book out of the bookstore bag, then turn around to find him in the doorway. He's put a fresh shirt on, and I make certain my disappointment doesn't show on my face before I hand him the book. In return, he gives me white box with a picture of a cellphone on it.

"Oh cool," he says. "You picked up my book for me. Thanks."

"No problem," I reply, staring at the box in my hands.

"These books are total garbage, but I can't stop reading them," he says, the familiar self-deprecation back in his voice.

"You shouldn't put yourself down for the things you like to read," I say, still unable to tear my eyes away from the box.

"You sound like Magne," he says, and I hear the crinkle of paper as he takes the other book out of the bag. "Meanwhile, you're being all cultured and reading critically acclaimed poetry."

I have to look up at that and he's grinning at me. I feel my lips curve in response.

Then he nods at the box. "Open it."

I slide the lid off and nestled inside is the exact phone in the picture. It's newer and fancier than anything I've ever been able to afford. He taps it with a finger and the screen lights up. "I went ahead and set it up for you," he says. "But you can change the settings to what you like."

"I can't take this," I say.

"Yes, you can. And before you say it's too expensive, I didn't buy it brand new. It's my old one. I *did* get you a new case for it, but I left it in my office."

I open my mouth to say it's too expensive, anyway, that I can't pay for a cell plan, and he reaches out to put his fingertips on my lips. I know my eyes must be huge, the way I'm staring at him. I desperately want to open my mouth farther, to draw one of his fingers in to suck on it. So I hold very still.

"It's on the farm's plan. All our farm hands are. Just, if you need to talk to Thorstein, text, don't call. He hates talking on the phone."

"Okay," I whisper against his fingers.

"Good," he says. Then he takes the box with the phone and puts it on the bed next to my bags of clothes.

He steps closer. "Now," he says. "I need you to stop being afraid of me." He puts one hand on my neck, palm against my throat. His fingers curl into the muscle on one side of my neck, and his thumb presses into the spot under the point of my jaw.

I freeze, holding utterly still, and stare at a point over his shoulder. I feel ice in my guts. And my cock gets hard. I'm so terrified I might piss myself, and so turned on it hurts.

With just one hand, he forces my head back and to the side, exposing the most vulnerable part of my throat.

"How is this supposed to make me less afraid?" I choke out, surprised that the words are even audible.

"Why are you so afraid?" he says, moving closer, so close I feel his body heat.

"You could kill me," I say. "You could snap my neck. Rip my throat out. You wouldn't even have to try very hard." I feel tears leaking from the corners of my eyes, and I feel so fucking weak. I can't fight back, and I'm not sure I even want to.

He leans over, opens his mouth, and presses his teeth to my neck. Just his unextended, almost-human teeth, but I've seen him change and I know he could have full wolf teeth extended before I could even begin to plead for my life.

"You can kill me," I say, and this time, I don't mean that he's capable. I mean I give him permission.

He takes his teeth away, leans his face into my neck instead, lets his hand slide away to rest on my chest. "I *could* kill you," he says. "But I need you to know that I *won't*. Can you try to believe that for me?"

"Okay," I say, not sure I'm making sound come out of my mouth. "I'll try," I whisper.

"Good," he says, and pulls me into a hug. "And I need you to stop flinching every time I touch you. You're going to give me a complex."

I laugh and it startles me.

"I like hearing you laugh," he says.

I don't know what to do, so I stand quietly while he embraces me and then, finally, I find the courage to lift my hands away from my sides, to rest them on his back.

He makes a quiet noise in his throat. "Werewolves are very tactile," he says. "We communicate with body language and touch almost as much as with words. More, sometimes." He shifts so we fit close together, strokes his hand down my back, and the fear ebbs away. The desire has gone nowhere, though, and there's no way he hasn't noticed my boner pressing against him.

When he relaxes his arms, I step away, find my back against the tall dresser near the door. He looks at me, studying my face. Then he frowns a little, inhales deeply though his nose. He steps closer, and I have nowhere to go.

"Justin," he says, and his voice has a roughness it didn't have before.

"Yeah?" I say. I make myself meet his eyes, but I can't read whatever's in them. It's intense, whatever it is. Raw. He moves closer and his chest brushes mine, his forehead rests on mine. He puts his hands on the dresser behind me, caging me with his arms, and I feel flushed all over, even though he's barely touching me.

"Fuck, Justin," he says, his voice gone extra low and rumbly.

I press my palms back against the solid surface of the dresser, press my back against it. He tilts his head, inhales deeply beneath my ear, his face tucked against my neck.

"Fuck," he says again. "Why do you smell so fucking good?"

I know my breathing is ragged, loud. I feel like I'm gasping for air, almost like I'm panicking again. His body is so close, I feel his heat, feel his chest bump gently against mine as he breathes, and his cedar-musky smell fills my nose. I think I whimper.

Then he's pressing against me, from his shins to his collar bone, every muscle leaning into mine, grinding my back, my ass into the hardwood of the dresser behind me.

His body fits perfectly against mine, his added height making each curve and angle nest, and I don't even realize when I reach out, wrap my arms around him, and make fists in the back of his t-shirt. I know he can feel my hardness against him, and I don't care.

I feel his against me.

For a long time we stand that way, pressed together, our harsh breathing synchronizing until we're both panting into each other's necks. I want to kiss him, but I can't move. I'm afraid if I move, he'll come to his senses and shove me away. That he'll never even look at me again.

Finally, he shifts so his forehead rests on mine again, his hand cups the side of my face. I think he's trembling but that might be me.

"*Kjaereste,*" he whispers. Then, the thing I was afraid of happens. He steps back, away from me. I force myself to let go of his t-shirt, to drop my hands to my sides.

He brushes my cheekbone with his thumb, and then he says, "I have to go." And he turns, walks out of the room and down the stairs. I hear the front door close, hear his car start. Hear the spit and ping of gravel as he hits the gas too hard pulling down the long driveway.

It's a long time before I can move, before I can stumble to my bed, push everything on it to the floor, and crawl under the covers. I curl into a ball, and I can still smell him on me, can still feel his every muscle pressed onto mine, feel his hard length next to mine, trapped between our bodies.

"Bjarni," I whisper, and uncurl enough that I can pull my fly open, take myself in hand and jerk off. I don't linger. I don't want to think. But it's his face, his burning blue eyes, I see when I spurt all over myself. My chest aches. My heart aches. My stomach hurts.

Finally, I make myself get up and take a shower, stuff my clothes into the hamper in the bathroom – the second hamper Bjarni added just for me because the room is big enough for chairs and cabinets and still has extra space, so why not? I can smell my own semen on the clothes, so he certainly will, and I don't care if he'll smell what I did. I go back to my room, crawl back into bed, and eventually I fall asleep.

I wake up when he comes home, when I hear the crunch of tires on gravel and the purr of the Mitsu's engine. I listen as he opens the door, tosses his keys in the dish on the table in the front hall, and takes his shoes off. I hear every floorboard and stair creak, and I hear the slight hesitation outside my bedroom door.

And as he passes, I smell him. I smell his soap, his sweat, his spunk. And I smell the woman he's recently fucked. She wore patchouli perfume and drank gin.

I'm not sure I manage to keep in the whimper that tries to creep out of my throat. I *know* I don't keep the tears in, but at least they just run freely and don't rip out of me with sobs. I feel jealousy and anger and self-hatred. And I feel empty. And hopelessly in love.

He goes to his room, and then to the bathroom. The shower runs for a long time, so long I smell the steam seeping out and filling the hall, cedar-scented from his soap. Finally, the water shuts off and a few minutes later, he goes to his room. It's a long time – five minutes? ten? – before I hear his door close. Like maybe he's standing there, looking towards my door, waiting for me to come out.

I think, maybe, I hear him sigh before his door closes, hear him mutter, "Fuck," his favorite word. And then the door does close, and I'm left to lie in bed in misery.

I know I'm not exactly a great catch, but apparently, I'm so repulsive he had to run out and find a random woman to go to bed with.

But he *wanted* me. I could feel it. I could *smell* it. He wanted me, but he didn't *want* to want me.

I lie awake until the tears stop, then I wipe my face, turn onto my back, and stare at the ceiling until sleep finally, mercifully, comes.

Except my dreams are full of the smell of him, the feel of him against me. Only in my dreams, he kisses me.

Chapter Six

IN THE MORNING, I stay in bed as long as I can, waiting for Bjarni to leave. Eventually, though, I have to get up. I get dressed, pull my new boots out of their box, and put them on.

Then I take the cellphone out of its box and shove it into my pocket without looking at it. When I get outside, I'm not sure where to go. I know I'll be working with Thorstein, but I don't want to go to the farmhouse, because Bjarni will probably be there. And to get to Thorstein's house, I'd have to go past the farmhouse.

Lucky for me, I've left it so late that Thorstein comes looking for me.

"You sleep in?" he says, looking down at me from the back of an enormous blond horse.

"I didn't sleep well," I say.

He looks at me more carefully, then kicks one leg over the horse and slides to the ground. I'm pretty sure he does it backwards, swinging his leg over the horse's neck and dismounting with his back to the saddle, but the horse doesn't seem to care. It just reaches its head down and grabs a mouthful of grass and stands there chewing, looking at me out of one eye.

"You okay?" Thorstein says.

"Yeah," I say, and he raises an eyebrow. "Okay, not really, but I will be."

"You and Little Bear had a fight," he says.

"Why do you call him that? Little Bear?"

"Don't change the subject," he says, crossing his arms on his chest and looking very stern. The crinkles at the corners of his eyes show he isn't, really.

"It wasn't a fight," I say. "I don't know what it was." I can't look at his eyes anymore, at the kindness on his face, so I stare at my feet. My boots look really, stupidly new compared to his, even though they're the same kind.

"He hurt you," he says.

"He didn't mean to."

He touches my chin with one finger, so I have to look up at him.

"Bjarni can be thoughtless," he says. "If he's ever shitty to you on purpose, you let me know."

I shake my head slightly. "It's okay, really."

"I need to know, Justin," he says, his voice kind but firm. "It's my job to deal with this kind of crap, not yours. And I've known my brother a long time; I know exactly how he can be."

I look back at my feet. "So why do you call him Little Bear?" I ask, and he laughs.

"Because it's his name," he says. "Bjarni is the diminutive form of Bjorn, which means 'bear.' So, Little Bear." He's smiling when he says it.

"Then why does he call you Big Bear?"

His smile widens and I see his dimple, but just the one. "Because my middle name is Bjorn."

I have to look at his face, to see if he's shitting me.

"Dad really liked the name," he says.

"Even though you're werewolves and not were-bears?"

He laughs. "We weren't born werewolves. But yes. It's a bit weird, but there you go." Then he gestures at the horse. "You ready to work?"

I nod. "What are we doing today?"

"Fences," he says. "Did you buy gloves?"

"Oh," I say. "Yeah." I run back up the steps to get them from where I left them on the table by the door. Bjarni's keys are still there and seeing them makes my stomach turn over. I push the feeling away.

When I get back outside, Thorstein is on the horse again. He moves one foot out of the stirrup, moves his leg forward, and holds out his hand.

"Um," I say.

"Never been on a horse?"

"Never."

"Put your foot in the stirrup, take my hand, and on the count of three, stand up in the stirrup and swing your other leg over behind me."

"What if it… he… moves?"

"Chuck here is bomb-proof," he says. "And lazy. He's not going anywhere. Come on."

I shove my gloves into my back pocket and move closer. This horse is almost as tall at the shoulder as the top of my head. How am I supposed to get up there? Chuck turns his head and looks at me, snorts, and bends down for another bite of grass. I notice there's no metal bar from the bridle in his mouth. A bit? I think that's what it's called.

I suck in a deep breath and somehow manage to get my foot up into the stirrup, and suddenly I'm sitting behind Thorstein, clinging desperately to his shirt.

"Hold my belt if you need to," he says. "In no time, you'll be riding hands-free."

"I doubt that," I say.

"We'll see."

Then he nudges Chuck with his leg and turns him around and we're off at a steady ground-eating walk.

"Chuck is very wide," I say, squirming to find a more comfortable position.

"He's a Belgian draft horse," Thorstein says. "He was supposed to be put to work plowing and logging, but he hates being in harness. For whatever reason, he's fine with a saddle, so saddle horse he is." He pauses, looks at me over his shoulder, and adds, "It's probably obvious that I need a bigger riding horse than most people." He turns back. "Though even I find Chuck a bit big around the middle," he says. "And as soon as my new colt is old enough to ride, Chuck gets to retire."

"'Retire' isn't a euphemism, is it?" I say. "Like 'put to sleep'?"

He laughs. "No. He'll be living out his old age in the paddock in front of my house, eating grass and having everyone who visits bring him apples and carrots."

We ride in silence for a while until we reach a big field, so large I can only just make out the fence on the opposite side. Thorstein turns Chuck to walk alongside the fence.

"We just moved the highlands to another pasture, so now we check all the fences to make sure they didn't do any damage while they were here."

"Highlands?" I say.

"Cattle," he answers. "Cute little hairy beasts. Good temperament, but sometimes they get over-enthusiastic scratching their asses on the fence posts." He points to the fence and gently pulls Chuck to a stop, kicks his leg over the horse's neck, and slides to the ground.

"Like that," he says and lifts a rail to put it back into place. "Hop down and get me the hammer and the biggest nail you can find from the saddlebag."

I stare down at the ground, which seems awfully far away.

Thorstein says, "Lean over the saddle, kick your leg over Chuck's ass, and slide down on your stomach."

I do as he says and manage not to hurt myself on the way down. My legs wobble when I hit the ground and Thorstein chuckles.

"You're going to be sore by the time we're done," he says. "I told you I'd put you to work."

I dig out a hammer and a huge nail and hand them to him, then hold the rail in place as he bashes the nail in.

"If it gives me thighs like yours, I'll put up with it," I say, and he laughs.

Back on Chuck, we continue along, stopping a few more times to re-set rails, hammer huge nails, and attach bits of fence back together with strong wire. I mostly hold things in place while Thorstein does the fixing, and I suspect he could probably do this job alone, but I'm enjoying myself too much to care. And it feels strange, to allow myself to relax and just take pleasure in hard work.

About halfway around the field, while I'm struggling to cut a piece of wire with the wire-cutter, Thorstein says out of nowhere, "You really like him, don't you?"

I force myself to finish cutting the wire, to not stammer out a lame excuse. "Like who?" I say, and Thorstein raises an eyebrow.

"Bjarni," he says.

I look away, over the field, watch a couple of swallows dipping and swooping over the grass, hunting for insects. Thorstein follows my gaze and for a moment we just watch the birds.

"I'm a werewolf, remember," he says gently. "I can smell how your emotions change when I mention his name."

"I know," I say, eyes following the birds. "I do like him," I say, and it feels like a confession. "I more than like him." It makes me feel lighter to tell someone. "But I know he'll never feel the same way. It's okay. I'm a grownup; I can deal."

He sighs and rubs Chuck's forehead. The horse blows air out through his nose and closes his eyes, leans into Thorstein's scratching fingers. "You have some idea of how we grew up," he says. "Even if Bjarni was interested in guys, he could be so far in the closet he doesn't even know himself. If he was gay or bi, he'd have had to be, to survive our father." He looks at me kindly. "I'm not saying you should get your hopes up," he says. "But I can tell he thinks of you as a friend at the very least." He stares back at the swooping birds.

"I think he feels towards you the way I feel about our whole pack," he says.

I look at him, at his profile as he watches the swallows fly. He's all hard angles, there's not a single thing soft about him, physically, but he's so kind, so gentle, so patient. If I can trust anyone, I can trust Thorstein.

"How's that?" I whisper.

One corner of his mouth quirks up but he doesn't look at me. "He wants to keep you safe. To protect you." Then he does look at me, his blue-green eyes paler than the sky. "He wants to take care of you."

I don't look away this time. "I don't want someone to take care of me," I say. "I want someone to help me learn how to take care of myself."

When Thorstein drops me off at Bjarni's front door, my legs are so sore I can hardly stand. When I walk, I could swear I've gone permanently bowlegged.

"You'll get used to it," Thorstein says. "For now, take a bath as hot as you can stand it, and stay in as long as you can. And take painkillers before bed."

I know from the lights that Bjarni is in the living room, which I have to pass by to get to the stairs. I can hear a video game, so I walk as quietly as I can. He still hears me.

"Hey, Justin, want to play a game with me?" he calls.

I stop, turn towards the living room door. He's sitting on the huge leather couch, beer on the coffee table in front of him, game controller in hand.

"I'm under orders to take a very hot bath," I say.

He sets the controller down and gets up. "Did he have you on a horse all day? That was just mean."

"I'm fine," I say, turning for the stairs. "It was nice to be outside."

"You're going to be sore."

"Yeah." I stare up the staircase, which seems a lot longer than it was. I make myself take the first step, ignoring Bjarni as he follows me.

"Don't you check your phone?" he says. "Or did you forget you have one?"

I kind of did forget. It's been in my pocket all day, set to silent. I pull it out, look at the screen. Three texts, all from Bjarni. One was from last night.

i'm sorry, is all it says.

This morning, he sent, *want me 2 bring u brkfst?* And later, *you ok?*

"I didn't see your messages, sorry," I say, and pull myself up the stairs by willpower and much use of the banister.

"I was shitty to you yesterday," he says. "I shouldn't have just left like that. Without saying anything."

"It's fine," I say. My stomach hurts again. I don't want to talk about this. I make it to the top of the stairs and turn towards the bathroom. Bjarni gets there first, and when I get to the door, he's already got water running in the huge clawfoot tub and he's rummaging in a cupboard.

"What are you doing?" I say.

"Running you a bath, he says, and stands up, holding a big plastic bag triumphantly. "I knew I had Epsom salts."

"I don't need you to baby me." It comes out angrier than I meant it to.

"I know," he says. "I just –" He shakes his head and walks over to the tub, dumps a generous amount of Epsom salts into the water, and tests the temperature with his free hand.

"I'm sorry, Justin," he says. "I just didn't know what to do."

My stomach clenches and I want to turn and walk away, but I can't move.

"Didn't know what to do about what?" I say, more boldly than I feel, letting a bit of anger into my voice again, even though in my belly I just want to curl into a tiny ball on the floor.

He sets the bag of salts aside and moves a step closer. "About you," he says. "About –" He makes a frustrated gesture. "About *wanting* you."

I refuse to look away. I told Thorstein I wanted to take care of myself, so I might as well start now. "Running away and picking up some random woman in a bar seemed like the appropriate solution?" I say.

He steps closer again. "No," he says. "But it seemed like a really good way to forget. To…" He flares his nostrils. "To make you hate me."

That was not exactly what I expected. "You find me so repulsive you'd rather I *hated* you?" I say. I will *not* fucking cry. "Do you want me to leave?"

"No, I don't want you to leave," he says. "I thought if you hated me… it… You wouldn't be hurt." His fist strikes the doorframe and I jump. "It was stupid, and I'm sorry. I should have stayed and dealt with how I was feeling like an actual adult."

I step around him to turn off the water before it gets so full it'll overflow when I get in. And I flinch away when he touches my back.

"Don't," I say, and turn to face him.

"Justin," he says. "Please let me apologize." He doesn't touch me again, but he doesn't move away.

"How," I say, reluctantly, but only a little, "should you have dealt with this immense problem?"

He bites his lip, the most uncertain gesture I've ever seen him make. It makes him look younger. "I guess I should have kissed you, like I wanted to. Instead of running away."

"What?"

"Justin, I've never wanted another guy before, never even *looked* at another guy. I *like* fucking women. But you…" He lifts his hand like he's going to touch my face, but he doesn't. He drops it back to his side.

"Guys that look like you don't want guys that look like me," I say. "Can you leave so I can get in the bath before the water gets too cold to do any good?"

"What do you mean 'guys that look like you'? You're… There's nothing wrong with the way you look."

"We both know that even if you were gay, you'd be way out of my league," I say, suddenly just tired.

"You're wrong," he says. "You're totally fucking wrong."

"Whatever." I pull my t-shirt over my head and stuff it in the hamper. The smell of my clothes from yesterday billows out in a puff of air and I hear Bjarni inhale. I hold very still for a moment, then I decide to just pretend that everything is perfectly normal. Keeping my back to him, I strip off my socks, my jeans, and finally my boxer briefs.

I tell myself I don't care what he thinks of me, and I turn around to get into the tub. I lift my chin and try to meet his eyes, only he's not looking at my face. His gaze is running up and down my body.

"Allfather on a fucking pogo stick," he says, softly.

I try to step around him, but he doesn't get out of my way.

"Please go," I say, and I mean it to come out firmly, but it's barely audible.

He meets my eyes finally. "You're so fucking beautiful."

No words will come out of my mouth. Tears burn in the corners of my eyes, but I refuse to let them out. He steps closer and I don't step back. He puts his hands on my face, cups my cheeks. "Justin," he says. "*Kjaereste.* You're fucking beautiful and don't ever let anyone tell you otherwise." Then he crushes his lips to mine, pries my mouth open with his, and kisses me hard, teeth and tongue. And he leaves, closing the door softly behind him.

The bath helps soothe my tired, aching body, even if it does nothing to help my confusion.

I lounge until the water starts to cool, then I scrub my hair, notice it's grown a little longer, maybe doesn't look quite so tragic, and scrub myself with the new bar of soap I got when Raine took me shopping. It's handmade from goat's milk, and it smells like the forest.

I hear Bjarni's footsteps on the stairs as I'm finishing toweling off. His tap on the door is much quieter and more hesitant than I'd ever expect from him.

"It's not locked," I say.

He opens the door. "Hey," he says.

"Hey."

He holds up a bottle. "I thought maybe… I studied massage therapy for about five minutes a few decades ago. When I was trying to find creative ways to piss off my dad," he says. "I'm actually pretty good at it. Though it turns out they don't let you specify that you only want to massage hot chicks."

I don't know how to answer that. Of course, I want his hands on me, but is that really a good idea? No matter how much it might turn out he's attracted to me, he still prefers women. I can hardy expect that to change.

"Even with the hot bath and Epsom salts, you're going to be sore tomorrow. A leg massage will help," he says.

I still don't know what to say. I managed, for a moment, to stand up for myself, but I don't know how anymore. I'm too tired. Too confused.

Maybe he senses my weakness, because he flashes his toothy grin and pulls a chair away from the wall and points to it. "Sit," he says, and I sit. He moves another chair, sits himself, and lifts one of my feet into his lap. Then he opens the bottle, squirts some oil onto his hands and digs his thumbs into the pad of my foot.

"Oh, my God," I whisper, and he chuckles, low and rumbly.

"Feels good, doesn't it?" he says.

His hands are very strong and sure as he rubs my foot, then my calf. He sets that leg back on the floor and lifts the other one, repeating the process. I feel like I'm melting into my chair, like my skin is on fire. I clutch my towel closed at my groin, try to ignore the burning heat there.

Bjarni moves his chair closer and kneads the muscle above my left knee, then the long muscle along the outside of my thigh. He doesn't look at me; his head is tilted to one side, his eyes closed, as he digs his fingers, his thumbs, the heels of his hands into my thigh, sliding up under my towel to reach every bit of muscle that might be left sore from riding.

Then he moves to my right thigh.

"Stand up and turn around," he says, when he's done with both legs.

"What?" All I can force out is a hoarse whisper. Then I say, "I'm not sure I *can* stand up." But I do as he says. He stands behind me.

"This works better lying down," he says. "You're going to have to take the towel off."

"What?" I say again.

"Your ass muscles are going to be sore, too," he says. "Take the towel off so I can massage them."

I'm not sure I'm breathing when I undo the towel from my waist, pull it off my butt, and hold it bunched in front of my crotch. I'm so hard it hurts. My balls ache. I bite back a moan when Bjarni's oily hands dig into my ass muscles, knead them until it's almost too much.

His hands slide up my back, thumbs pressing into the muscles there, too. Then he leans over my shoulder and growls into my ear, "Can I buy you a beer?"

Chapter Seven

IFIND IT HARD TO CONCENTRATE on dinner because every time I shift position on my chair and a sore muscle twinges, I think about Bjarni's hands on me, slippery with massage oil. Trying to fall asleep isn't much better.

The next day is a day off, which is a good thing, because I barely get myself down the stairs. I have no idea how I'd be able to do any useful work with my legs feeling like they do. Even the thought of walking to the farmhouse for breakfast is too much.

But halfway down the stairs, I realize my stomach is growling because I smell bacon. Here, in Bjarni's house. And in the kitchen I find Bjarni, dressed in sweatpants and an extremely threadbare t-shirt, turning over bacon in a cast iron pan.

"How do you like your eggs?" he asks, before I can even comment on the apron he has on over his t-shirt. It has a picture of a fork and spatula and the saying "You're going to want my meat in your mouth" printed on it.

"Over easy," I say, and he grins.

"Can't guarantee they won't get broken," he says and I shrug. "I made you tea," he points at a steaming mug on the table, where a teabag floats in brown water. I fish it out with a spoon and take a sip. It's actually not bad.

"I didn't know you even had a kettle," I say, sinking into a chair and unsuccessfully biting back a groan.

"I don't. I had to use a pot."

I look at the stove, where a small saucepan, steaming slightly, has been pushed to the back burner.

I sip my tea again, feel the steam soothe my sore eyelids.

"Didn't sleep well?" he says, putting a plate loaded with bacon, hashbrowns, and two perfect over-easy eggs in front of me.

"Bad dreams," I say.

"You want to talk about it?"

I shake my head. "Just running, pain, the smell of beer and meat. Oil and gas. I kept waking up, right when I might have seen his face, or heard his voice."

He sits down with his own plate of food.

"Why did you make me breakfast?" I say. "You hate cooking."

"I don't hate cooking," he replies. "I just don't have anyone to cook *for*, usually." He stuffs a whole slice of bacon in his mouth, chews, swallows. "And I'm trying to apologize."

I don't want to talk about what he's apologizing for. I don't even want to think about it.

"I thought you apologized yesterday."

"I don't think I can apologize enough." He scoops up a forkfull of hashbrowns.

"Well, stop," I say. "It's weird." I eat a piece of bacon, which tastes so good I immediately eat another one.

"Not gonna stop until I'm certain you've forgiven me," he says.

I don't know if I *can* forgive him, even if I can hardly blame him for just being who he is. So I don't say anything, but I do enjoy the breakfast, even though it's way more food than I usually eat in the morning. Or all day.

"Any plans for today?" he says.

I shake my head. "Go for a run," I say, though I'm not sure I'd get more than a couple of steps. "Read. Raine gave me some art history books to study." I eat the last bit of hashbrown and get up to do the dishes. I ignore the burning in my leg muscles. It could have been a lot worse.

"You?" I take his empty plate.

"Drink beer and play video games," he says.

"Ambitious."

He snorts. "You want to join me?"

"Will you come for a run with me?"

"I only run in wolf shape," he says. "And you don't have yours yet."

"Where do you run in wolf shape?"

"The forest by the salmon hatchery if I want a really good run," he says, and I wince at the thought of what happened to me there. "Or our wood lot, if I just need to burn some energy quick."

I rinse the plate I'm holding and add it to the stack on the dish rack. Bjarni gets up and starts drying. "So we'll go to the hatchery and I'll run on two legs while you run on four."

"Are you okay to go back there?" he asks, taking the cast iron pan out of my hand and setting it on the stove, turning on a burner to dry it.

I shrug. "I might as well find out."

"How about this?" he says. "You go for a quick run, while I gather snacks. Today we drink beer and play video games, and tomorrow we go to the forest and have a really good run. I'll show you the best places to go once you're a little more wolfie."

I hang up the dish towel, arranging it perfectly flat so I can avoid looking at him. Yesterday he told me I was beautiful, and now he wants to spend the weekend with me.

"Please," he says. Something in his voice makes me look up at him. "This is going to sound really lame, but it's nice to have someone I can hang out with. I grew up with cousins in and out of the house all the time, so there was always someone to play with, to watch movies with, to share chores. But no one to spend time with because they *wanted* to, only because they had no choice."

"I grew up only being allowed to play with the kids from my parents' church," I say, crossing my arms over my chest like I'm meeting a challenge. "And when I finally made a friend in junior high, I suddenly found myself homeschooled."

"Okay, you win." He laughs. "It's possible your childhood sucked more than mine."

I laugh, too, and it feels like a release, like I'm letting go of a whole lot of shit I was holding in.

"So? Pretend to shoot stuff with me all day and we'll get some proper exercise tomorrow? I bet your legs will thank you for a day of rest."

The game he chooses turns out to have as much climbing around in ridiculously detailed CG environments as it does shooting. It's really a single-player game, so we take turns with the controller. Mostly I do the exploring parts, and Bjarni does the shooting. The few times I try to shoot the bad guys, I end up getting us killed.

"It doesn't matter," he says, when I swear in frustration at dying again. "We just start again at the last save point."

"And then we have to raft down the damn rapids again."

"You're getting better," he says.

"I'm really not."

"What you need," he declares, climbing over my legs, "is another beer."

"I'm going to die six times before you get back," I say. Somehow, the little video game character, a dude way cooler and better looking than I'll ever be, is still alive when Bjarni climbs back over my legs and cracks open the two bottles of beer – some kind of dark brown local microbrew that is far too easy to drink.

He tries to hand me my beer but I'm busy trying to keep from dying so he holds it to my mouth.

"Drink," he says.

"I can't see. You're in my way."

He tips the bottle before I'm ready and it pours over my chin and down my neck.

I look at him. He looks at me, eyes wide. And maybe it's the look on his face, or maybe it's because I've already had several beers – and even the werewolf metabolism can't keep up with the rate I've been downing them – but I burst out laughing.

I don't even know when the last time was that I drank enough to even feel a little buzzed. It feels good to let go a bit, knowing that I'm still safe.

I laugh until my sides ache and when I can finally breathe, I realize Bjarni's been laughing right along with me.

He takes the controller from me and sets it on the table. "Let's try that again," he says.

"I have hands," I say. "I mean they're free now. My hands. For drinking."

"We need practice," he insists. "For next time." He takes both of my hands and presses them into my lap. Then he lifts the beer bottle, puts it to my lips, and tips it. I manage one swallow before it runs down my chin.

"Oops," I say.

He sets the bottle aside. "Got your shirt wet," he says.

"I better get a clean one." I don't move.

"I'll help." He grabs the hem of my t-shirt and pulls it over my head before I can stop him. Then he picks up the beer bottle and tries to pour beer in my mouth again. And misses. It runs down my chest and pools in my belly button.

"You're wasting beer," I say. "I like that beer."

"You can have mine," Bjarni says. Then he grins a wicked grin at me. "I'll have yours." And he ducks his head, right down to my stomach, and licks the beer out of my belly button, traces the path of malty liquid across my abs and between my pecs. He pauses, then licks my neck, my chin. And ends up with his lips on mine, probing my mouth with his tongue.

"Bjarni," I say, maybe to protest, maybe just to say his name.

"Did I get it all?" he says.

"Pretty sure you missed some." My voice is rough, barely audible.

"Where?" He examines my chest, tracing the path of the beer spill with one finger.

"Everywhere," I say. Then I look into his eyes. "But mostly here." And I grab his hair with both hands and kiss him. He doesn't startle, doesn't pull away, doesn't even hesitate. He meets my tongue with his own, tilts his head and opens his lips wider to kiss me deeper.

When we pull apart, we're both breathing hard.

"Fuck," he says. It's partly moan, filled with wanting.

"Bjarni?" I hate how hesitant my voice is, how afraid I am that he's going to get up and leave again.

"Mmm?" He's nuzzling my neck, and it's sending little zaps of tingling electrical pulses down to my crotch, by way of both nipples.

"Are you doing this because you're drunk or –"

He sits up, cups his hand around my cheek. "I'm not drunk," he says. "Buzzed, definitely. Drunk, no."

"Do you –" I can't finish the sentence.

He strokes my hair, mouth curling into a half-smile. "Come upstairs," he says.

"What?"

He gets up and holds out his hand, and when I take it in one of mine, he pulls me to my feet. And he's right. I'm not drunk either. Just buzzed. And happy.

He keeps hold of my hand and leads me upstairs, into his bedroom. It's late enough in the day that the sun has moved from the back of the house to the front, and most of the room is bathed in light. He shuts the door but leaves the blinds open. Only a thin curtain blocks out the view, and it's not enough to keep out the sun.

For a long moment, he just stands, holding my hand, looking at me.

Then he says, "Why don't you think you're good looking?"

I look away, at the window. I can just see the brown sheep grazing through the gap in the thin fabric. "I have eyes," I say. "I've seen myself in the mirror."

He shakes his head. "Hasn't anyone ever told you you're wrong? That you're…" He pauses, lets go of my hand to put both of his hands on my face. "You're so lovely," he says. "I don't understand why you can't see it."

When he kisses me this time, it's soft, so soft it's almost not a kiss. He just brushes his lips on mine, across my cheek, finds the spot under my ear that makes me shiver.

His hands slide over my chest, the callouses on his fingers catching on my nipples, and I can't suppress the moan that comes out of my throat.

"You like that?" he whispers in my ear. He rubs both nipples with the pads of his thumbs and I arch towards him, wanting his body pressed against mine. "Gods, I wish my nipples were that sensitive," he says, and ducks his head to flick his tongue across one, to suck on it until I moan again.

"Bjarni," I say, and my voice squeaks on the final syllable. He straightens up, looks into my eyes.

"Justin," he says.

"Don't stop touching me," I say. I'm begging, and I don't care. "Please."

His hands stroke my back, tucking me close, pausing only to strip off his shirt so our chests are pressed together. "I'm here," he says. "I've got you."

I find his mouth with mine again, dare to push him back a step, towards the bed. He growls deep in his throat, and I push him back another step, and another. He pulls me down onto the bed with him and we sit on the edge, side by side, mouths pressed together, hands stroking bare skin.

"Stand up for a sec," he says. I don't ask why, I just stand. He hooks a finger under the waistband of my sweatpants, pulls it away from my body, and slides the pants down my legs. He frowns when he sees I'm still covered, then takes my boxers off the same way.

I look down at him, he looks up at me. My boner twitches and the corner of his mouth quirks up.

"Come here," he says, and pulls me closer to bury his face in my crotch. He inhales, deep, and moans. "You smell so fucking good." I feel his breath on my pubic hair. He pulls me back down to sit beside him again, turns to face me, to stroke his hand down my face.

"I want you, Justin," he says, his voice mostly growl.

I can't make words come out, so I just kiss him, put my hand on his chest to push him back on the bed, lean over him. I try to tell him with touch what I don't dare say in words. I kiss his neck, nibble his earlobe, trace the strap muscle of his neck with my tongue. I feel each muscle in his chest with my hands and follow with my mouth. I find one of his nipples with my lips and when he hardly reacts, I bite.

I start to move away, but his hand cups the back of my head and holds me there. "Do that again," he says. "Harder." So I bite down on the tender flesh – I find it endearing that his nipples are soft pink – dig my teeth in as hard as I dare and he arches his back, tightens his fingers on my scalp, and makes a strangled noise in his throat.

When his grip on my head eases, I bite his other nipple, more sure of myself, and he moans.

Then I trace the outline of each of his abs with my fingers, and my tongue, kiss and nibble across his belly, and have to stop when I reach the waistband of his sweatpants.

I slide off the side of the bed, tug at his pants until he lifts his hips so I can slide them off. He's not wearing anything underneath and for a moment all I can do is stare at him.

I mean, yeah, I'm gay, so I like dick, but penises in general are pretty stupid looking. But Bjarni's isn't. He's big, and he's uncut, and so swollen his foreskin has pulled all the way back, leaving his tip exposed and already glistening with a drop of moisture.

Finally, I nudge his knees apart, kneel between them, and curl my fingers around his length.

"Fuck," he says, all breath. He pushes himself up onto his elbows to watch me. I meet his eyes, and run my tongue up the underside of him, watch his eyes close.

He shifts his weight to lean on a single elbow so he can run his fingers through my hair.

I kiss the inside of his thigh, lick the crease where his leg meets his pelvis, nip the sensitive skin.

"Extend your wolf teeth," he says.

"I don't have wolf teeth yet," I say.

"Try." His fingers scrape against my scalp, and I think about being a wolf, about big canines descending from my gums, claws sliding out of my fingers. I think I can feel my jaw rearranging to make room, but I still almost shriek when claws really do appear, sliding out of the ends of my fingers and digging into Bjarni's hip where I've been holding it. I carefully uncurl my fingers from his cock before I make him bleed somewhere unforgivable.

"Bjarni," I say, hearing how my voice is slurred trying to talk around teeth too big for my mouth – and they aren't even nearly as big as they will eventually be.

"I knew you could do it, *kjaereste*," he says.

I'm terrified, suddenly, of myself, but he just looks at me calmly, pride in his gaze, so I turn my head, open my mouth, and set my teeth against the inside of his thigh.

"Bite me," he says. I bite him, timidly. "Harder," he says, and I sink my teeth in until I feel the skin break, taste his blood. And then I let go, lick away the blood and watch fascinated as the little puncture wounds close and scab over.

I look at his face again and his eyes are half-closed, his lips curved upwards. I make sure my claws and teeth slide away and return to human before I curl my fingers around him again, push myself up on my knees, and slide my lips over him.

He's too big to fit his full length in my mouth, so I keep my hand on the base of him, stroke while I suck. He sits up more, watching me, stroking my hair gently.

"You should grow your hair out," he says, rough-voiced. "Just enough to give me a good grip."

If he's thinking about me blowing him again when my hair is longer, then maybe this isn't a one-time, drunk afternoon thing. Maybe I can have more.

I pause, and he groans. "Don't stop," he says. I slide my lips over him as far as I can, feel him in the back of my throat. And then I swallow, and for just a moment, before my gag reflex threatens to kick in, I'm able to take more of him. He groans louder.

"Justin, fuck." His fingers tighten in my too-short hair. "I'm gonna fucking come." And he does, flooding my mouth with heat and salt. I keep sucking until he stops throbbing, then slide off him, taking every drop of moisture into my mouth.

When I lift my head and look at him, he says, "Swallow."

I swallow, and he studies my face.

"Come here," he says, and I get up, sit on the edge of the bed again. He puts an arm around me, drags me with him to lie full-length on the bed, lays my head gently on a pillow, and kisses me so hard our teeth crack together.

He moves to my neck, growls in my ear, "You made me break my one unbreakable sex rule."

I go still, and he shifts so he can look into my face. I'm anxious again, but he's smiling. "My partner always comes first," he says.

"Why?"

"Because I'm a selfish prick and if they don't, I might not bother once I'm done."

Does that mean he's going to fall asleep now? Leave me hard and hot and wanting him desperately?

But he kisses me again, rolls a nipple between finger and thumb until I cry out, nibbles my skin from chest to belly, and curls his fingers around my erection. His hands are big, and my cock's not as impressive as his, and for one desperate moment I'm afraid he'll be disappointed. Then his tongue finds me, his mouth slides over me, and I try to say his name, but halfway through it turns into a moan.

"I fucking love how you say my name when you're turned on," he says, and I grab his hair with both hands.

"Don't stop," I say. He obliges, puts his mouth on me again, sucks until I feel like I'm going to die if I don't get release soon. Instead, he lifts his head again.

"How did you do that?" he says. "Where you somehow… fit more of me in your mouth?"

I pant, trying to catch my breath. "You have to suppress your gag reflex and… kind of… swallow."

"Swallow," he says, looking at where he's slowly stroking me, making me squirm.

"It takes practice," I gasp. "It'll definitely make you gag the first few times. You might bite me by accident. Or throw up."

"Do you want me to try?"

"Fuck yes."

So he tries, and he gags, but he doesn't bite me, or throw up, and then I can't stop. The orgasm hits me so hard I see grey at the edges of my vision, and I think I yell out his name, but I'm not even sure.

When I can finally relax, he looks up at me from between my thighs, like he's waiting for something.

"Swallow," I whisper, and he grins. I can see the white fluid, *my* fluid, seeping between his teeth. Then he swallows, crawls back up the bed to hover over me, and finally lie next to me, and tucks me close.

"I didn't know guys could give blowjobs like that," he says. "I didn't know *anyone* could give blowjobs like that."

He kisses the side of my face. "I think I've been missing out."

"I wanted to make you feel good," I say. "And sucking cock is about the only thing I'm good at."

"I don't believe that," he says.

We lie together for a little longer, then he gets up. "I'm gonna have a shower."

I feel cold where his body heat was, but I'm so relaxed I don't even move to pull a blanket over myself.

When he comes back, rubbing his hair with a towel, he nudges me gently and I open my eyes. He's still naked, strong, beautiful, and I smile so hard my skin feels tight.

He smiles back. "Your turn," he says. "I left you lots of hot water."

I get up, unsteady and limp, gather my clothes, and go to the bathroom. I want to shower quickly, but I'm too tired, too sated, and I linger under the water.

When I get out, dry off, and walk naked into the hall, Bjarni's door is closed. I stare at it, like I've been gut-punched, and try to work up the courage to knock, or to just walk in. But finally, I go to my own room, get into my narrow, cold bed, and curl into a ball. I only remember that we missed dinner when my stomach rumbles, but I ignore it and wait for sleep to put me out of my misery.

Chapter Eight

I LAY IN BED AS LONG as I can stand it the next morning, hoping he'll be gone when I get up, or at least playing video games in the living room again, so I can slip out the kitchen door at the back.

But he's sitting at the kitchen table, drinking coffee, and looking at something on his phone.

"You okay?" he says. "I made you tea, but I'm pretty sure it's cold by now."

"I'm fine," I say, and fish the tea bag out of the cup. It is cold, and too strong, but I drink it anyway.

He doesn't say anything and when I look up, he's frowning. "You're not fine," he says. At least he doesn't accuse me of lying.

I put my teacup down, carefully, lining the handle up with the edge of the counter. I don't want to tell him I was hurt that he shut me out, that I wanted to curl up with him and fall asleep. Together. I don't want to sound childish. I rub my face with both hands.

"Bad dreams again," I finally say, which is true, even if it isn't what's bothering me.

"Did you remember anything else?"

I shake my head.

"Are you sure you want to run in the woods today?" he says. "We can stay in and play games again. Or I can show you the quickest way to the wood lot."

"I'll be fine. I need the exercise."

He leans back in his chair, studying me.

"What?" I say, turning my back on him to rinse my cup. I don't hear him get up, don't know he's there until his hands are on my hips, pulling me back against him. His breath is hot on my neck.

"Are you mad about last night?" he says, and for a moment I think he's realized that shutting me out of his room was mean. But then he says, "Do you want to pretend it never happened?" He slides his hands around to my stomach, up under my shirt and onto my chest. "'Cause I'm not sure I can do that."

I don't answer. I stare out the window over the sink, to where there's an area surrounded by high chain link fencing. Three dogs stand by the gate, watching the house. They're different kinds of dogs, but all very large.

He must notice where I'm looking. "They were Dad's guard dogs," he says. "I don't know what to do with them, so they stay in the farmhouse at night, and run around out there during the day."

"Why would a werewolf need guard dogs?"

"Dad was paranoid someone would try to take over his position as pack leader."

His fingers find my nipples and I try to jerk away. He goes still, then moves his hands away, leans back enough to turn me around so he can see my face.

"Justin?" he says. I can't meet his eyes, so I look over his left shoulder. "I thought… yesterday was pretty amazing. Am I wrong? Did you – ? Was I – ?" He stops, then steps abruptly away. "I'm sorry," he says and turns for the door.

"Bjarni." I finally force the word out. He turns back. His face is blank, unreadable, like he knows I'll be able to tell what he's feeling if he lets any expression show.

I take a step towards him, and another. "Yesterday was good," I say. "Very good. Don't go." I get close enough to lay a hand on his chest, feel him breathe, feel his heartbeat. "I'm just… I'm…" I close my hand into a fist, bunching up his t-shirt between my fingers.

"Are you still afraid of me?" he says.

I swallow hard. I can't say no, but I don't want to say yes, because I'm not afraid of him the way he thinks I am. I'm afraid of wanting him too much.

He grabs my wrist and swings me around, backs me up to the wall and pins me there, one hand on my throat, thumb and fingers digging in.

"You are," he says.

I make myself meet his eyes. He's frowning, scowling.

"Don't do that," I say.

"Because it frightens you?" he asks.

And before I can think clearly enough to regret it, I say, "Because it turns me on."

He rubs his thumb up and down my neck, staring at me. I don't think he expected that. He presses closer, puts his mouth against my neck.

"Does it?" he says, voice deep and growly.

I press the hand not trapped between us back against the wall, as if the solidity of the building can give me courage.

"Can't you feel how hard I am?" I say, pushing my pelvis against his, shocked by my own daring.

He pushes back. "Oh, is that for me?" he says.

There's a knock at the door and we both go still, listening as it creaks open.

"Hi, Colleen," Bjarni calls when he recognizes the footsteps. He moves away, adjusts his pants, and points from me to a chair. We're both sitting, bulging trouser crotches hidden by the table, when she reaches the kitchen.

She gives Bjarni a funny look when he doesn't get up to help her with the plates she's balancing. "I had to leave the front door open," she says.

"What's all this?" Bjarni gestures at the plates she's set on the table.

"One or the other or both of you keep missing meals, and Hilde and I can't eat it all. So, room service." She puts her hands on her hips and looks from one to the other of us. Then she shakes her head. "Men. I don't know how any of you survive on your own."

"Bjarni made breakfast yesterday," I say.

"Did he, indeed? I didn't know he had anything in his refrigerator."

"I'm not helpless," he says.

"No," she answers. "Just lazy. I wonder what put that bee in your bonnet." She looks pointedly at me, but when I don't say anything, she unwraps the plates, puts one in front of each of us and says, "Eat." Then she leaves and closes the door loudly on her way out.

"I might have to start locking the door," Bjarni says.

I'm too busy staring at the huge pile of chocolate chip pancakes on the plate in front of me to answer. "How am I supposed to eat all this?"

"With homemade maple syrup?" he says, and gets up to fetch syrup, butter, and cutlery. His bulge is gone, I note, a little disappointed. Then again, so is mine.

I manage about half the stack before I have to stop. Bjarni eats all of his and makes a start on finishing mine.

"Are you going to be able to run after that?" I say.

"I'll run slow," he answers, grinning.

When we get to the salmon hatchery parking lot, it takes me a long time to make myself get out of the car. Bjarni waits patiently, sitting behind the wheel.

"We don't have to do this," he says.

"*You* don't," I say. "I do." I open the door and put one foot on the gravel. "It's like that thing they say about horses."

"What's that?" He sounds amused.

"If you fall off, you have to get right back on, or you'll lose your nerve."

"Or, in my case, you just never ride a horse again."

I pause, about to put my other foot on the gravel, and twist around to look at him.

He looks back and gives me a self-deprecating smile. "I used to ride rodeo. Steer roping, mostly," he says. "It was the one thing I did that *almost* made Dad proud. Until I went over my horse's head and landed crotch-first on a steer's horns."

I wince and he laughs.

"So, if you're wondering if your symbiont will regenerate your family jewels in case of a horrific accident, the answer is yes." He snorts at the expression I must be making. "Very slowly and painfully."

"You don't have any scars," I say, then suddenly realize what I've said and blush fiercely, like my whole body's on fire.

He tries unsuccessfully to keep his grin from getting any wider. "Once you're fully a wolf, it takes a lot to make scars permanent. And I guess my symbiont wanted me fully functional, so my junk healed perfectly."

I can't help but hunch over a little at the thought of damaging and having to re-grow that particular part of my anatomy.

"Unfortunately, it provided Thorstein with his favorite threat when I do something he doesn't like." He makes his face very stern and deepens his voice even more. "If you do that, Little Bear, I'll rip your testicles off, and you can spend the rest of your life growing them back."

His imitation of Thorstein is good enough that it makes me laugh, and that reduces my anxiety enough that I'm able to get out of the car and start stretching.

The parking lot is empty, so Bjarni strips off his clothes and leaves them on his seat. He doesn't seem bothered by the gravel under his bare feet.

"Stop staring at me, *kjaereste*," he says, cocking an eyebrow at me. "You're turning me on and running on all fours is not easy with a giant stiffie catching on all the undergrowth." He leers. "It won't tuck in properly if I'm aroused."

"Sorry." I turn away and start whistling, staring pointedly at the sky. "Here I am, very much not looking at your huge cock."

"You better start running, pretty boy, or I'm going to do something dirty to you with my huge cock."

"Promises, promises," I say, but I head for the path along the river. I start slow because I haven't been for a proper run since the last time I was here – and I *won't* think about what happened then. And besides, my legs still haven't recovered from spending all day on a giant horse. And my belly is full of pancakes.

I listen for Bjarni behind me and almost have a heart attack when he appears in front of me instead, in the middle of the path, on all fours and looking decidedly wolf-like.

The thing about werewolf wolf shapes, though, is that they're not *really* wolves. Like, the symbiont alters you physically, so your joints bend differently, and proportions shift. Teeth and claws and tail and hair kind of extend rather than grow.

Werewolves in wolf shape look more like B-movie latex prosthetic werewolves in a lot of ways than they look like natural wolves. They'd be mistaken for huge wolves in the dark of night, sure, but in full daylight it would be hard to see them as anything but monsters. Or us. I should say *us*. My symbiont will make me look like that eventually, too.

And Bjarni *is* monstrous. But he's also beautiful, especially when he turns to run along the path in front of me. He's like liquid gold – because the hair he's covered in, not enough to call him truly furry, is the same dark blond as his human hair, and it shines in the sunlight that filters down through the trees. And if I thought he was beautiful to watch in motion in human shape, he's even more breathtaking in wolf shape, no movement wasted, every muscle and ligament working in perfect harmony with the rest.

Maybe it makes me a pervert, but Bjarni's almost as hot in wolf shape as he is as a human.

I have to stop and walk before I'd like, and Bjarni notices immediately, and slows to walk alongside me. Absently, I stroke his hair with one hand, running my palm across his shoulders and along his spine.

"Are you *petting* me?" he says, somehow managing to speak clearly with a muzzle full of huge teeth.

I almost snatch my hand away, but instead I raise my eyebrows and say, "Yes."

"I'm not a dog," he says.

"No, you're an extremely sexy man who turns *into* a dog." I turn away and stare along the path, pretend not to notice his indignant look.

"Wolf," he says. "Sort of. And if you keep doing that, I'm going to have to turn *out* of a wolf and drag you off into the bushes."

I don't take my hand away, but I do stop stroking his back and just rest my palm on his shoulder. "Have you ever –" I say but stop myself.

"Have I ever what?"

"Never mind."

He looks up at me, stares for a moment, and then a knowing look comes over his face, and a wicked smile.

"You want to know if I've ever fucked anyone in wolf shape."

I don't answer. Put that way, it sounds crude.

He chuckles, which sounds really weird coming from his giant wolf body.

"A couple of times," he says. "But she was *also* in wolf shape."

"Does that matter?" I say.

He doesn't answer right away, and when I look at him, he appears to be considering the question.

"I don't know," he finally says. Then, looking at me out of the corners of his eyes, "Would you fuck me in wolf shape? Like this?"

The path here is flat and smooth, so I can take my time looking at him, studying him. "If I had my wolf shape," I finally say. "I probably would."

"But if you didn't?"

"I'd be too scared," I admit.

"You're more afraid of me like this?" he says, voice soft and growly.

"I'm more afraid of what your teeth and claws might do to my sensitive bits," I say. "I'm not eager to find out what it feels like to re-grow them."

"That's fair," he says. Then, "Note to self: do not seduce Justin in wolf shape." He looks sidelong at me again. "Yet."

When I feel a bit rested, we turn back, and I break into a slow run again. "You don't have to wait for me, you know," I say. I wave my hand. "Go run back and forth, or something."

"You sure?"

"I'm fine. Don't hover."

Then he launches suddenly away, off to one side into the woods. I hear crashing for a heartbeat or two, then nothing.

I'm concentrating so hard on keeping my breathing even that it takes me longer than it should to hear him calling me.

"Bjarni?" I call back, dropping to a walk, then stopping. He's off to my right, closer to the river.

"Don't come over here, Justin. Go back to the car."

I smell blood.

"What? Are you okay?" I step off the path, anxiety clawing at my guts again. An animal trail leads off in the direction his voice is coming from. Fear churns in my belly, but not fear for myself, fear for him. What if he's hurt and doesn't want me to see? There's enough blood I can smell it, thick on the air, so he *must* be hurt.

"I'm coming," I say. "Stay where you are."

"No, Justin," he says. "Go back to the car. You don't need to see this."

I keep going. His voice is closer. He sounds… I don't know how he sounds. Not afraid, exactly. Anxious, maybe. Very concerned with me not seeing whatever it is. Does he sound hurt? Maybe. Scared? No.

He's crouched in a sort of cleared space on the riverbank, where the action of the water has left a gravelly beach. He gets up when I stumble over a half-hidden branch, catches me when I almost fall, and I see…

For a horrible, horrible moment I think *he's* done this, left this blood splattered over moss and leaves and rocks. But of course he hasn't. But *someone* has. Some werewolf. And not just blood.

"Oh my God," I say, and grab Bjarni's arms to keep my feet. He's already holding me, but I still sway unsteadily, almost fall.

On the gravel, face down, lies a half-naked young woman, and spread out around her, ripped and torn, a glistening pile of different colors of flesh. I stare and stare and horror grows and all at once I realize it's her entrails, ripped out and… partially eaten?

Claw marks rend her back and her jogging pants are around her ankles, her legs spread.

I twist desperately away from Bjarni to vomit violently into the bushes. Then he's there, arms around me again, keeping me from falling into my own puke.

"Shh," he says. "I didn't want you to see this, sweetheart." He strokes my hair, my face, tucks me against his chest so I can't see. He leads me back down the animal trail, but I can still smell her, smell beer, smell oil and gasoline. But no, that's *my* memory and fuck I'm going to pass out.

I don't lose consciousness, but it's close. I *do* puke again. And again. And Bjarni finds me a fallen log to sit on, holds me, rocks me back and forth until I can think again. So much for being able to take care of myself.

"What happened to her?" I say. "Was it – ?"

"A werewolf? Yeah." He kisses the top of my head, and I realize he's in human shape, already was when I found him in the clearing. "I smelled… I thought it was an animal. Fresh kill. I can't be sure, but I think he tried to change her, and when she died he…"

"Started to eat her?" I cover my mouth with my hand and manage not to throw up any more chocolate chip pancakes.

"I think he got angry. Lost his shit and tore her apart."

"And –" I stop. I can't say it. "Her joggers were pulled down."

"Don't think about it, *kjaereste*. She was probably already dead, so he didn't hurt her any more than he already had."

"We have to tell Thorstein," I say.

"Yes, we do."

"And we have to call the police."

"Yes."

"But your clothes and our phones are in your car."

"I can run there and back very fast. But I don't want to leave you by yourself."

"Go," I say. "I'll be okay."

"You won't," he says. "You can't lie to me."

"I *will* be okay," I say. "I *have* to be. I'll just sit here until you get back. I'll… I'll recite the Periodic Table of Elements so I can't think of… of *that*."

He kisses the side of my face. "Do you know the Periodic Table of Elements?" he says gently.

"Some of it."

He rests his forehead against mine. "Stay here," he says. "This time, please do as I say."

I nod.

"Okay," he says. "I'll be right back." And then he's gone, changing shape as he runs, I think, but he's out of sight so quickly I can't be sure.

For a little while, I do as he said. I sit on the log and wait. But I have to know. I don't know if I can tell, but I need to know if the werewolf that attacked this woman is the same one who attacked me.

I make sure to follow the exact path back to her body as we took away from it, and when I get there, I try to step only where I'm sure Bjarni stepped.

It's not as horrifying, seeing her the second time, because I know what to expect. And because I let my vision go blurry and don't look right at her.

Seeing won't do me any good, anyway. I didn't see who attacked me, or if I did my brain hasn't seen fit to remind me of it yet. No, what I need now is my sense of smell, and even without my wolf shape, even so early in my development as a werewolf, my sense of smell is better than human. I crouch where Bjarni crouched, next to the woman but not so close I'm touching any part of her, attached or not.

And I breathe in, long and slow. The overwhelming scent of blood almost sends me scrambling to puke in the bushes again, but I manage to detach it from where the blood originated. Blood on its own doesn't bother me; I'd be a pretty crap werewolf if it did.

I breathe in again, let my nose filter the air for me. Blood, damp, maple trees in sunlight, fear – hers and mine – moss, wet gravel, river, cheap beer, cigarette smoke. I have to stop, to breathe, to make sure this is the here and now I'm smelling and I'm not falling into my own memory of terror again.

But no, it isn't my memory. It's here. Cheap beer that came out of a can. Cigarettes. Stale and fresh sweat. Werewolf musk. I go back to the sweat. Could I identify it to an individual if I smelled it again? Maybe. I don't know. I smell her, too, human, afraid. I almost throw up again when I realize I can smell what he did to her, after she was dead.

And then, under it all, oil and gasoline, mildew and damp cloth. I turn my nose towards it, open my eyes. In her mouth, an old rag, once white but stained dark.

And Bjarni's arms are around me again, pulling me away again.

"Fuck, Justin," he says.

"In her mouth," I say, and then let the blackness hide the terror again.

Chapter Nine

I'M ONLY OUT FOR A SECOND, and I don't know if Bjarni even notices, because apparently we're still moving, back to the fallen log where I was supposed to wait for him.

He sits, slides to the ground so his back is to the log and pulls me down with him. He settles me between his legs, leaning me back on his chest, and wraps both arms around me.

"Thorstein's coming," he says. "And my Uncle Seamus. He's a cop. Technically, he's Magne and Hilde's uncle. Colleen's brother. He's… kind of our werewolf liaison, not attached to any one unit, though of course the human cops don't know he's a werewolf, or that we even exist. He'll be the one questioning us. He's a werewolf, too." He stops suddenly. "Fuck, I'm babbling."

I shift so I can lean my cheek on his chest. He's warm, and solid. "Have you seen a dead body before this? Like a person? Dead?"

"Yeah," he says. "A few times, but not brutal like this. Most recently, my dad."

"I'm sorry."

"I'm not. He deserved what he got."

I just breathe for a few minutes, try to absorb his calm. "I've never seen a dead person before," I say. "I've never even seen a badly hurt person. I mean, I've seen people get beat up. I've *been* beat up. But not like that. Some werewolf I am."

"Death and violence don't have to be part of a werewolf's life, *kjaereste*. We just got unlucky."

"But you hunt in wolf shape."

"That's different," he says. "It's a social event, and it's not brutal. And it's not required, either. Lots of werewolves sit out the hunt."

I turn my face closer to his chest, like I can hide from him. From myself. "I hate how weak I am," I say.

I feel his breath on my hair, his lips on the top of my head. "You're not weak," he says. "You're kind. You're sensitive. You're gentle. But you're very, very strong."

His hand strokes my arm and I relax under the soft touch.

"I had to know," I say. "If it was the same werewolf."

"I know. I'm not mad at you." He kisses my head again. "I have no right to tell you what to do, anyway. You're an adult."

"You rank higher than me," I say. "In the pack."

"We don't really have ranks," he replies. "My dad tried to structure things that way, but it's not really how it works. Just some of us have more forceful personalities."

I sigh. "Does this mean the forest won't be safe for werewolves to run in anymore?"

"What, because of the psycho killer or because of the cops?"

"Either."

"Seamus will make sure the cops get what they need the first time. Thorstein will keep looking for the killer. We're narrowing it down. We'll find him. There aren't that many of us it could be."

"Is it against werewolf law to change people?"

"It's discouraged. Usually, the whole pack is involved to some degree, because bringing in a new wolf affects all of us." He suddenly squeezes his arms tighter around me. "Doing it against someone's will, or without asking at all, is *definitely* not okay."

"What will happen to him, when he's caught?"

"That will be for the Elders to decide, but he hasn't just changed someone. Now he's killed. And... molested."

Not long after, there are voices, and crashing in the bushes, and I start to get up, but Bjarni holds me still. Then there's a middle-aged guy with greying hair, the most ordinary-looking guy I've ever seen, staring down at us. I see uniformed police officers behind him.

"It's that way," Bjarni says. "The puke is his." He points to me. "It's a fucking mess, Seamus."

"You two, okay?" The man, Seamus, looks at us with no expression on his face.

Bjarni looks up at him, his lips curling back from his teeth. "Would you be?"

"Depends on what you saw."

"No, we're not okay. I knew her. Fuck."

"Try not to be an asshole, kid," Seamus says. "I'm on your side. I'm here to help."

Bjarni sighs. "I know. I'm sorry. I tried to keep Justin from seeing it. Her. He thought *I* was hurt."

Another voice calls out, from the direction of the river. "O'Malley, get the fuck over here."

"You knew her?" Seamus asks, and Bjarni just nods. "All right. Don't go anywhere."

"I'm so tired of being afraid," I say, squirming around so I'm leaning with my back to Bjarni's chest again.

"I'm sorry, *kjaereste*," he says. "It shouldn't be this way. We're supposed to look out for each other, all of us. Not have one of us start trying to make his own wolves."

"Do you think he wants to start his own pack?" I ask, and Bjarni goes still.

"Shit," he says. "Shit. That could be it. I've been narrowing down who it could be based on the bits of evidence we have, on what you remember. But if someone is pissed that Dad's gone and Thorstein isn't running the pack the same way… Shit."

He shifts to get his phone out of his pocket, starts typing a text, arms still wrapped around me so I can see the screen of his phone as clearly as he does.

justin had an idea, he types and sends.

"I'm right here, Little Bear," Thorstein says. He steps over the log, his phone in his hand, and sits on the fallen tree. Bjarni leans his head against his brother's knee and Thorstein strokes his hair briefly, then leans forward, elbows on knees.

He looks at me. "What are you thinking?"

I twist around to face him properly. "I don't know," I say, suddenly wondering if I have anything at all to add. "But it's the same guy. I'm sure of it. Bjarni thinks he was trying to make her — to make another wolf, and it didn't work." I look at my hands, clenched tight around Bjarni's forearms, my fingers digging into his skin. I force them to relax. "But what if he's trying to make his own pack?"

Thorstein cocks his head, like he's actually considering my idea. "To what end?" he says.

"I have a list of possible suspects," Bjarni says. "Maybe one of them doesn't like how you're changing things."

"And wants to what? Challenge me with his own followers? Drive the rest of us out? A bunch of brand-new wolves isn't going to be very useful for that."

"I don't know," Bjarni says. "Maybe he's hoping others will join him if they think he's some great leader. Or maybe he's not very smart and doesn't realize he can't make thinking creatures do what he wants against their will."

"Except he can, a bit. If he uses compulsion to make his new wolves do simple things, he might convince them that he can make them do anything."

"Compulsion?" I say.

"When a wolf is new, for the first few months, any pack member who contributed blood to the wolf's making, or who has the same symbiont, can compel the wolf to do things. It's supposed to be a way of keeping the new werewolf safe until they can look after themselves." Thorstein laces his fingers together and looks at his hands.

"It only works for simple things, like 'stay here,' or 'stop,' or 'get away from that.' Things that would keep a wolf from getting himself killed," Bjarni adds. Then, reluctantly, he says, "Dad liked to make new wolves kneel and show him their throats."

"Could he…" It's hard to force the words out past the fear threatening to choke me again. "Could he do that to me?"

Bjarni's arms tighten around me.

"Could he?" I repeat, trying to keep the hysteria out of my voice.

"Yes," Bjarni says quietly.

"But only very simple commands," says Thorstein. "And you'll outgrow it in a few months."

I think about that, or try not to, because it scares the shit out of me. Then something else occurs to me. "If he's making his own werewolf pack, why did he leave me in the woods?"

"I found you right when you were recovering from the effects of your first full moon. He was probably waiting for you to wake up, and I got there first."

"It turned out to be a good thing for you, that he changed you right before the full moon. He probably thought it would make you vulnerable, easy to convince, but it also meant he had to wait for you to come out of your moon madness first." Thorstein rests his hand briefly on my head and I lean into it, feeling no need to flinch away.

Seamus O'Malley – Detective O'Malley, as it turns out – comes back then, keeping me from having to think more about the possibilities of my attacker being able to order me around.

"We're calling it a wild animal attack," he says, but the look he gives Thorstein shows that he knows exactly what killed the woman. "We're going to ask Natural Resources to patrol more often for a while, and temporarily close the area to the public."

Thorstein nods. "Jamieson will be in charge?"

"As always," says O'Malley. "So you have nothing to worry about. Except what you were already working on." He looks at me. "You're Justin, yeah?"

I nod.

"Welcome to the family," he says. "I'm sorry it's under such shit circumstances."

"Thank you," I mumble.

He looks at Bjarni. "Tell me how you knew her."

"She…" He stops and his arms tighten around me, then relax. "I picked her up in a bar once. We went to her place. I never saw her again after that."

"You remember her name?"

"Of course I remember her name. It's… It *was* Delia. She never told me her last name."

O'Malley scowls and nods. "You boys can go home, then. We'll finish up here." He looks pointedly at Thorstein and says very quietly, "I'll let you know if we find anything you can use."

Thorstein nods, gets up, and they grip forearms. Then Bjarni nudges me and we get up, too, and each repeat the gesture.

O'Malley gives me a tired smile when it's my turn. "You're stronger than you look," he says, when he lets go of my arm.

When we reach the main path, Thorstein says, "Take him home, Little Bear. I'm going to scout around a bit." Then he heads off away from the parking lot.

It's good that we were almost back to the car, because I'm shaking so hard, I don't think I could have walked far.

We drive quietly for a while, then Bjarni suddenly says, "I killed him."

"What?" I say, startled out of my dark thoughts of running and claws.

"My dad. I killed him."

I can only stare at him for a few long heartbeats. "I thought… Thorstein told me your grandfather killed him. In self-defense. Because your dad thought he was too old, too much of a burden."

Bjarni stares straight ahead, but I can read his face a little. Fear. Of what? Being found out? Of how I'll react? Also grief, and anger. And burning hatred.

"That's what we agreed to tell the Elders," he says. "And Dad did think those things. He did intend to… to euthanize Granddad. So it was true enough they believed it." He shifts his grip on the steering wheel. "But that isn't what happened.

"Dad was torturing Thorstein. He found a way to control him. He was… he was strangling him. Magne was trying to help, but there was nothing he could do. Dad thought I was in the house, and I just walked up behind him and broke his fucking neck."

He swallows and his eyes dart sideways, but he can't quite look at me.

"I couldn't take it anymore. His abuse, his need to control everyone around him. He took away Thorstein's freedom, he drove Magne to leave. I should have fucking done it sooner."

"And your grandfather?"

"He saw it happen. He came up with the cover story and told the other Elders."

I bite my lip. It hurts, and it's terrifying, that he's killed someone. But he did it to protect his brothers, and to escape abuse.

I touch his shoulder and he startles, swerving the car into the other lane before correcting it.

"You did what you had to do," I say, keeping my voice gentle. Keeping my fear from bleeding into my words.

"Thorstein better hope he finds your attacker first," he says, voice utterly cold. "Because if I find him, I won't just snap his neck. I'll spread his fucking entrails out like he did to Delia, and I'll watch him die slowly."

Then he's suddenly pulling the car over, stumbling to the side of the road, and on his knees, throwing up in the ditch.

I follow, and hold his hair back, wrap my arm around his shoulder and whisper comforting words into his neck until he's done.

When we get home, Bjarni locks the front door, then goes to lock the back, too, while I climb the stairs, suddenly too tired for words. I'm in my room, staring at my bed as if I have no idea what to do with it, when Bjarni says, "Hey."

I look up and he's leaning in the doorway. "Hey."

"Come here." He holds out his hand and I step towards him. It's a small room and one step is all it takes until he can pull me closer. He holds me to his chest and strokes my back. "I wanted you to have a good weekend," he says.

I lean my head on his shoulder, press my hands against his back. "It started out pretty good," I say.

"And ended up pretty shit," he replies.

"Unless you're the psycho killer," I say, "that wasn't really your fault."

"Do you think I did it?" His body is tense. "Because I knew her? I only fucked her once."

"Of course I don't think you did it."

He relaxes a fraction. "Do you think I *could* have done it?"

"Killed someone? Maybe. Probably. But not like that."

He relaxes a little more.

"I should probably have a shower before bed," I say. "I feel like her blood is on me, even though I didn't touch it. And I taste like puke."

"Me, too, on all counts," he says.

"You go first. I'll just stand here and try to find the energy to take my clothes off."

I feel the rise and fall of his chest next to mine, feel his heartbeat beneath the palm of my hand.

"Let me take care of you," he says, his voice ragged. "Just for tonight."

I lift my head from his shoulder and look at him. He has that raw look in his eyes that I can't quite read. I nod and a hint of a smile pulls at his mouth.

"Shower first," he says, and leads me to the bathroom, where he turns on the water, fiddles with it until it's the right temperature, and undresses us both. He helps me into the tub and under the spray, then climbs in after me. His hands are gentle as he works shampoo into my hair, rubs soap over my skin, and makes sure all the suds are rinsed away.

I take the soap from him when he's done and do the same for him. His hair takes more time than mine to wash and rinse – I swear it's already longer than when we met.

I want him, badly, and my body responds accordingly, but I'm too weary to do more than make a soft noise in my throat when he curls his fingers around my length and strokes me.

"Too tired?" he says.

"Shellshocked, maybe," I say.

He shuts off the water and we get out of the tub, towel each other off.

"Thank you," I say. "Thank you for being nice to me." It sounds lame, but I don't care. This is what I need most right now: someone to treat me kindly.

"Are you hungry?" he says, when we're dry.

I shake my head. "Yes, but I don't think I could keep food down."

"Me neither," he says. We walk out of the bathroom, naked, hand-in-hand, and when I turn towards my room, he stops me. "I don't want you to be alone right now," he says. Then he adds, quieter, "*I* don't want to be alone right now," and he leads me into his room, locks the door behind us, and pulls me into bed. He tucks the blankets over me, spoons me close and whispers, "You're safe, Justin, I promise."

I'm sure I'm going to lie awake a long time, and if I manage to sleep it will be full of nightmares. But I drop off quickly and have no dreams at all that I remember.

It's not even dark yet when I wake up, and I can see fragments of the setting sun, dim through the curtain and the trees. I can tell Bjarni is awake, too. I roll over to look at him.

"Feel a bit better?" he says, touching my cheek.

I nod. "You?"

"Yeah." His thumb strokes along my cheekbone. "We're going to find that fucker."

I nod again. I'm afraid we never will, but I have to trust that he can't stay anonymous forever. He'll slip up, and Thorstein will find him, or Bjarni will. I'm not sure which of them I hope will be successful.

I want to just lie here forever, safe in Bjarni's arms, in Bjarni's bed, but I know that can't happen. Even if he still wants me, he is who he is, and sooner or later he'll go looking for someone more exciting. Someone more female, probably.

He pushes himself up on one elbow, looks down into my face, and I think he's going to tell me it's time to leave. But instead, he bends over me, traces my lower lip with his tongue, and then kisses me, gently. His hair falls forward and tickles my chest.

I open my mouth to his tongue, let my fingers slide into his hair. It feels like strands of fine silk and shines in the waning light. His eyes almost glow to my wolf vision.

His hand moves from my face to my neck, and I feel that thrill of almost-fear as he squeezes my throat, not hard, but enough that I notice. I let my hand wander down his back to his ass, grip it hard and arch towards him when his hand leaves my throat to brush across my chest, rough over my nipple.

He lifts his mouth from mine to look at me. "Is this okay?" he says. "After this morning? Do you want me to back off?"

I pull his mouth back to mine and slide my tongue against his. For a moment, he lets me kiss him, but then he pulls away again.

"I need an answer, *kjaereste*. I don't want to push you if you need some time."

"That was my answer," I say, trying to pull him to me again.

"In words, Justin," he says, kissing the end of my nose.

"Make me forget this morning," I say.

His mouth quirks up on one side. "On one condition," he says.

"What's that?" I twine one leg around his, try to pull him tighter against me, and he obligingly shifts position so our bellies press together, trapping both our erections between us.

"Explain to me why gay guys like ass fucking."

"Butt stuff can be nice," I say, suddenly self-conscious.

"Butt stuff?" The slight curl of his lips grows. "That's... almost cute."

"It sounds nicer than 'ass fucking'." I say.

"Okay."

"And it includes more than just fucking."

"Such as?"

I hold up my hand. "Fingers, for a start. Tongues. Toys. Lots of things."

"And it feels good?"

"It can. It should." I nudge him away slightly, reach down to stroke him. "But it's going to take a bit of work before you'll be able to shove this anywhere but my mouth."

He grins and half-closes his eyes. "Am I too big for you?" he says, letting a cocky grin come over his face.

"Yes," I say. "But we can change that."

"I don't want to hurt you." He opens his eyes all the way, meets mine.

"You won't," I say.

"You're sure it feels good?"

"Fuck yeah. Can I demonstrate?"

"You want to fuck me?"

"Yes, but even though I'm not monstrously huge, I'd probably hurt you if we jump straight to that. But we can work up to it." I bite my lip. What if he doesn't want to take time, to spread this out over many nights? Or at least a few? "If you want to."

"How do we start?"

"You have lube?"

He leans over me to reach the nightstand, pulls a tube out of a drawer. He says, "I'm a healthy, sexually mature male; of course I have lube."

I snort. "You want to go first?"

"Do you remember my unbreakable rule?"

"The one I've already made you break?"

He leans down and takes my lower lip in his teeth, stretches it away from my gums, then kisses me. "Yes, that one," he says.

"Okay," I say.

"Tell me what to do," he says, sitting up and stroking one hand from my neck down to my belly.

"Put some lube on your finger," I say. "And… you know."

"Which finger?"

"Doesn't matter."

He looks at me a moment longer, then takes the tube, squirts a blob of lubricant onto his middle finger, and nudges my legs farther apart. He slides his hand between my thighs, between my ass cheeks, until he finds my anus with the tip of his finger. He watches my face carefully, then massages me gently, spreading the lube.

"That good?" he says.

"Fuck, yes."

He shifts position again, so he can take my cock in his other hand, stroke me slowly as he presses his finger against me, into me. I arch my back to give him a better angle.

"Once you're in," I say, "you should be able to feel my prostate."

"Like 'turn your head and cough'?"

"Yeah, if your doctor is hot and looking to get sued."

He laughs and suddenly I'm pushing against him, my body responding without thought.

"There," I say. "Oh God." It feels so good. I haven't had anyone touch me this way in a long time.

"That does look like you're enjoying it," he says, teeth flashing.

"Two fingers," I gasp.

"What?" he says, glancing up from where he was watching his hand stroke me, his other hand slide back and forth as his finger moves inside me.

"Two fingers," I say.

"Right," he says, sliding his finger out. He has to let go with his other hand to add lube to his fingers and I think I whimper. But then he's got two fingers full length inside me, pushing in and out, his other hand stroking me again.

"I'm so close," I whisper. My hands clench in the bedsheets and I can't stop myself from pushing my pelvis up in time to his movements. He's synchronized the stroking of his hand with the push of his fingers, and I want to yell out his name. Instead, I say, "Three."

"Are you sure?" he says but doesn't hesitate. I'm coming as soon as his three fingers, thick and strong, are all the way inside me, massaging me, bumping against my prostate. I spurt all up my belly and onto my chest and I *think* the sound that comes out of me is his name.

"Yeah, I want to try that," Bjarni says when I'm still. He slides his fingers out of me, grabs a tissue to wipe the lube off, to wipe my semen off his other hand. I start to clean my belly, but he stops me. "Not yet," he says.

So I push him onto his back, duck my head to take as much of him into my mouth as I can, and then lube up my finger and rub it against him.

I lift my head and say, "Tell me when you're ready."

"I'm ready," he says immediately. I slowly push my finger inside him, feel him tighten up.

"You have to relax," I say, letting my lips brush the tip of his cock as I speak.

He breathes slowly, in and out, and when I feel him relax, I slide my finger into him. I massage him from the inside and almost laugh at the look of ecstasy that crosses his face.

A couple bobs of my head, a couple gentle thrusts of my finger, and he says, "More."

I slide in two fingers, feel his hand in my hair.

"Don't stop," he says. I push into him faster, harder, suck harder and let him just feel my teeth. "Fuck," he moans. "Fuck." Then, "More. Three fingers."

I do as he says, slide three fingers into his ass, push in and out as I move my other hand on the base of his erection, fit as much of him in my mouth as I can.

"Fuck yes," he says, then he tugs my hair, pulls my mouth off of him, and spurts white fluid onto his belly and chest. He hands me a tissue to clean my hands and pulls me up onto him so our slippery chests and stomachs slide and stick together.

Chapter Ten

HE KEEPS ME TUCKED against him until it gets dark, and I wonder how it can only just be night. Then he stirs and sits up.

"Back in a sec," he says, and I prepare myself to hear the shower, prepare myself to be asked to leave. But I only hear the sink, and when he comes back, he's holding a hot, wet facecloth that he uses to wipe off my chest, my stomach, anywhere that's sticky or crusty with our combined jism.

"That feels nice," I say, relaxing under the heat of the cloth and the gentleness of his touch.

When we're both clean, he stretches out beside me, pulls the blankets up, and tucks me against him again.

I'm starting to drift into sleep again when Bjarni says, "Justin." His voice is deep and growly, rumbling in my ear. I swear my own chest vibrates with the sound.

He leans so close I feel his lips move against my ear. "Justin, I want you to be mine. *Only* mine." He sounds fierce, possessive, and I start to get hard again. I turn my head so I can meet his eyes. Even in the dark they seem to be lit from within. His lips are slightly parted, and I lean towards him, not thinking of anything but those words he just said. But then I remember Thorstein telling me how Bjarni can be thoughtless and selfish, even if he doesn't mean to be.

"I want…" I say and stop. I'm afraid of what he'll say. I *know* what he'll say, and even knowing, it will hurt.

"What do you want, *kjaereste?*" he says, his warm breath tickling my face.

I look away, then back to his eyes. "I want you to be only mine," I say.

All my muscles tense like I'm waiting for a blow, but it doesn't matter. It still feels like a gut punch when his eyes slide away from mine, and he says, "Yeah, that might be a problem."

I hold very still, close my eyes so I don't have to look at his face when he rips my heart out.

He tucks his head against my shoulder. "I really like fucking women," he says. "And I don't have any plans to stop."

"No," I say. "Of course not." At least, I think I say it out loud. And so calmly I surprise even myself, I sit up, swing my legs over the side of the bed, and pull away from Bjarni's arms to stand up.

"Justin," he says.

I walk out the door and close it gently behind me, walk to my own room, and lock the door. Still very calmly, I start to get dressed. Boxers, track pants, t-shirt, socks, hoodie.

I hear Bjarni's door open, hear his footsteps in the hall. He taps softly on my door, and I ignore it. "Justin?" I stand very still, wait for him to leave, listen to him go down the stairs, collect his keys from the table by the front door, leave the house.

When he accelerates away, he hits the gas too hard and gravel pings off the living room window. Only then do I move again. I leave the house, not sure if I even shut the door behind me, and put my runners on sitting on the front steps. Then I jog along the path to the farmhouse, cut across the lawn, and find the path to Thorstein's house, then down his driveway. Bjarni isn't going to come up this way, so I don't have to worry about running into him.

On the wide, well-kept driveway, I break into a proper run, find my rhythm, and speed up, as if I can outrun the feelings that threaten to steal my breath. I can't stop, can't slow, or thinking will catch up with me and then I'll cry, and if I start to cry I don't think I'll ever stop.

So it's a really good thing Thorstein's paying more attention than I am when he pulls into his driveway and catches me in the headlights. He slams on the brakes, and I stop myself by slapping both hands onto the hood of the car, not caring that the hot metal is uncomfortable on my palms.

The interior light goes on as he opens the door. "Justin?" His voice is calm and gentle. I suppose he must get angry sometimes, but he's never failed to be kind and patient with me.

"I'm just going for a run," I say. "Sorry."

But he's a werewolf and I, at least, can't lie to a werewolf, even if I haven't said the lie out loud.

He sighs. "Get in the car," and I don't even think about *not* getting in the car. We drive up to his house and when he shuts off the engine he looks at me and sighs again before opening his door. "Come on," he says, and I follow him up the steps onto his front porch.

He points to a wide, comfortable-looking bench under the front window. "Sit." I sit. He goes inside and I hear voices – his and Raine's – but I can't tell what they're saying. In a moment, he comes back out carrying three stubby glasses each holding a measure of deep amber liquid. The color reminds me of Bjarni's hair, and I have to hold back a whimper.

He hands me a glass and says, "Drink."

I take a sip and the smooth, smoky liquid – some kind of probably very expensive whisky – burns all the way down my throat.

The door opens again and it's Raine, carrying a quilt that she wraps over my shoulders. She sits on one side of me, and Thorstein sits on the other, and they both lean against me, holding me between them in a warm, comforting sort of pressure. Thorstein hands Raine a glass and all three of us just sit, sipping and staring at the lawn.

Then Thorstein says, "Want to tell me why I almost ran over you in my own driveway?"

If I talk, I'm pretty sure I'll start to cry.

"Is it Bjarni?" Raine says. "What has he done this time?"

"You don't like him, do you?" I say, swallowing the lump in my throat and taking another sip of whisky.

She snorts. "We're friends and I love him like a brother, but no, I don't always like him."

She pulls her legs up onto the bench and leans her head on my shoulder. She's so strong I forget she's actually shorter than I am. "But you're also my friend," she says. "And I also love you like a brother, and I don't think there's ever been a time I didn't like you."

"I'm so stupid," I say.

"You're not," Thorstein says. He sees that my glass is empty and takes it from me, setting it on the porch railing where it catches the light from the moon just peeking over the trees. "Talk to me."

"It's nothing. It's not like I didn't know he would do exactly what he always does."

"Talk," he says again, only this time it's more of a command, and I find myself babbling out everything that's happened between me and Bjarni since the day he found me in the woods. And I find myself including way more detail than I probably should, but once the words start, I can't hold them back.

And when I get to tonight, to that totally expected gut-punch of a conversation, the tears I thought were maybe kept at bay start to slide down my face.

"I'm so fucking stupid," I say, and it comes out too close to a childish wail. I pull my knees up, curl into myself, and try to keep any more stupid noises from coming out of me. It works, but then I start shaking instead. Thirty-three fucking years old and I'm crying like a jilted schoolgirl because a guy I *knew* would never want only me told me exactly that.

Thorstein puts his arm around me, and Raine snuggles closer, and they hold me while I shake and cry and neither of them says anything. Finally, when I can breathe properly again, Raine hands me a box of tissues and Thorstein says, "You're not stupid, Justin."

Raine adds, "You're just in love."

That makes me look up. "What? No. I can't be in love." But of course I already knew I was, knew it days ago. I look from Raine to Thorstein. "Shit," I say, and finally admit it out loud. "I *am* in love with Bjarni."

Raine looks over my head at Thorstein. "You do know you used compulsion on him?" He looks surprised. "Do you think he would have told you all *that* otherwise?"

"Did I?" he says. Then, "Fuck, I did." He slouches back against the bench. "Well, now we know whoever changed him was himself changed by Dad. Or I was involved. Or Bjarni. Or Granddad, I suppose, but he hasn't participated in blood-sharing since we left Norway."

"Does that help?" Raine says. I stare from one to the other of them, trying to follow the conversation.

"It doesn't hurt," Thorstein says. "We can rule out any wolves who married into the pack, and any who were already here when we arrived."

He tightens his arm around my shoulders, then lays his palm on the back of my neck. It reminds me so much of how Bjarni comforts me that I almost start crying again.

Raine touches my knee. "What do you want to do, sweetie?" she says. "Do you want us to walk home with you?"

"I can't go back there," I say. Then in a whisper, I add, "He's not there anyway. He went out."

Raine hugs me, and Thorstein says, "You can stay here tonight. Tomorrow we'll move your things over to the farmhouse."

"Won't Colleen and Hilde mind?" I say.

"I very much doubt it," Thorstein replies. "Colleen loves having people to fuss over, and Hilde's not home much, anyway."

"Is that okay?" Raine says.

I nod. "I just can't go back."

"You don't have to do anything you don't want to, Justin. Not here."

I wake up at what feels like way too early an hour, to pounding on the door. I jump out of bed to answer and realize I'm not at home. Not in my room at Bjarni's. I'm in Thorstein's guest room. It's decorated in deep greens and greys and browns, with a hand-stitched quilt on the bed and a woven rug on the hardwood floor. It's homey and comfortable. Comforting.

I can't help but step closer to the window to listen. The room is over the front porch, and it's really hard not to hear, anyway.

The door opens and Bjarni's voice says, "He's gone, Bear. I can't find him."

"Bjarni." Thorstein, calm and soothing, as always.

"I screwed up, Thorstein," Bjarni says. "I really fucked up this time and he's gone. The front door was open when I got home, and his bed wasn't slept in last night." He sounds desperate. Afraid.

"Bjarni," Thorstein says again, only a little exasperated this time.

"I really fucked up," Bjarni says.

"Yes, you really did," Thorstein says. "You really fucking did."

"What?"

"He's here, Little Bear. He's fine." Thorstein lets out a noisy breath. "Well, not *fine*, but safe."

"I told him –"

"I know what you told him. You could have been kinder."

"I didn't want to lie to him." Bjarni's voice is rough, and I can hear something like anguish in it.

"Of course not. But maybe you should have thought about that before you let things get so far." Thorstein's voice has dropped to what I've started to think of as his pack-leader voice, the one you ignore at your peril, even when he's being very kind.

"And maybe, just maybe, you could have *not* gone out looking for a quick lay the very same night you told him you wanted him to be yours."

Bjarni's voice comes out like a sob, almost. I want to lean out the window to look at him; I can't imagine him so fragile. "I *know* that, Bear. I fucking know. I screwed up." I hear footsteps on the porch, like he's pacing back and forth along its length. "And it… it wasn't even true. I was just *afraid*." He paces some more. "I went to a bar –"

Thorstein cuts him off. "I don't want to hear about your latest conquest."

"Just *listen* to me," Bjarni says. "I sat at the fucking bar and drank a fucking beer, and three gorgeous women gave me their phone numbers and I didn't want any of them. Not even a little. I left and I threw the bits of paper in the first trash can I passed."

More pacing, then he suddenly stops. "I thought I might be… dysfunctional. But then I thought about… and no. Everything works just fine. I just didn't want those women. I wanted… I'm…"

Thorstein's sudden laugh makes me jump. "You're an idiot, is what you are," Thorstein says.

"No," says Bjarni. "They were fucking hot and not a fucking stirring.

And all I could think about was getting home to make sure Justin was okay."

"Bjarni," says Thorstein.

The pacing starts again, faster, more frantic.

"Bjarni!"

The pacing stops.

"You're in love, you dumb fuck."

"I know."

Silence from Thorstein. I can imagine him, arms crossed, filling the doorway as he leans on the frame, watching his brother with one eyebrow raised.

I have to sit down, and the bed is too far away. I slump onto an old trunk under the window.

"I'm… in love." Bjarni starts pacing again, but more slowly. "With Justin." Soft footsteps, back and forth, a sound like maybe he's sat down on the bench under the window, almost directly below me. "And it scared the shit out of me."

"Because of Dad?"

"Yeah."

"He's gone, Little Bear. And no one here is going to do what he would've done, for wanting another man."

"I didn't fuck anyone last night," Bjarni suddenly says. "I went out to… to do that, but once I got to the bar, I didn't want to. I… I called Katie and she just told me to go home. She told me I was stupid. That I was afraid of what it meant to want Justin. So, I just drove around for hours. And I finally went to see Granddad."

Katie… The Katie who owns the gallery with Raine? Who I work for now? I know they slept together once, months ago. Was he trying for a booty call? Or are they friends?

"What did Granddad say?" Thorstein's voice is gentle, non-judgmental.

Silence for a few moments, then Bjarni's voice, soft, wondering. "I'm in love with Justin."

I'm pretty sure some kind of sound comes out of me, and I hope it isn't loud.

"Bjarni," says Thorstein. "Go into Great Valley to pick up the feed order. Raine and I are going to move Justin's stuff over to the farmhouse while you're gone. Give him some space."

"No, I need to talk to him, Bear. You can't expect me to carry on as if nothing has happened."

"I agree, you do need to talk to him." Now heavier footsteps, the creak of wood like Thorstein's sat next to his brother. "But you also need to give him time to figure out what *he* wants. What he wants when you're not looming over him, because if you think you're having trouble thinking rationally around him, imagine how hard it must be for him to think with you around."

"I don't *loom* over him."

"You loom over anyone shorter than you."

"Whatever."

"Little Bear, you also need to figure out what *you* really want, and what you're willing to give up to get it."

"What do you mean?"

"Justin deserves to be loved by someone who isn't going to run off and screw any halfway attractive woman who passes by. He deserves happiness, Bjarni. He's had a shitty life, and he deserves someone who'll be faithful to him, who will always try to make his life a little bit better."

Silence for a moment.

"And what do you think I deserve?" Bjarni says, self-contempt heavy in his voice.

"You deserve happiness, too, Little Bear. And I'm not Dad. If Justin makes you happy, and you make Justin happy, then you should be together. But *first* you both need to figure out what you want. Clear-headed."

"Okay."

"And you really hurt him. You're going to have to work hard to regain his trust."

"Yeah." Bjarni's voice is quiet again, subdued. "Okay. I don't know how to do that. But okay."

I watch him leave through the slit in the curtains, and he turns back once to look up at the house, to search the windows, maybe. I hope he can't see me.

When he disappears into the trees between Thorstein's house and the farmhouse, I get up and go out into the hall, sit on the top step. A moment later, Thorstein comes in. He's only wearing boxers and he looks like a fucking statue, all sculpted muscle and gleaming white-blond hair.

Raine sits on the top step beside me and bumps my shoulder with hers. "Pretty, isn't he?" she says.

"How do you stand it?" I say, summoning a smile from somewhere.

"I'm horny all the fucking time," she says, and laughs.

Thorstein looks up at us, eyebrow raised, and snorts. He leans on the wall at the bottom of the stairs and says, "How much of that did you hear?"

"All of it," I say, wondering if I'm about to get chewed out for eavesdropping.

"What do you want to do?" he says.

"You still want us to move your things to the farmhouse?" Raine asks.

"Yeah." I stare at my hands. Then I look up at Thorstein. "Do you really think I deserve all those things you said?" It's dumb, but tears are burning the backs of my eyes again. I refuse to let them out.

"Yes, I do." He pushes away from the wall. "Come on, let's have breakfast."

"I'll be down in a bit," Raine says, standing and heading back down the hall. I'm still dressed from last night, so I go down to find Thorstein running water into an old-fashioned percolator. A kettle is already on the stove, and a big fancy coffee machine that can make pretty much anything you can imagine occupies the end of the counter.

"Why don't you use that?" I point at the machine.

"It's Raine's," he says. "To be honest, I'm a little bit afraid of it."

I stare at him until I notice his eyes crinkling at the corners as he tries to hide a smile.

"You don't know how to use it," I say.

"Nope."

"Let me. One of my many failed jobs was barista at a fancy coffee place on Grand Avenue. I was pretty good at it."

"If you were good at it, why was it a failed job?" But he steps aside and gestures at the machine.

"My parents found out I worked there and kept sending their

missionary friends in to visit. The manager laid me off because it was the only way to keep them from harassing the staff."

He puts a hand on my shoulder and squeezes, and I prepare myself to flinch. But I don't. It feels nice.

He doesn't seem to be aware that he's almost naked, and I try very hard not to look at him. He's not his brother, and he's so huge I feel like a child next to him, but he *is* extremely attractive.

And he doesn't try to hide the scars on his wrists, which I know he doesn't like people to see. It makes me feel better, knowing he's so comfortable around me.

"What do you want me to make you?" I poke at the machine, figure out what all the functions are, and turn to look at him.

"Coffee." He laughs. "And a mocha for Raine."

So, I make an americano and a mocha, while Thorstein fetches milk and cocoa when I ask. And he doesn't hesitate when I ask for Earl Grey tea and vanilla extract, so I make myself a London fog.

But the time Raine comes down, dressed in yoga pants and a t-shirt, long hair damp and twisted into a loose bun, Thorstein is cooking bacon and toasting bread for bacon sandwiches.

It's so nice and normal and comfortable that I wish I could just stay here with them, but I know they value their privacy. And I imagine me being in the next room every night might affect their sex life in a not-good way.

Raine hands Thorstein a pile of clothes. "Don't torture the poor lad with your masculine beauty," she says.

He replies, "Are you sure he's the one being tortured?" and wiggles his eyebrows at her. But he pulls on the jeans and long-sleeved t-shirt.

When we're clearing up the dishes I start to say, "I want..." but feel myself tearing up. Thorstein just waits, drying each dish as I rinse it, and putting it gently on the appropriate stack in the cupboard.

I try again. "I want those things. I want someone who only wants me." I focus on the plate in my hands, making sure to get all the bacon grease off. "And if Bjarni can't do that, then..." I stop. I almost choke on the words. "Then I'll just have to find someone who can."

Thorstein dries the plate as slowly and contemplatively as I washed it.

"Don't give up on him yet," he finally says. "But make him realize what he's going to lose if he decides to carry on as usual."

"What do you mean?" Dishes done, I rinse the sink and wring out the cloth. I dry my hands on the towel Thorstein hands me.

He leans on the counter. "Don't give in and do whatever he wants you to. Make him wait. Make him earn your trust back." He scratches an eyebrow. "Stay in the farmhouse for now. Once you start working in the gallery, stay at Raine's the days you work." He frowns thoughtfully. "If you want to start this week, I'll drive you in Wednesday night."

"Okay," I say, feeling an odd sort of relief settle over me. I don't want to be so far away, but I also do. In Riverbend, nobody knows me except Katie and Magne. And I guess Elias, the bookstore guy. I can be anonymous, and just go to work, and relax, and figure out what to do.

"Maybe stay in Riverbend a week or two," Thorstein goes on. "Get to know the city. Have some fun."

"Katie would *love* to take you out drinking or dancing or whatever," Raine says. "And shopping."

"But –" I start.

"You can work for me anytime. Our busiest season isn't for a few weeks yet, and then I'll work you so hard you won't have time to think." He grins.

Chapter Eleven

I THROW MYSELF INTO three days of hard work on the farm, weeding the kitchen garden and mucking out stalls and learning – sort of – to ride a horse by myself. It goes quickly and I only see Bjarni in passing. I can't meet his eyes and he doesn't try to touch me, and it hurts, but it's also a relief.

On Wednesday after supper, I'm waiting on the farmhouse steps with a duffle bag containing my few clothes and toiletries when Raine appears, not with Thorstein in the big BMW like I expected, but on foot on the path to their house.

She's scowling and her whole body posture shows annoyance.

"Oh dear," says Colleen from one side of me.

"What's Thorstein gone and done now?" Hilde says from the other side.

"Do you think they had a fight?" I say.

"As close as they ever get to fighting," says Colleen. "Which isn't very."

Raine reaches the bottom of the stairs and scowls up at us. "He's insisting on driving Justin all by himself," she says. "He doesn't want me to go into town at all anymore, because my fucking wolf symbiont is taking too long."

She stomps up the stairs.

"He's worried, is all," Colleen says. We all trail inside where Raine paces back and forth in the living room. Hilde flops onto a chair and I perch on the arm of the couch.

"I know," Raine says. "I know. It's just frustrating. I *hate* being treated like an invalid." She blows out a lungful of air and flops onto the couch next to me.

"He's treating me like I'm nine months pregnant on top of being immunocompromised," she says. "Hovering and asking me if I feel okay."

Then suddenly she goes still, and just as suddenly stands up. "Oh fuck," she says. She looks around at us, eyes wide, almost panicked. "Oh, fuck fuck fuck."

I have no idea what's going on, but apparently Colleen and Hilde do.

"How late are you?" Colleen says.

"Only a week," Raine says. "Oh shit."

"What?" I say, and nobody answers.

"Shit," she says again. "How am I going to get to a pharmacy if he's the one driving Justin into Riverbend?"

She's pacing frantically, and Hilde jumps up and stops her, one hand on each of Raine's arms. "You're making me dizzy," she says. "In the upstairs bathroom, under the sink, there's a whole stack of tests." She smirks. "I have three boyfriends; you don't think I'd be caught without, do you?"

"Thank you!" Raine says and hugs the other woman and is gone up the stairs.

"Tests?" I say, feeling slow and stupid.

"Pregnancy tests," Hilde says, shaking her head like yes, I really am stupid.

"Oh," I say. "*Ohhh*."

Now it's Colleen's turn to pace, but she's slow and measured, not frantic, like she's using her footsteps to measure out the time it will take for the test to do whatever it does.

"Thorstein doesn't want kids," I say. I remember him telling me that while we were out checking the pasture fence.

"No," Hilde says. "He *wants* kids, he's just afraid to have any, because…" and she bares her teeth and hooks her fingers like claws and says, "Grr." She shrugs. "Because he doesn't want to pass on the *berserkr* nature. He doesn't want his children to have to go through what he did," she finishes.

"They wouldn't, though, would they?"

"No," says Hilde, and she squeezes my wrist sharply and when I look at her, she shakes her head, tilting her chin at her mother. Fortunately, I get *her* hint. This topic isn't a good one to address in front of Colleen. It's too close to revealing horrible things about her late husband that she'd probably rather not think about.

We lapse into silence, and it seems like an eternity before Raine comes back down the stairs. She looks dazed.

"Well?" says Colleen.

Raine doesn't say anything. She just hands over the little plastic test.

"Eep!" shrieks Colleen, and then claps her hand over her mouth. She hands the test to Hilde.

"I'm going to be an auntie," Hilde says, grinning.

"Who's going to be a what?" says a deep, smoky voice from the doorway. Raine whirls around but it's just Bjarni.

Hilde hands him the test.

"Did you just make me touch something Raine pissed on?" he says, but he looks at the stick. "I have no idea what this means," he says and hands it back.

"It means you're going to be an uncle, dumbass," says Hilde.

"I'm pregnant," whispers Raine.

I get up from the couch, touch her on the arm tentatively. "Is that good?" I ask softly.

She turns and hugs me. "Yes," she says. "For me, absolutely fucking yes." Then she pulls back to look at my face. "For Thors… I don't know."

"Well, you're about to find out," Bjarni says. We all hear the rumble of the BMW's big engine, the crunch of gravel on the driveway.

"Stay here," Raine says. "All of you." She looks pointedly at Bjarni who grins, pulls her close when she passes by, and kisses her cheek.

"Congratulations," he says, and she smiles.

We all watch her go out the door, then crowd the window as she walks slowly down the steps and over to the car. She says something and

Thorstein gets out. He looks at her, head cocked to one side, and says something in reply.

She bites her lip, then hands him the pregnancy test. He stares at it, tiny in his huge hands. She points out something on it and he nods, and just keeps staring. She touches his arm and says something else, something that takes a bit more time. She looks like she's laying out a careful argument and he just keeps staring at the plastic stick in his hand.

Then she stops talking and he finally looks up at her. There are tears in his eyes and his face is so full of joy I feel tears start in my eyes, too, and have to swallow a lump in my throat. Whoever is standing next to me puts an arm around me and pulls me close.

Then Raine smiles and Thorstein smiles back, touches her face in wonder, and pulls her into his arms.

"Now he's really going to be insufferable." It's Bjarni, his voice almost in my ear. It's his arm around me, his shoulder I've tucked my face into, his shirt I'm drying my tears on.

I pull away suddenly and he steps back.

"Can I talk to you before you go?" he says. "In private?"

"Okay," I say, and follow him to his office, where he closes the door. I look out the window and watch Thorstein and Raine walk up the steps hand-in-hand, hear the clamor of congratulations from the living room.

"I'm going to be an uncle," Bjarni says. I turn and look at him and he's grinning.

"That's what you wanted to talk to me about?" I say. I know it's not, but I'm finding it hard to breathe and I just want to get this over with.

"No," he says, and looks at his feet. Both hands are stuffed in the pockets of his jeans and his feet are bare, his toes dirty.

"Justin." He takes a step closer and stops and I can't keep staring at his feet, so I look up and meet his eyes. "I haven't —" he starts, then stops. "I didn't cheat on you."

"Of course you didn't," I say. "We'd have to be together for you to cheat on me."

There's hurt in his eyes, but it's nothing like how he hurt me. I lift my chin and don't look away.

"I mean that night. I didn't sleep with anyone but you."

"You were going to."

"I –" He can't deny it. "*Kjaereste*. I fucked up. Bad. I know." He runs both hands through his hair, turns away and stalks across the room. "But I don't want… I don't want anyone but you." He turns back, pleading with his eyes. I just keep looking at him, making my face as blank as I can.

"Please," he says, taking a hesitant step closer. "I know I have to earn your trust back. Just… tell me how. Tell me what I need to do."

I don't trust myself to say anything. There's a huge lump in my throat I can't swallow.

He reaches out like he's going to take my hand but stops halfway and lets his arm drop.

"I want to be with you, Justin. Only you. I want –" He hisses and makes a frustrated gesture. "I want to be your boyfriend. I want the whole fucking world to know I belong to you, and only you. Just… please tell me what to do."

I sigh, turn away, and look out the window. Thorstein and Raine are sitting on the steps, leaning against each other. I can only see them from the back, but they look totally in love. I want that for myself, more than I can say.

"I don't know, Bjarni," I say. "I don't know what to tell you." I turn back and meet his eyes again. "But you can start by…" I hesitate and bite my lip, afraid that what I'm going to say will sound stupid.

"What, *kjaereste*?" His voice is soft, pleading.

"You can court me," I finally say.

He blinks. I don't know what he expected, but definitely not that.

"*Court* you?"

I nod.

"How do I do that?"

"I don't know," I say. "But that's what I want." I clench my teeth together, than force my jaw to relax. "Show me what I mean to you. What I *really* mean to you." My nostrils flare; I'm afraid he's going to make fun of me, or just refuse.

"Okay," he says softly. He takes a step closer, and this time he does take my hand. "I'll court you." He brings my hand to his lips and kisses the back of my fingers. "I'll prove to you that you can trust me. That I value you.

That you're the only one I want." He kisses my fingers again and his tongue flicks across my knuckles.

I want to bury both hands in his hair, to pull him closer and kiss him, but I make myself stand still. I can't help tightening my hand a little on his, though.

"Justin," he says. "*Kjaereste*." He turns my hand over and kisses my wrist, my palm. I don't want him to stop, but I *need* him to.

There's a soft tap on the door and he lets go. I stuff both hands in my pockets to stop their trembling.

"It's open," Bjarni says and the door cracks, then swings wide.

Thorstein says, "You ready to go?" and I nod.

"Text me when you're settled in?" Bjarni says.

"Okay," I say. "I will."

Thorstein drives even more smoothly, and faster, than Raine. I wait until we're on the highway, arrowing towards Riverbend, before I say, "What does *kjaereste* mean?" I stumble over the pronunciation, not quite managing the soft vowels or the extra consonant after the "k," but I guess I'm close enough.

The side of Thorstein's mouth curves up. "Where did you hear that?" he says, though I suspect he already knows.

"When Bjarni stopped calling me 'sweetheart' he started calling me that instead."

"It means 'dearest' or 'beloved.' It's what we say instead of 'girlfriend' or 'boyfriend' in Norway." He glances at me, then back at the road. It's just starting to get dark and there isn't much traffic. "It's a term of endearment," he adds.

"Oh," I say, eloquent as always.

"Did he try to convince you not to go?"

"No," I say. "He asked me how to… how to make it up to me. How to get me to trust him again."

He nods. "Good."

I feel a smile grow on my face and settle back in my seat. "I told him he had to court me."

"Did you?" He turns to look at me again and I see my smile mirrored on his face. "Good for you." He looks back at the road and snorts. "I wonder how long it'll be before he asks me how."

I laugh. It feels good. I find myself looking forward to the week ahead, to work and time all to myself.

"He asked me how and I said he'd just have to figure it out for himself."

He laughs, too.

In Riverbend, he comes into the small apartment building with me, pointing out where the mailboxes are, and the laundry room, and unlocks the apartment door and hands me the keys.

He looks around. "She really didn't bring much stuff to the farm," he says.

"She said I shouldn't need to buy anything."

"Shit, that reminds me," he says. "Colleen sent a box of groceries. It's in the trunk."

I walk around while he goes back outside, opening cupboard doors and looking in the fridge. There's meat in the freezer, and bread, and ice cream, and in the fridge, I find carrots, milk that's still good, and a few other things.

Colleen's groceries turn out to be a big produce box full of meat wrapped in butcher paper, cotton bags full of vegetables, and jars of homemade pickles and preserves. All products of the farm, I think.

"Thank you," I say, suddenly feeling overwhelmed. "All of you." I look up at Thorstein and he's smiling softly.

"Raine's bus pass and instructions for how to get to the gallery are on the fridge door," he says. "And if you need *anything*, even if you just feel lonely, you can call Magne. He's only a few minutes away by car, the way he drives."

I nod.

"You're going to be okay," he says.

"Will you let me know if you find out anything more about… about the guy who attacked me?"

"Absolutely. And we will find him. I promise."

When he's gone, I sit for a few more minutes, staring into space, then

I get up and lock the door, put the kettle on, and unpack the groceries and my clothes. It doesn't take long. I pull out the big poetry book, then go to investigate the books Raine left on her bookshelves to find something a little lighter to read.

It's almost all paranormal romance, which suits my mood perfectly. I find a paperback titled *The Wolf's Best Mate* that has two wolves and two bare-chested men on the cover that looks like it has the perfect combination of humor, heartbreak, and smut, and take it to the bathroom where I turn on the taps in the tub. It's not a huge bath, but it has a sloping back that looks comfortable to lounge in.

I fetch my tea, add a big dollop of lavender bubble bath that I find under the sink to the tub, and am about to get in when I remember I promised to text Bjarni. I turn off the water and get my phone.

Here safe, I text. I don't know what else to say.

miss u, he sends back. I bite my lip. I can't do this yet.

Got a book & cup of tea, I type. *I'll be ok*. I send it, then relent a little and add, *Sleep well.*

Sleep well kjaereste, he replies.

I stare at my phone for a while, trying to decide if I should say anything else. Finally, I set my phone aside and climb into the bathtub where I let what turns out to be an extremely steamy, very engaging story about two gay werewolves distract me from the real world.

I make it to work a little bit early, and Katie's already there. She gestures at a huge bouquet of flowers that takes up most of one of the design tables.

"Poor delivery guy was standing outside the door when I got here," she says. "He didn't want to just leave them."

"So is it a grateful customer, or did one of your one-night stands fall madly in love with you?" I ask. It's weird, but I already feel completely at ease with her.

She grins. "Actually, I think one of my one-night stands fell madly in love with *you*." She plucks the little gift card out of the middle of the bouquet and hands it to me. It says "Justin Leyendecker" in precise block letters.

I stare at her.

"I assume it's from Bjarni," she says. "Though it's possible you have an admirer I don't know about." Then she pokes my arm. "Open it."

I open the envelope and slide out the card. It's not his writing, of course – he'd have ordered the flowers over the phone or online – but I recognize the sentiment. *I'm going to court you so hard*, it says, and is just signed, *B.* I feel a flush creep up my neck and tuck the card into my back pocket.

"How long should I wait to text him?" I ask, when Katie gets back from unlocking the front door and putting out the "Open" sign.

"Days," she says, and grins. She turns on the cash register and starts up the computer. "At least till lunch," she amends. "Make him sweat just a little." Her grin widens. "Please."

"You're friends, aren't you?" I ask.

"Sure, but that doesn't mean I can't enjoy torturing him."

I look at the flowers, touch the petals of something deep red – a lily, maybe – and say, "The other night, when he phoned you…" I can't finish the question.

She leans her hip against the counter and cocks one perfectly plucked eyebrow at me. "You want to know if he was looking to get laid."

I nod, but don't meet her eyes.

"He wasn't," she says. "Not by me, anyway. He was freaking out because he suddenly wasn't wanting to fuck every woman in sight. Because all he could think about was you."

"And you told him he was stupid." Now I do look up, to see sympathy on her face.

"I told him he was *acting* stupid. That he should go home to you." She crosses her arms. "He called me again a few hours later. He'd been driving around all night. Just driving and feeling guilty. I told him he *should* feel guilty."

"Thanks," I say.

"No prob," she replies. "Bjarni can be a dick. Like, big time. But deep down he's a good guy. And I really think he's smitten with you." She smacks my shoulder. "Which does *not* mean you should give in easily. You're a better catch than he is. Make him work to get you back."

I blush again at the thought of being anything resembling a good catch. "You don't think he'll… get bored and move on? Go back to Bjarni-as-usual?"

"Not a chance," she says. "He wants you and as long as he thinks he's got even a tiny chance, he's not giving up. Now," and she gestures at the huge bouquet, "Help me figure out where to put this."

We find a spot where it sets off some richly toned floral paintings to good effect, and then rearrange the ceramics that were on the plinth now occupied by flowers.

The phone rings and she leaves me to move things around on shelves and, after a few experiments, I find an arrangement I think looks good, contrasting a group of brightly-colored vases with a large monotone lidded container, and managing to squeeze in some deep purple abstract glass pieces, too.

"Hey, that looks pretty good," she says and smiles. "I think you'll do okay here."

And that's pretty much how the day goes. Various small tasks that I feel nervous about, but manage to do pretty well, and by the end of the day I feel good about it all. I have a sheaf of printed-out artist bios to read tonight, with the instruction to remember at least one detail about each for tomorrow.

"There *will* be a test," Katie says, and laughs at my expression. "I'd at least like you to be able to match each name with their work in the gallery by the end of tomorrow. You can work on remembering more for next week."

And with that, I'm done my first day. And I realize on the bus ride home that not only did I forget to thank Bjarni for the flowers, I didn't think about him all day.

$$Chapter\ Twelve$$

THE REST OF THE WEEK is pretty much the same. I work at the gallery on Friday and meet some of the regular customers who seem to like me well enough, though it's Katie's advice they ask on framing choices and which limited edition prints would look best hanging in the same room.

"They'll ask your opinion once you've got a little more experience," she assures me.

On Saturday I sleep in then go for a run. I still can't run for as long as I'd like, and end up walking half the way home, but I'm feeling better, less lost. I'm almost back to Raine's building – my building now, I guess – when I pass a convenience store. On a whim, I stop in and buy a cheap notebook and a pack of ballpoint pens with the emergency five dollar bill I stuck in my pocket just in case.

In the apartment, I shower, put on clean sweats and an old t-shirt that was Magne's and sit at the kitchen counter on a stool with the notebook open in front of me.

I think back to my wasted years in university and the poetry classes I took. I didn't do as well as I hoped in those classes, only Bs and one B+, but I enjoyed them, and my professors made me think maybe I wasn't totally shit at it. And then I stopped trying to write when a guy I had a crush on made fun of me for it.

I wonder what happened to those old notebooks I kept, full of awful attempts to write poetry about unrequited love and gay sexual awakening. I wonder what happened to the few possessions that were in my crappy apartment in Great Valley. I thought about calling my old landlord to ask but haven't been able to make myself do it. Even if he didn't throw out my stuff, he'll still want his rent, and the thought of all that money I don't have makes me sick.

I stare at the page in front of me and start writing down random words. After half a page I realize they're not random at all; they're words and phrases that describe Bjarni. I close the notebook and think about making something to eat. Then I open it again, and jot down fragments of a half-forgotten dream.

I dreamed my lover
with lips of barbed wire
snagged my tender flesh
and pushed me away.

And all I could do
was turn back to him
and cut myself again.

Yeah, pretty crap, but it feels good to let something out that I was holding in. And maybe it'll keep me from having *that* particular dream again.

My phone vibrates and I glance at the screen. Bjarni. Of course. It's like he knows when I'm thinking about him.

picnic lunch 2moro? it says. I stare at it but can't make myself answer. I can't deny I miss being near him, but it's also so nice to be away, to be able to think clearly.

12 on brdwlk? comes another text. *can pick u up.*

Then, *please.*

I sigh, and give in. *Meet you there*, I send.

ok, he replies.

There are butterflies in my stomach for the rest of the day and I can't seem to settle down to read or even watch tv. So I clean the apartment, even though it doesn't really need it. I make dinner, shower, go to bed early with Raine's gay werewolf romance novel. And to my surprise, I fall asleep quickly.

I've hardly had any dreams since I've been here – even the one that sparked the lousy poem was from before that – but tonight I'm not so lucky. The nightmares come back, though this one doesn't start out terrible.

It starts with running in wolf shape, like a *real* wolf, a natural wolf. I'm running under a full moon, in a forest that smells like healthy trees and sounds like owls and insects and rushing river. I stretch my legs and streak between grey tree trunks, and it feels amazing.

Then something barrels into me from the side, knocking me off my feet and I'm human again, barefoot, in torn track pants and shredded t-shirt, bloody and scared. I can't see what knocked me over, but I smell it. Smell him. Musky and unwashed, cigarettes and cheap beer. Raw meat. Gasoline and oil. The dry leaves on the forest floor crackle as he gets closer.

Werewolf. He's half-shifted, toes and fingers sharp with claws, and this time I see his face, but it's all werewolf muzzle and big teeth. I can tell his eyes are watery blue and his hair dirty blond maybe, or light brown. I can't tell what his face would look like as human.

He's naked, and muscular, but with a pot belly and the look of someone who hasn't bothered to exercise enough to maintain the muscles once he built them. He's got an erection, and that scares me more than his half-shifted, sweat-smelling werewolf shape.

"Useless little fuck," he growls at me. I recognize his voice now. This is the wolf who changed me, who hurt me, and now he's back to... to what?

"You have to do what I tell you," he says. "So no sense fighting it." He moves closer and I see the oily rag in his hand. "Don't move," he says, and I can't move. His claws lay me open, tear slashes across my chest and I scream. That's when he stuffs the rag into my mouth.

"Now what should I do with you?" he says, and I try to force my limbs to move, to get me away. It's only a dream, but it's also a memory, and what will come next twists my guts in knots.

"Too bad you're not a girl. You're pretty enough, I thought you were when you ran past me."

I shake my head, try to spit out the rag.

"Bet you're a fucking fairy, aren't you?" he snarls. "Just my fucking luck. It's your kind I want *out* of my pack." Then he looks down at himself, at his hardness bobbing in front of his soft belly. A nasty smile grows on his face. "I hear faggots are good at sucking cock and the moon has given me quite the stiffie this time around. Are you good at sucking cock, pretty boy?"

I try to scream again, to scramble away. To wake up.

"Shut up," he says, and I stop trying to scream.

He pulls the rag out of my mouth and grabs my head with both hands. I start shaking uncontrollably and he laughs.

"Suck me off," he says. "There's a good girl."

I can't pull away, can't scream, can only let him pull my head closer to his crotch, pry my mouth open with a thumb that tastes like stale tobacco and engine grease.

His stench – sweat and werewolf musk and piss and I don't know what else – makes me gag and suddenly I'm awake, scrambling out of bed and trying not to puke on the rug. I don't make it to the bathroom, but at least I vomit on the hardwood where it will be easier to clean up.

And at least the dream ended before I had to put my mouth on that man's dick, but the memory of it happening is back, and keeps me heaving long after there's anything left in me but foam. Even then I keep gagging, tears and snot streaming out of my face. Even when it eases off, I stay crouched, unable to move, shaking.

Finally, I make myself get up, stumble to the bathroom, wash my face and hands, rinse my mouth. I don't want to face cleaning up the mess I've made in the hall, but I can't leave it there to stain the hardwood floor, so I dig a bucket and mop out of the cupboard in the hall, and clean.

I go back to bed, curl up in a miserable ball, and shake. I'm alone, and I'm scared. But I have more information about my attacker, about the werewolf who killed that woman in the park, and it doesn't do me any good if I don't tell anyone.

I reach for my phone. It's two in the morning. Should I wait until a more reasonable hour? I open the text messenger app, find Thorstein's name, and type. It takes a long time, because my hands won't stop shaking, and what do I say, anyway? I had a dream, and it made me remember?

In the end, I say, *I know what he looks like. Not his human face, but I can describe him. A bit.*

I expect a text back, if I get any reply at all at this hour, because Thorstein doesn't like talking on the phone, but my phone vibrates with an incoming call almost immediately.

"It's Raine," she says when I answer. "You're on speaker, sweetie. Tell us what you remember."

So I describe the dream and the memory it brought back and when I get to where he forced me, I can't finish the sentence.

"It's okay, Justin," says Thorstein's voice. "That's enough."

"You're sure it's not part of the nightmare?" Raine says. "You really remember it?"

"Yeah," I say. I choke on the word. "I remember."

"You want me to send Magne over to keep you company?" Thorstein again, strong and gentle. "He can be there in five minutes."

"No," I say. "It's okay. I'll be okay." I don't know if that's true, but I wanted to be strong, to take care of myself, to have some space to think. I *have* to do this.

When I hang up, I keep my phone clenched in my hand like a security blanket. If I need it, help is only a few clicks away. But I'm determined not to need it.

I stare into the dark, trying not to remember. I should go into the living room, turn on the tv. But I can't move.

My phone vibrates. Bjarni.

t told me, he says. *hv narwd dwn suspex. u ok?*

I don't answer.

justin?

I don't answer.

My phone rings and I ignore it. It rings again. And again. And goes silent.

If he was hurt, scared, alone, and wouldn't answer my calls, what would I do? I sigh. I'd find a way to get to him, to make sure he was okay.

I hit the return call button.

"Justin," he says. "Fuck. Are you okay? I'm coming to get you." I hear keys jingling.

"No," I say. "Don't come."

"*Kjaereste*," he breathes. He sounds… afraid? "Let me… let me take care of you."

"No," I repeat. "It was just a dream. I have to be able to get through this myself." Why do I have to do this myself? I don't know, I just know I can't run away anymore, and I can't let someone else look after me forever.

"Please," he whispers. That one word, so hard for him to say. I don't know if he realizes how difficult it is to say "no" when he says "please."

"Just…" I suck in a deep breath.

"What? What do you want me to do?"

"Just talk to me," I say.

"Okay," he says. I hear his footsteps, the creak of leather – he must be in his living room, sitting on the couch. "What do you want me to talk about?"

"Anything. I don't care. I just want to hear your voice."

His breathing, ragged like he's worried and trying not to show it.

"How about if I read to you? Do you like fairytales?"

"That would be nice," I say.

"Hang on," he says. Leather creaking as he gets up, footsteps. He's going upstairs. "I'm still here," he says. "Just finding the book." Sounds like he's flipping through books on a bookcase. "Okay, got it. I've had this book since I was a kid. Granddad used to read it to me. Asbjornsen and Moe. Have you heard of them?"

"No." My voice is barely a whisper.

"They're like the Brothers Grimm of Norway," he says. I hear him sit, on his bed maybe. Hear pages turning. "Shit," he says. "I forgot it's in Norwegian."

"That's okay," I say. "I just want to hear your voice."

"Maybe I can translate," he says, turning more pages. "Here, this is a good one." He clears his throat and says, "*Det var en gang*," his accent deepening with each word, so that when he adds, "That means 'There was, once.' Like 'once upon a time' in English fairytales," even his English is more touched with foreign sounds than usual. I want to drown in it.

He continues reading, first saying the lines in Norwegian, then translating them to English. I'm so lost in his voice that I don't realize how much time has passed until I hear birds singing, and a cock crows somewhere on the farm, just audible to my werewolf ears through the open phone line.

When he pauses at the end of a story, I say, "Thank you. I think I can sleep now." It helps that when I roll over, I can see the faint light of dawn creeping in though the blinds in the kitchen and making stripes on the hall floor.

"Any time," he says softly.

"Goodnight, Bjarni."

"Are we still on for a picnic?"

I poke my watch were it rests on the bedside table and it lights up with the time. Just after five. I can still sleep a few hours and hopefully not be a total wreck.

"Yeah," I say.

"See you in a few hours, *kjaereste.*"

This time when I sleep, I don't dream, like the rising sun keeps the monsters at bay. In real life, I know my particular monster is out in daylight, that he assaulted me, forced me, in daylight, but my sleeping self feels safe, at least.

I feel like crap when I finally crawl out of bed at eleven. My stomach muscles and ribs ache from throwing up, and there's a headache lurking behind my eyes.

But I brush my teeth and wash my face and don't look too closely at myself in the mirror. I pick out my newest, nicest pair of jeans – the ones I bought at the men's consignment that Raine said make my butt look good – and add a t-shirt that she swore made me look thin and toned instead of merely skinny.

It might be chilly near the river, so I add an army-surplus jacket, stuff phone, wallet, and keys in my pockets, and put on my hand-me-down sneakers. Once I actually make some money instead of getting advances on pay I haven't earned yet, I'll get a good pair of proper runners for running in, and something more casual for everyday. For now, these will do.

I have to run to catch the bus, and then I end up getting to the ferry dock, where we agreed to meet, early, but he's already there, leaning on the railing, with an honest-to-God picnic basket at his feet. His back is to me, and I walk slowly, studying how his jacket stretches across his back, how his ass and thighs look in his perfectly-fitting jeans, how the sun makes his dark blond hair shine as the breeze off the river lifts strands away from his shoulders.

He turns before I'm ready, and I can't catch my breath. I hope I'm not gawping at him as stupidly as I feel.

"Hey," he says. His voice sends an electrical zing through my chest, and I should be dismayed at how this man can destroy me with one almost meaningless word.

"Hey." I stop, stuff my hands in my pockets, suddenly not knowing how to act.

"Did you sleep?"

I nod. "A bit, yeah." I bite my lip. "Sorry I kept you up."

"Don't apologize." He brushes the side of my face with the backs of his fingers. "I'd have driven here to read to you in person if you'd let me."

"Thanks."

He nods, drops his hand away and picks up the basket. "There are tables and benches down that way." He nods along the river, and we start to walk.

After a few minutes of silence, he says, "Can I hold your hand?"

I look up at him in surprise, then look across the river. "Maybe on the way back," I say.

"Okay," he says. "How was work? At the gallery?"

"It was good," I say. "I like Katie." I look at him out of the corners of my eyes and he's got a tiny smile.

"Katie's pretty great," he says. A few more steps and he adds, "I guess you know we slept together once."

"I know," I say.

"It was months ago. It's not going to happen again. We're friends, that's all."

"I know," I say again. I drag a smile out from somewhere. "Katie doesn't do repeats, anyway."

That startles a snort out of him. "No, she doesn't," he says. "I didn't used to, either."

"What changed?" I don't know why we're talking about this. I don't care how many people he's slept with in the past; I just don't want to hear about them. And I don't want it to happen again.

"You," he says. "I met you."

"Oh."

We walk a little more, then he says, "I've got the list of suspects narrowed down. I know you maybe don't want to think about what happened, not so soon after remembering… that."

"It's okay. I want to find him and put it all in the past."

"I'm pretty sure there are only about five people it maybe *could* be. Three it's most likely to be."

He touches my hand but doesn't try to take it in his. "Thorstein's going to put out word that he's pretty sure he knows who it is, see how they react. If it doesn't work, if he doesn't take the bait… you're going to have to try to identify him."

I shudder. "I figured," I say.

"I'll be there," he says. "Thorstein will be there. Magne, too, probably. We thought Freysblöt, when the whole pack gathers to celebrate first harvest, would be the best time. That's at the equinox. The Elders will be there, too, so if we find him, they can deal with him right away."

"That's the day after my birthday," I say, quietly. "At least it will be over."

"Hell of a birthday present," he says. "But yeah, at least it will be over." He stops me, turns me to look at him. "I'm so sorry all this happened to you, *kjaereste*. I'm so fucking sorry."

I put my hand flat on his chest, feel his body heat, his heartbeat, his strength.

"Don't be sorry," I say. "If it hadn't happened, I'd have lost my apartment anyway, and I'd be in a men's shelter, or homeless. Or dead." I suck in my lower lip, bite it hard to make myself keep talking. "And I'd never have met you."

Then I turn and keep walking. It's a few steps before he follows, but he has longer legs and catches up easily.

"Wait," he says. "You're counting meeting me as a *good* thing?"

"Sure," I say. "Why not?"

"Even after I... after I hurt you?"

"*That* was not a good thing, no." I step off the sidewalk to let a little old lady on a scooter pass by from the other direction, then resume walking. "But you're a pretty good kisser." He makes a strangled noise. "And, aside from swearing, you're pretty good with your mouth in general."

He drops behind again, then catches up to steer me off the path to a picnic table under a maple tree with a view out over the river. His hand lingers on mine.

"You think maybe I could try some new things with my mouth sometime?" he says.

I sit across from him at the table and let him capture one of my feet between both of his.

"I'll consider it," I say. Then I frown. "What new things are you talking about?"

He picks up my hand, brings it to his mouth, and wraps his lips around the tip of my index finger. I feel his tongue slide against me as he sucks my whole finger into his mouth. Then he slides his lips away and lays my hand back on the table. My jeans are suddenly too tight, and I desperately need to adjust myself.

"You'll just have to wait and see," he says. "But I've been doing some reading. There's a nice little shop on Crosstown Drive called Venus & Son."

I snap my mouth shut, because it's apparently been hanging open, and stammer out, "The sex shop?" I've never been there, but even in Great Valley I'd heard of it.

"Mmm," he says, pulling sandwiches, chips, and bottles of iced tea out of the basket. "They're very friendly and knowledgeable." He grins and a pale blush touches his cheekbones. "They didn't even make fun of me for being a grown man just figuring out he likes other men." He tilts his head. "Or one other man in particular."

He may only be blushing a little, but I have a burning flush creeping up my neck that's going to hit my face at any second.

"You went into Venus & Son and asked for advice on…" My voice stops working.

He hands me a sandwich.

"On how to pleasure my beautiful boyfriend, yes," he says. "Assuming he ever forgives me for one colossal screw-up."

I stare at the sandwich in my hands as if I don't know what it is. "Your boyfriend?" I say, and I look up at him.

"If you want," he says. The blush is gone as if it was never there, and his toothy, cocky grin is firmly in place.

My mouth is hanging open again. "Oh my God," I say.

"I don't know if going to a sex shop and asking a very gay man for help with choosing sex toys counts as courting, but I'm pretty sure it should."

I finally muster enough brain power to stop gawping at him and concentrate on unwrapping my sandwich. It appears to be home-baked bread, thick with Colleen's home-churned butter, and layered with the farm's amazing smoked ham and some kind of pale, hard cheese. I realize how hungry I am, but before I take a bite, I say, "I suppose that counts." Then, "Did you buy anything?"

I hide my mortification behind my sandwich. *I'm* the gay guy; I'm supposed to be the one comfortable with sex shops and butt stuff, and here's Bjarni, realizing he doesn't know as much as he'd like and asking an expert – a *stranger* – for advice.

He shakes his head. "Not any toys. I wanted to wait until we could go together. I did get a couple of books, though." He takes a bite of his sandwich.

From somewhere I manage to find a little boldness and say, "They make these little vibrators."

He stops chewing, eyes wide.

"For sticking up your butt."

He chokes and grabs for an iced tea, gulps, swallows.

"We could try those," he says.

On the walk back, I let him hold my hand, and when he offers a lift home, I don't say no. But I don't ask him up to the apartment. I'm not ready for that yet, and I realize I'm enjoying making him grovel. Just a little.

"At least let me kiss you," he says, when I'm about to get out of the car.

I lean over the gear shift, slide one hand into his soft silky hair, and pull his mouth to mine.

My lips are swollen and throbbing by the time I pull away, say, "Text me when you get home?" and head inside.

Chapter Thirteen

I BARELY MAKE IT IN THE DOOR, dazed and happier than I've been in a while, when I get a text from Katie.

b outside @ 9, it says. *E&me taking you dancing.*

On Sunday??? I reply.

Gallery closed Mon, she says.

Clubs are open?

Always a club open somewhere.

I want to say no, to spend the evening making lists of words that might turn into poems in my notebook, and to read more of Raine's smutty romance novels. And yeah, to stare out the window and think about kissing Bjarni Thorvaldson.

But I know trying to convince Katie to let me stay home when she believes the best thing for my broken heart is to flirt with hot men in a club would be an exercise in futility. Even if I admit to her that my heart is considerably less broken than it was.

So I just reply, *I'm not wearing leather or latex.*

LOL, she answers. *wear tite jeans & t.*

I don't plan to change out of the clothes I wore to have a picnic lunch with Bjarni.

I turn sideways on the couch and stretch out. I have plenty of time for a nap, and I'm probably going to need the rest if, as I suspect, Katie and Elias are actually going to make me dance and not just let me sip a drink in a corner and observe.

I'm drifting off, remembering the feel of Bjarni's hair on my fingers, the flick of his tongue against mine, when my phone vibrates again.

home, the text says. *desperately want to kiss u again.*

My lips curve into a smile and I don't even have to force it. I don't want to encourage him too much, to start back on the same too-fast trajectory we were on before, except part of me doesn't care about slow and careful. Part of me wants to say "fuck it" and jump back in head first. I already know that next time I see him, I'm probably going to end up sleeping with him again. But I'm not sure I want *him* to know that. Not yet.

Finally, I type, *Me too.* Then, feeling cheeky and wanting to maybe worry him a little, I add, *Katie & Elias are taking me out tonight.*

My phone rings and I'm smiling when I answer.

"You know Elias is like the gay version of Katie, right?" he asks. "Fucking someone different every night and breaking hearts all over the place?"

I want to answer, "Don't you mean the gay version of you?" but maybe that's unfair. Maybe he really has changed.

"He's already been warned that I'm off limits," I say, allowing amusement to color my tone. I don't tell him that if I weren't in love, I'd be happy for Elias to take me home for a one-night-only fuck.

"By whom?"

"Do I hear a little bit of jealousy?" I tease.

"You hear a lot of jealousy," he says, letting a growl into his voice. I think he's joking, but I'm not sure.

"You have nothing to worry about. I don't cheat."

He's quiet, and I wonder if he thinks I was implying that he *does* cheat, that I still believe he's going to pursue women. I didn't mean it that way when I said it.

"I know, *kjaereste,*" he says. "I trust you. I just want to be there. *I* want to be the one to take you out. I want to be the one everyone else is envying because I'm with the sexiest man in the place." If I didn't hear the heat in his voice, I'd think he was exaggerating.

"You really think that?" I say, hating that I need the validation, that I crave the thrill I feel when he tells me I'm attractive, or beautiful.

"That you're sexy?" He blows out a lungfull of air. "Didn't I mention how good your ass looked today? In those jeans you were wearing?"

"No," I say. "I don't recall you saying anything about my ass."

"Your ass looked really good today," he says. "*You* looked really good. Tired, but fucking gorgeous." I hear him take a sip of something, imagine how the muscles in his neck look when he swallows. "Does it count as courting you if I tell you how incredibly beautiful you are every day?"

I laugh. "Do you have a little notepad where you write down everything that counts as courting and tick it off each time you complete something on the list?"

"Maybe," he says. "So does it count?"

"Only if you actually believe what you're saying."

"You know I can't lie to you," he says. "My werewolf."

"So I'm told," I say.

"You are beautiful," he says. "And so fucking sexy. And even if you do forgive me, if you let me be your boyfriend, your one and only, I will keep telling you you're beautiful for the rest of your life."

That gives me pause. That he's thinking – even just as a throw-away comment – of the rest of my life.

"I should try to take a nap," I say. "I don't think Katie will let me sneak home early."

"First tell me who told Elias you're off limits. Was it Katie?"

"Raine," I say.

"Speaking of Raine, Thorstein is walking around in a fucking daze right now."

"He's happy?"

"So fucking happy." His voice goes quiet. "It's really good to see."

"He'll be an amazing father."

"He will. He raised me, you know?"

"I didn't," I say. I mean, I wouldn't even have guessed, since their dad only recently died.

"Our mother died when I was three," he says. "I don't even remember her. Dad was feral with grief. He'd disappear into the woods for weeks at a time. Granddad made sure we had food, but he had his own shit going on, I guess. Thorstein was left to deal with me."

"How old was he?" I'm trying to imagine Bjarni at three years old, and I can't.

"He was ten. Can you fucking imagine? A ten-year-old kid who just lost his mother, whose father is gone most of the time, left to raise his three-year-old brother?"

"Shit," I say.

"Yeah. Thorstein and Mom were really close, too. He was devastated and wasn't even allowed to grieve. And I was a fucking terror. I don't know how he managed to keep me alive. He lost most of his childhood to being my surrogate father, because Dad couldn't fucking take care of his own kids. I think that's when Dad started to go off, too, to get paranoid and power-hungry."

"I never met your father, but I think I hate him," I whisper.

"I'm glad you never had to meet him," he says. "I'm glad he's dead."

"I wish you'd had a better father," I say. "I wish we both did."

"At least I had Thorstein. And I know he'll be a fucking great dad because he's always been as much a father to me as a brother." He sighs. "For Magne, too."

"How does Magne feel about being an uncle? I hope someone told him."

Bjarni laughs, a genuinely happy sound. "I think he's almost as happy as Thorstein. He's probably already shopping for a whole wardrobe of 'World's Best Uncle' t-shirts."

"That kid's not going to be able to avoid having a really great childhood."

There's a happy pause, then Bjarni says, "Listen, Justin. Have fun tonight. I mean it. Dance with some hot guys, drink some girly drinks. Relax. I promise I won't be too jealous sitting here at home by myself."

"I'm not really the dancing type, but I'll try."

"And maybe..." He sounds suddenly uncertain. "Are you coming back to the farm after work Friday?"

"Yeah," I say. "I kind of have to, what with the full moon coming up and me still being a brand-new werewolf."

"Can I pick you up? Drive you home? Maybe stop somewhere for a burger?"

"Are you asking me on a date?" I say, teasing. It feels so good to be able to tease him.

"Yes, I am," he says, all serious, and I can't tell over the phone if he really is serious or if he's teasing back. "And if that goes well, I'd like to take you somewhere really fancy next time."

"That sounds nice," I say. "But what kind of fancy? Like what do I wear?"

"If I can swing it," he says, "You'll need a dinner jacket. No jeans."

"Will I need a tie? I don't own a tie." I don't own a dinner jacket, either, but one problem at a time.

"No tie. Just nice pants, matching jacket, dress shirt. Probably what you wear to work at the gallery would be fine."

"I don't wear a jacket at the gallery," I say. "Will you tell me where we're going and when, so I can wardrobe consult with Katie?"

"If I can get reservations, I'll tell Katie and she can take you shopping. I want it to be a surprise."

"Okay," I bite my lip. I can never seem to figure out how to approach the topic of money. Or my severe lack thereof.

"Do you need another advance? To go shopping?" he says.

I think of the pitiful amount of cash left in my wallet after I had to buy clothes for the gallery and boots for the farm. I don't know what it will cost to buy fancy-restaurant-level clothes, but it won't be cheap. And there's not going to be much of that cash left after going to a club tonight.

I guess I'm quiet so long he figures out my dilemma.

"I'll transfer you some more," he says.

"I don't —"

"No arguments," he says. "I know Thorstein, and he's going to be working your ass off in a few weeks. You'll make it all back in no time."

"I don't have my new debit card yet," I say. The thought fills me with dread, because I also don't have my new credit card, which means I haven't been making payments. And I only have a temporary driver's license.

"I'll talk to Magne," he says. "Don't worry about it."

"You don't have to take me anywhere fancy," I say.

"I *want* to," he answers. "I want to take my beautiful boyfriend to the fanciest fucking restaurant in Riverbend and have everyone stare at us when we walk in."

I snort. "You just like having everyone look at you."

He snorts back. Then he says, gently, "Justin, you deserve fancy restaurants and expensive clothes. And I want to be the one who gives them to you. Now try to sleep a bit before your sex-crazed boss and her equally sex-crazed gay friend drag you away to dance your cute little ass off."

"Fine," I say.

"Good," he says. "I'll text you tomorrow. And Justin?"

"Yeah?"

"You're beautiful." And he hangs up.

At nine o'clock a taxi pulls up to the curb with Katie and Elias in the back seat, leaving me to climb in the front. Luckily, the driver isn't the chatty type, so I'm spared having to say much more than, "Hello."

Standing on the sidewalk in front of a place with neon purple lighting in an unreadable font, Katie drapes an arm over my shoulders and says, "Tonight's on us. You try to pay for your own drinks, I'll fire you."

"Yes ma'am," I say, and she swats the back of my head.

"So, this isn't technically a gay club," Elias says, "But it's queer friendly and lots of queer folks hang out here, so don't be afraid to flirt with whoever catches your eye."

"I'm happy sitting in the corner with a fruity drink," I say.

"Is that fruity as in 'contains fruit'," says Katie, "Or fruity as in gay?"

"Both," I say. "And it better have a paper umbrella in it."

Inside, the music is so loud it's like the whole building has a heartbeat, and despite my usual inclination to head for the corner farthest from people, I let Katie and Elias pull me onto the dance floor.

The thumping beat and the flashing lights work their magic and pretty soon, I'm forgetting how ridiculous I probably look. I close my eyes for a moment, letting the energy of all those human bodies moving around me wash through me, and when I open them, my friends are nowhere in sight.

But there's a guy – killer-cheekboned and bare-abbed – dancing in front of me. He meets my startled look with a grin and wink and leans over to yell above the noise, "Can I have this dance?" in my ear. I don't say no and before I know it, his hands are on my waist and he's pulling me closer. For a moment, I let him. I enjoy the feeling of his strong fingers digging into my hips, of his breath on my neck.

But when he moves to press his pelvis against mine, I step back and shake my head. "Sorry," I say.

He gives me another grin. "Boyfriend?" he yells in my ear.

I nod.

"Too bad," he says. He tucks a business card into my hip pocket. "In case you change your mind." And then he's gone, absorbed back into the crowd.

And he's not the only hot guy, or beautiful woman, for that matter, who comes over to dance with me, to offer a phone number or a place to crash when the club closes. Finally, Elias drags me away to a table at the edge of the dance floor and brings me a drink. It's got pineapple, and a paper umbrella, in it.

"So, you look like you're having fun," he says, grinning.

I raise the drink in salute and sip it. It's cold and sweet, and fucking perfect. "Thanks," I say.

"How many did you get?"

I must look blank, because he grins and holds up a handful of bits of paper, napkins, and business cards. "How many phone numbers?" he yells.

I shrug.

"I got twelve," he says. "Plus a very dirty proposition involving the back alley. Might be a personal record."

"Eight, and two offers of blowjobs" I say, after counting. I leave the bits of paper on the table. "They're all yours."

He laughs and shakes his head. "Put them back in your pocket and throw them out later. That way you won't insult anyone."

I shove the numbers back into my pocket and contemplate keeping them. Not to actually phone anyone, but to tease Bjarni with.

"Where's Katie?" I yell and Elias turns away to survey the room. Finally, he points. Katie's dancing, surrounding by good-looking muscular men, and she looks entirely in her element. As we watch, she pulls one of them closer to say something in his ear, and he slides a hand around her waist. He replies and she laughs.

And then he looks up, over her head, sees something he doesn't like, and steps back. Two guys, bigger than any of the men surrounding Katie. They look like maybe they belong to a biker gang or something.

"What are they doing here?" Elias says. He's suddenly alert, on edge.

"You know them?" I say, leaning closer so he can hear me.

"No, but they sure don't look like they belong."

Katie doesn't look too happy about them either, as they try to dance – or gyrate, really, because I don't think what either of them is doing could be called *dancing* – on either side of her. The other men she was dancing with edge away, finding other attractive people in the crowd to flirt with.

One guy, who has a recently healed scar across his cheek, and several days' worth of stubble on his chin, leans over to say something in her ear and she shakes her head and goes to move away. She steps back, right into the second guy, who's even more unkempt looking than the first. He puts a hand on her arm, fingers digging in.

She tries to pull away but can't.

"Fuck," I say, pushing away from my stool and abandoning the rest of my drink on the table.

"Be careful," says Elias. "I'll go get the bouncer." Neither of us is anywhere big enough to take on even one of the guys harassing Katie, but I'm not going to just sit there and watch.

I make my way across the dance floor, which is suddenly very easy, because people are unconsciously making room around Katie and the two men. For a second, the building's ventilation system brings me their scents and I recognize it: werewolf.

I take Katie's other arm and pull her so sharply towards me that the guy holding her is startled into letting go. I push her behind me and find myself face-to-face – more or less, because I have to look way up – with two irritated werewolves that are way bigger than me. They're not Thorstein-big, but then who is? They're each at least close to Magne-big.

"Leave her alone," I say, and I'm pretty sure they can't hear me over the music, but they'll understand the sentiment. I wish I'd thought to text

Magne before coming over here. At least he could avenge my inevitable pulping.

"You're in my way, little man," says one of them, voice loud and angry, even with the blaring music.

Where the hell is Elias with the bouncer?

"I said leave her alone," I say. I feel Katie's grip on my shoulder.

"I can handle these asswipes, Justin," she says, but I can tell it's all bravado in her voice.

"Yeah, pretty little faggot," the other werewolf says. "I'll just bet she can handle us," and he makes a lewd gesture.

"Both of us," says the first one.

"Leave her the fuck alone." I let my voice fill with the anger I've always pushed aside, when someone bigger and stronger than me has pushed me around. I don't care if they flatten me. I've had the shit kicked out of me often enough, and I don't care anymore. If I back down, I won't be able to face myself in the mirror. I'm done running.

One of them sneers and cocks back a fist. And is suddenly on the floor with a boot on his neck. I look up in surprise just as the other guy smashes a fist into Magne's face.

Katie drags me back a few steps.

Magne shakes his head and drops of blood spatter from his nose. He grins, all teeth, and looks so much like Bjarni I have to check the color of his hair. Before the other guy can react, Magne's hand is on his throat, forcing his head back, fingers digging in and cutting off the guy's air.

"You wanna get the fuck out of here," Magne says. "And keep on going right out of the county if you don't want any more trouble." He pushes his face close to the guy and for a moment, I think he's going to put his werewolf teeth on the guy's throat. But we're in a public place, and he only sneers, "And believe me, you don't want any more trouble than you're already in."

He lets go of the guy, who stumbles back, clutching his neck. He drags his friend to his feet and they both head for the door just as the bouncer finally arrives.

Magne holds up both hands. "I was just leaving," he says. He's bigger than the bouncer, only just, but he backs away anyway, aiming a grin at me and a wink at Katie.

We re-group at our table, fresh drinks in hand. "Should we go?" I say. I can't imagine we'll be able to re-capture the magic we found before those werewolves showed up.

"What was Magne doing here?" says Katie. I have a feeling I know, that maybe Bjarni asked him to keep an eye on me, and I'm not sure if I'm happy about it, even if he did just step in exactly when he was needed.

"I've never seen anyone take a punch like that," says Elias. "I think I'm in love."

"Magne's very, very taken," says Katie, "Or you'd be getting in line. Behind me."

"He's also very, very straight," I say. I'm ready to head home. I need to tell someone that there are strange werewolves around – assuming they're not members of Thorstein's pack, which of course I can't know for sure. But I guess Magne will already have taken care of that. But I also want to growl at Bjarni for sending his brother after me.

"Well, I want to dance some more," says Elias. "It's barely eleven. And how likely is it that something like that will happen twice in one night?"

I sigh and eat the pineapple out of my drink. I have no desire to leave by myself, so I guess I'm going to have to wait to talk to Magne and Bjarni. I wonder if I can figure out how to get them on a conference call so I can yell at them both at once.

I wonder where I suddenly found the courage to think about yelling at either of them.

Though I never quite get back into the same happy state I found before the werewolves showed up, I do enjoy a couple more hours of dancing and flirting, and I'm feeling pretty good when the club finally closes, and we stumble out into the early morning. I half expect Magne to be leaning against the wall by the door, waiting, but he's not.

We walk a few blocks to get clear of the crowd and Katie hands me her phone, grinning like a cat who not only got the cream but figured out how to get it directly from the cow.

I take it, look at the picture that's up on the screen, and stare. It's me, dancing with Elias, taken from the back. And my ass does look pretty good in these jeans.

Then I notice it's displayed in the text app, and she's just sent it to Bjarni with the message *Lookin after ur man*. Her phone chimes and I see his reply before she takes it back from me.

fuuuuuuuck, was all he said.

"Are you sure that's me?" I say.

Elias leans over Katie's shoulder to look. "That's definitely your ass," he says.

Katie taps at the screen, then hands it back to me. Another photo. My eyes are closed, and my arms are over my head, pulling up my t-shirt to expose a strip of belly muscles. I have a dreamy look on my face.

When Katie takes her phone again, Elias grabs her hand to look at the screen. "If I didn't know your boyfriend would flatten me," he says, "I'd ask for a copy of that one to add to my GILF file."

"Your what?"

He just smirks and gets into the front seat of the cab that pulls over for us.

"It's like MILF or DILF," Katie says, with a disgusted snort, "Only the 'G' stands for 'guys'."

"Oh," I say. She climbs into the back seat and just as I'm following her, I hear her phone chime. She starts giggling uncontrollably.

"What?" I say.

She doesn't answer, so I snatch her phone out of her hands to see that she's sent Bjarni that photo, too, and he's replied.

An eggplant emoji, followed by the splashing water emoji.

A flush burns its way up my neck until I'm sure I'm going to catch us all on fire.

Chapter Fourteen

THE REST OF THE WEEK goes pretty much like the last one, only on Wednesday I get whisked off to Charles's Consignment by Katie, to buy clothes she deems suitable for whatever fancy restaurant Bjarni plans to take me to.

She picks me up in her Civic just after lunch and when we get to the shop, she and the owner – a tall, thin, dark-complexioned man who really is named Charles – park me in front of a mirror at the back of the shop and tell me not to move.

The two of them walk around the store together, talking about me like I'm a mannequin they're dressing for an extra-special shop display.

"With his coloring," says Charles, "we don't want too much saturation or brightness. Do you know what his date will be wearing?"

"No idea," says Katie, "but I'll see if I can find out." I hear her tapping on her phone. "What do you have that will bring out his eyes?"

They come back to where I'm standing and peer at my face, tilt it towards the light to better assess my eyes.

"What color would you call that?" says Charles. "Greenish brown?"

"Hazel, I think," says Katie. "I've seen them look different colors depending on what he's wearing or how sunny it is outside."

"Remarkable."

They leave me standing there and wander off again, pulling out and putting back items of clothing as they go.

"He says dark blue," I hear Katie say, and I glance up to see her holding up her phone to Charles. "Navy?"

"Mmm. More of a midnight, I think. It would look black in the shade."

When they finally come back, what seems like several hours later, but is probably only about forty-five minutes, it's with a rolling rack hung with jackets and matching trousers, and a whole lot of dress shirts in different colors.

I allow myself to be pushed into the change room, and dutifully try on each thing as directed.

"No, not that one," says Charles, as I emerge wearing the first outfit.

"The shirt isn't bad," says Katie, so they hang it on the "maybe" end of the rack.

"I want his eyes to fall out," I say. "When he sees me."

Katie takes the shirt off the rack and hands it to Charles. "Not quite eye-falling-out caliber," she says, and he puts in on the rack of rejects.

Eventually, I realize they're looking less at the fit of the things I try on, and more at the cut and color.

"He has broad shoulders for such a thin creature," Charles says.

"He's not as skinny as he looks," replies Katie.

"So I see." Charles looks at me contemplatively in the mirror. I'm wearing a charcoal-grey jacket and trousers that I think are lightweight wool. I pointedly don't look at the price tag hanging off the cuff. Katie informed me that I wouldn't have to pay until everything is tailored and ready next week, so I refuse to think about money until then.

"Yes, I think the grey looks good," Charles finally says. "But that shirt just won't do."

"It's a very neutral grey," says Katie. "It should go with his date's midnight blue, but what about a warmer-toned shirt? Maybe that russet raw silk you dismissed earlier?"

"Hmm... You might be right."

I look from one to the other of them, feeling very much like my opinion doesn't count.

"Take that shirt off," Charles says and when I go to step back into the change room, he adds, "Don't be silly. You're only taking your shirt off." Then he pauses. "We need to find you an undershirt."

I finally speak up. "I'd rather use the change room," I say.

He frowns but seems to realize I'm not just being shy. Maybe he'll think I have some horrible disfigurement I don't want anyone to see, and in a way he's right. Besides the cut marks and thin scars on my wrists from coping – or not coping – with my parents, there are my werewolf scars that would be too awkward to explain. I mean, saying I was attacked by a wild animal, or a vicious dog wouldn't be too far off from the truth, but it's easier to just keep everything hidden.

I dutifully put on the sleeveless undershirt Charles gives me, before reaching for the shirt Katie hands me over the change room door. The fabric feels deliciously soft against my skin, and it seems a shame to wear anything under it. It's silk, but that soft, matte-finish kind rather than the shiny, slippery kind. I put it on and it feels so nice I almost don't care what it looks like. It fits my shoulders but is too big in the torso – that's what tailoring is for, I guess.

I step out of the room and Charles holds the jacket for me to put back on and then I turn back to the mirror. And stare.

"Oh, that's definitely it," says Katie.

"Mm. Yes, I think that will do," says Charles. He sounds almost smug. "Once everything is properly fitted."

The shirt is a sort of rusty, browny color that makes my hair look almost red, and catches the brown and gold in my eyes. But when I turn, the light shifts and gives the fabric a greenish cast, making my eyes go green, too. I look… pretty good, actually.

I'm then instructed to stand still while Charles wields chalk and pins and makes notes in a little book. And then I'm finally allowed to change back into my jeans and tee, and suddenly I'm ordinary again. But Katie has assembled a whole army of shoes for me to try on.

When she's satisfied that we've found a pair that suit the outfit, and will also work for gallery wear, I wander off to look at less formal things while she finalizes plans for me to come back for a final try-on after tailoring. She's going to take charge no matter what I say, so I figure it's just easier to step aside and let her do her thing.

I find a couple of shirts on the clearance rack that I can wear when the weather starts to turn colder, which will be soon, and I almost miss the pair of high-top Chucks buried under a pile of other shoes in the casual section. The bright leaf-green color catches my eye and I almost don't dare hope they'll be my size. But they are, and I think I have just enough cash left to buy them and the shirts, assuming I won't need any more groceries this week.

"You got your wish, sweetheart," Katie says as we leave the store. "Bjarni's eyes are going to fall out when he sees you in that outfit. Please, please tell me I can be there to watch."

"I looked okay?" I say.

She smiles. "I saw you checking yourself out in the mirror," she says, poking my arm. "With it altered to fit you perfectly, you're going to be the hottest boy in hot town."

"Okay, I'll take that as a 'yes, you looked okay'."

"He's going to spontaneously combust when he sees you, Justin."

I have to smile at that and try to imagine what he actually *will* look like when he sees me all dressed up. "I hope so," I say. Then, "I really need an actual haircut."

"Ooh, please let me make an appointment for you," she says. "Please please please."

I look at her sidelong. "Will I be able to afford it?"

"You can't go to a corner barber for a date at –" She snaps her mouth shut.

"Where?" I say. "You know where he's taking me, don't you?"

"I'm sworn to secrecy," she says. "But it's very swanky, and you need a proper haircut, from a proper men's stylist." She grins at me. "I know a guy who is stupid expensive but will give you a smokin' deal because you're my friend."

And stupidly, the thought of having a friend – several friends, in fact – makes me feel warm inside, and reduces the anxiety at the thought of having to spend more money I don't have to make my head look like I didn't have an unfortunate accident with a pair of clippers. At least it's grown out enough that there's hair to actually *style*.

The next two days speed by, and I learn how to write up framing orders and discover I have a decent eye for color, to the point that one of our regular clients, an old lady I only know as Mrs Walker, declares that I have chosen the absolute perfect mat colors for the watercolor painting she brought in. It's a small thing, but it feels pretty amazing.

Then, while I'm in the back eating my sandwich on Friday I get a text from Bjarni.

hv to take raincheck on burgers, he texts. *t wants m @ farm so hell pick u up @5.*

My stomach sinks a little, but really, it only means an extra forty-five minutes or so.

OK, I reply. *I guess I can wait to kiss you.*

make him stop & buy u food, he texts.

I let a smile curve my lips and contemplate how best I can tease him. I discard several replies as too bold or too risqué, and several others as just dumb.

Finally, I text, *Yes, dear.*

He replies with a kissy face emoji.

See you in a few hours, I send.

fyi, he replies. *i *am* going to kiss you.*

My breath catches, just a little, at the memory of the last time we kissed.

I guess that's ok, I reply, and add a shit-eating grin emoji.

Then more kissy face emojis. From both of us.

I know Magne has arrived at the gallery when I hear Katie out front say, "How's my favorite Thorvaldson brother?"

I hear him snort. "You just want me to have another show and make you some money," he teases.

"Of course, I do," Katie says. "But if you want to drive away assholes harassing me at a club, you're welcome to do that, too."

"Any time," he says.

I grab my jacket and hurry out front, where Katie's bringing in the sign and getting ready to close.

"Hey Justin," Magne says. "Ready to go?"

He leads me out to his truck – a pristine 1970s Chevy C10 that rumbles deep when he starts it.

"I need to stop by my apartment to grab my stuff," I say, and he nods, then points to an envelope on the seat between us. It's one of those big brown ones and looks kind of thick.

"That's for you," he says.

"What is it?"

"New bank cards and shit," he says.

My stomach lurches. "Oh," I say, and he looks at me funny, but doesn't say anything else. I leave the envelope where it is until we pull in in front of my building, and then I bring it in with me, reluctantly.

Magne grabs a box out of the back of the truck, and follows me in.

I drop the envelope on the kitchen counter and go to the bedroom to change into jeans and t-shirt and my new Chucks, and grab my duffel bag.

"You should probably open that," Magne says, nodding to the envelope.

"Yeah," I say.

"You don't like financial stuff." I guess it's obvious enough that he doesn't have to phrase it as a question.

"Not really." I force myself to pick up the envelope and slide it open. New debit and credit cards and another bank card I don't recognize. I put the first two in my wallet, along with the new driver's license and hell, even a library card. The rest of the envelope looks like paperwork I should probably keep filed away, if I had a place to file important paperwork.

Magne picks up the extra bank card and hands it to me. "Bjarni didn't explain this?"

I shake my head. "I get… really bad anxiety about money stuff." I sit on one of the kitchen stools and Magne takes the other one.

"He got you a personal line of credit," he says. "Used it to pay off your credit card because the interest is lower and so are the required monthly payments."

I feel like I'm going to throw up, so it's hard to follow what he's saying.

"All you have to do for now is pay the interest, and that comes out of your bank account automatically. Just make sure you don't spend your whole paycheck, and you'll be fine."

I swallow down the panic that threatens to steal my breath. "I don't have anything in the bank for it to come out of," I say.

"Yes, you do."

"Did he…?"

"He gave you another advance." He studies my face, maybe understands my dismay. "Thorstein will get it out of you once harvest starts in earnest, don't worry." He squeezes my shoulder. "You're going to be fine."

"What if I screw up again?" I say. My voice sounds small.

He shrugs. "Let Bjarni help you manage your money. It's what he's good at. And anyway, even part time, Thors will pay you well enough you won't have to worry. Not unless you get really reckless and start buying collector cars or something."

I laugh and he smiles. "Thanks," I say.

"Not a problem." Then he points at the cardboard box he's left on the counter, then one he brought in from his truck. "That's for you, too. Some stuff I thought you might be able to use."

"What is it?" He doesn't answer, so I open the box and look inside. Then I look at him. "I can't take this," I say. I reach in and pull out a laptop computer that looks almost new. Still in the box are charging cables, bluetooth keyboard and mouse and what looks like an external hard drive.

"Yes, you can," he says. "I like computers. I keep my shit up to date, so I end up with extras."

"But you could sell it."

He shrugs. "I usually donate my old gear to schools and literacy programs. This time, I'm donating it to you, since you lost all your stuff when you lost your apartment."

"My old laptop wasn't nearly this nice," I say. "Thank you."

"No prob," he says. "Now let's get on the road."

I remember, in the truck, how I wanted to yell at him for watching over me on Bjarni's behalf, but I can hardly do that now, after he was so generous. So instead, I just ask, "How come you were at the club Sunday night?"

"What, you don't think I'm the dancing type?" He laughs and shifts the truck as we pull out onto the highway, then settles back in his seat. "Thorstein told me our rogue wolf has been making his own pack, so I've been on the lookout. I picked up their trail when a buddy of mine told me a couple of strangers were throwing their weight around at a diner downtown."

He glances at me, then back at the road. He looks amused.

"You were following *them*," I say, accidentally emphasizing the last word.

He smiles but keeps his eyes on traffic. Friday night heading out of the city is busy, and there will be cops out getting ticket happy.

"Did you think I was following you?" he says.

It sounds dumb, now that he's asking. "I thought maybe Bjarni asked you to keep an eye on me," I mumble.

Now he does glance at me. "He *was* worried about you. After Saturday night."

"It was only a dream," I say. "And something I remembered."

"I know." He drums his fingers gently on the steering wheel. "He cares about you," he says. "He hasn't cared about anyone but himself for decades, so he might get a little enthusiastic sometimes."

"He cares about *you*," I say. "And Thorstein."

"Maybe."

"*Did* he ask you to keep an eye on me?"

"He asked me to check in on you once in a while. I said it wasn't necessary because Katie was already doing so."

"Is *everyone* watching me?" I say, dismayed, but also kind of touched.

He chuckles. "No one's going out of their way to spy on you," he says. "But yeah. Me, Katie, even Elias. We're here if you need us." He squeezes my knee briefly, then returns his hand to the steering wheel. "People like you, Justin."

"They do?" I mean, it's not like I think people generally *don't* like me, but it's still a strange thought. I've been running from my life so long I guess I haven't given people a chance to even know me, let alone decide how they feel about me.

"Yeah. You're a good guy. Friendly, kind." He grins with a lot of teeth and two dimples showing. "How you got mixed up with a colossal asswipe like my brother, I'll never know."

I look at my hands. "Bjarni's not so bad, under the jerk facade," I say. "I think… I think he's just afraid to let his guard down, you know?"

"Yeah, I get that," Magne says, voice softer. "But Dad's gone now, and he doesn't have to keep up the act."

"Maybe he doesn't know how to stop," I say.

That sidelong look again and the grin softens into a smile. "You're pretty smart," he says. "But listen. Bjarni and I don't get along. Put us in the same place for more than five minutes and one of us is going to end up bloody."

He pulls into the other lane to pass a Volkswagen van going way too slow, even for me, and I'm an overly cautious driver.

"One of the last times I saw him, I broke his nose," he adds.

"Oh," I say, and try not to stare at him. I mean, I know he's capable of violence, but Magne doesn't seem like he actually enjoys it.

"He deserved it," Magne says. "He even admitted he deserved it."

"What did he do?"

"He said something inappropriate about Raine. I'm pretty sure even Thorstein would have broken his nose if he'd heard it."

"Oh," I say again. "Maybe I'd have broken his nose myself. Or tried to."

He laughs. "I saw you put yourself between those wolves and Katie at the club," he says. "That was brave. Stupid, but brave."

"I couldn't just do nothing," I say. "I was hoping Elias would show up with the bouncer before anything too painful happened. Instead, you showed up."

"I'm pretty sure those guys were part of the rogue wolf's new pack. Or maybe the whole of his new pack," he says. "They're new, haven't developed their full wolf strength yet. Probably haven't figured out they don't have to do everything he tells them."

"Unless it's a simple direct order," I say.

"Sure," he says. "But even then, time and distance make a difference."

"What do you mean?"

"He could say 'dance a naked can-can' and they have to dance a naked can-can."

I can't help but laugh at the mental image.

He goes on. "But if he said, 'drive half an hour into Riverbend and dance a naked can-can in the Purple Kangaroo Club,' they'd start driving and within an few minutes the compulsion would wear off."

"What if they're really dumb and don't *know* it would wear off?"

"They'd have to be really, really dumb."

I think about that for a moment and find it somewhat reassuring that the guy who changed me can't make me do *anything* he wants, even if he *could* make me… well, yeah.

"Why were they in the club do you think?" I ask.

He considers that. "I think they were following you," he says.

"Me? Why me?"

He glances at me, and I feel a sickening feeling in my gut.

"To bring me back to him," I say. "To the guy who changed me."

"I think so," he says. "They just decided to have a little fun with Katie first because she was with you."

"To scare me into cooperating."

"Maybe, yeah."

"Will they try again?"

"I don't think so," he says. "I lost their trail, but they seemed to be headed out of town. All the wolves in Riverbend and a few other folks I know are keeping watch for them. I don't think they'll get near you again."

It's not as comforting a thought as I'd like, but then we're pulling off the highway onto the road that leads to the farm and my stomach lurches for an entirely different reason. Instead of fear, it's butterflies of anticipation I'm feeling. Because I'm almost back to Bjarni, who for all his irritating qualities, promised to kiss me. And he's a very good kisser.

Chapter Fifteen

Magne pulls into Thorstein's driveway, but once we're parked, we both head for the path to the farmhouse, me to drop off my things in my room, and him to say hi to his mom and sister.

Bjarni is waiting on the porch. "Thought I heard your truck," he says, cautiously reaching out to grip Magne's proffered arm. They look at each other warily and let go almost as soon as they touch. "Did you stop for something to eat?"

He's looking at Magne when he says it, but I answer anyway. "I forgot to mention it." I don't want him to think it's Magne's fault I haven't eaten; there's enough bad feeling between them as it is.

Bjarni's nostrils flare and his jaw clenches, but he turns away from his brother finally to look at me. His face relaxes and he smiles. "You hungry?"

"I had a big lunch," I say, which is true, but doesn't answer the question.

Magne and Bjarni both turn the same skeptical one-eyebrow-raised look at me, and I wait for my stomach to betray me. Miraculously, it stays quiet.

"I guess I could eat something, though," I say, and both brothers snort in exactly the same way. I look between them and can't help grinning. I don't think they have a clue how similar they are. "I know why you two don't get along," I say.

"Why's that?" Bjarni says, letting the corner of his mouth turn up.

"Because you're so much alike," I say, and step between them to go into the house.

"Take that back!" says Magne. I just lift a hand in a wave and head upstairs to drop my bag in my room.

When I come back down, they're all in the kitchen. Magne's sitting at the table with a cup of coffee, flanked by Colleen and Hilde, and Bjarni is at the counter, scowling and putting a thick roast beef sandwich together.

"Look who's gone all domesticated," Magne says.

"Behold the power of love," says Hilde.

"Fuck off, both of you," replies Bjarni.

"Children," Colleen says in her best irritated mom voice. She's smiling, though. That weird undercurrent I sensed the first time I had breakfast here is still there, maybe even stronger because Magne is here. I still can't quite figure it out, but I'm pretty sure it has something to do with their dad and his death, and the way they can't quite relax or saying anything negative about him because Colleen is still grieving, even if she seems fine.

Bjarni hands me the sandwich he's just made, which is when my stomach decides to grumble, loud.

"What a good wife you make, Little Bear," says Magne and Bjarni whips a squashed slice of bread at his head. Magne catches it, only barely in time, and flings it right back. Bjarni ducks and it hits the wall.

"Take it outside, if you're going to throw things," says Colleen and the brothers look at each other, like they're considering doing just that.

I swallow the bite of sandwich that's in my mouth so I can change the subject. "Are we going over to Thorstein's?" I don't say why, or that his request is the reason Magne is visiting tonight, because I don't know how much Colleen knows about my attacker or anything else that's gone on recently.

"Raine's coming over to watch that new Jane Austen adaptation with us," Hilde says. "So I expect you men will want to clear out."

"I like Jane Austen," I say.

"Well, you're an honorary woman, then."

I frown into the next bite of my dinner. I don't think one has to be a woman to enjoy certain things, even if society has deemed them "girly," but I'm not quite bold enough to say that I can be a man and like Jane Austen. Or that I can be a man and like fucking other men.

"You're welcome to stay and watch with us," says Colleen, and the moment passes.

"Thorstein says he's found a great new local beer he wants us to try," Magne says.

"You two go on ahead, then," says Colleen. "Let us have Magne to ourselves for a few minutes. He hasn't been home in weeks."

"I'll catch up with you," Magne says.

As we leave the house and step out into the yard, Bjarni takes my hand and laces his fingers with mine. It won't be dark for a while yet, but I wish it was, so I'd have an excuse to walk closer to him. Not that the dark is much hindrance to a werewolf, but I can always pretend my wolf vision hasn't developed yet.

Halfway through the trees between houses, he stops and pulls me around to face him.

"Hey," he says, as if we're just seeing each other and haven't already spent twenty minutes together with his family. He lets go of my hand to put both his hands on my hips, drawing me close, but not quite close enough that we're touching.

"Hey," I say back, resting my hands on his arms and relishing the feel of the tension in his biceps.

"Katie took you shopping?"

"I have to go back Wednesday to make sure everything fits after alterations. I guess I'll need a ride back early. Unless my car is fixed?"

"I was waiting till I could teach you how to fix it with me," he says. "But I can drive you back Wednesday. I'm sure Thorstein can find me some errands to run, so I won't even have to take time off work." His fingers dig into the muscles of my hips, and I find my eyes drifting closed. I slide my hands up to his shoulders.

"Hey," he says again. "Look at me."

I open my eyes.

"I fucking missed you," he says.

I smile. "You just saw me a few days ago."

"That was Sunday. That's… five days. An eternity."

"It kind of was."

"Forgive me yet?"

"Getting there."

He looks at me, expressionless, until I want to squirm, and then he bends closer to press his lips to that spot on my neck, right below my ear, and I shiver.

"*Kjaereste,*" he says, placing a kiss on my cheekbone, my jaw, and finally my lips.

My fingers tighten on his shoulders involuntarily and he pulls me closer, fitting our hips together, and slides his tongue into my mouth.

I want to melt into him, to let him sweep me away and do whatever he wants with me. Instead, I grab his hair and pull, forcing his mouth down on mine harder, and I push up on my tiptoes to press myself more firmly against him.

"Fuck, Justin," he whispers when he finally pulls away.

"Take me home with you tonight," I say, wondering if I'm making a mistake, if I should wait until I can be sure of him, but not really caring if I am. My body is on fire, awake in a way it hasn't been in a long time, and I feel the moon just starting to sing in my blood.

He tucks my head against his shoulder. "I wish I could, but the full moon is too close."

"Why does that matter?"

"It matters because you could be moon-drunk any time now, and by sometime tomorrow you'll be full-on moon-mad, convinced you're running on all fours in wolf shape." He pulls away to look at my face. "That's what the full moon does to new werewolves."

"But –" He puts a finger against my lips.

"No arguments." He steps away and laces his fingers in mine again and we resume walking. "I'll stay with you tonight, in your room, watch over you in case the madness hits early." He looks at me and smiles, but it's tense. "But no sex."

I frown.

"I mean it. You won't be capable of consenting, and I do not fuck anyone who doesn't, or can't, give complete and enthusiastic consent."

"So you're not a total dick after all," says Magne, suddenly appearing to follow us out onto Thorstein's lawn. Raine passes us going the other way and gives a wave and a grin and then is gone into the trees. My attention is diverted, and I guess Magne's is too, because I don't think either of us sees Bjarni move until his fist connects with Magne's face with a crunch.

There's a split second of utter silence, and then Magne's tackling his brother and they're rolling on the lawn, snarling, and I think I hear several more punches connecting.

"Stop it!" I yell. "Stop!"

They don't make any sound except the quiet snarls, harsh breathing, and grunts of effort, like yells or curses would distract from the fight. And that makes me think they're very serious.

"Stop!" I try to get close enough to them to… I don't know, separate them somehow, but only get knocked over for my trouble.

And then Thorstein's big hands are pulling me out of the way, pushing me towards the porch.

"What the fuck is wrong with you two?" he growls, and he reaches down, grabs dark hair in one hand and blond in the other, and drags his brothers apart. "I need both of you on my side, not fighting each other."

He suddenly jerks his hands close and Bjarni and Magne's heads crack together, and they sprawl at his feet, staring up at him. Magne's nose sluggishly leaks blood down his face and Bjarni's lip is split and his teeth stained red.

Thorstein turns away from them in disgust and I'm watching his face when some terrible thought passes over it and he suddenly sits on the steps, rubs both hands over his face, and says, "Oh, fuck."

"Thorstein?" I say, creeping closer to kneel in front of him. He doesn't look up, and his hands are trembling.

"I shouldn't have done that," he says. "I should not have fucking done that."

I'm too focused on Thorstein to see Magne or Bjarni get up, but they're there at once, each moving to sit on one side of their older brother, leaning against him, holding him between them.

"It's okay, Big Bear," Magne says. "I'm pretty sure we deserved it."

Thorstein sighs. "I just fucking did exactly what Dad would have done."

"Magne's right," Bjarni says. "We were fighting like idiots."

"You," Thorstein says to Bjarni, "are always looking for a goddamn fight." He turns to Magne. "And you always have to fucking provoke him."

Both younger brothers rest their heads on Thorstein's, wrap an arm around his shoulders.

"And I'm going to fucking turn into Dad."

"You're not," says Magne.

"No, you're not," agrees Bjarni.

Thorstein stares at his hands. "What if I do something like that to my kid?" he whispers.

"You won't," I say, putting my hands on his knees.

"But what if I do?"

"Did you ever hit me when I was a kid?" Magne asks. "I used to climb all over you, all over both of you, like my own personal jungle gym. And you never once lost your temper."

Bjarni says, "And I was way worse. I was a terrible little shit. And you were only a kid yourself. But you never hit me."

"Magne and Bjarni were being assholes," I say, ignoring the identical looks they shoot me. "And they're both grown ass men who should know better. *And* they can defend themselves." I lean forward. "You've never been anything but patient with me," I say. "Even when you have to show me the same basic thing six times in a row."

That earns me a small laugh, and Bjarni and Magne reach out at the same time to ruffle my hair.

"You're not Dad," Magne says. "And you never will be."

"Your kid's going to grow up safe and loved," Bjarni says.

Thorstein sighs. "I hope you're right."

"Now where's this fantastic new beer I heard about?" Bjarni says, and Thorstein laughs.

"Inside," he says. "I think we could all use a drink."

Thorstein's living room is comfortably furnished with tables and chairs and sofas made of some kind of beautiful gleaming wood and rich upholstery in forest colors.

He points Magne towards the kitchen sink and Bjarni towards the bathroom to clean the blood from their faces.

I watch Magne at the sink, wiggling his nose to make sure it's not broken.

"Why did you say those things?" I say, on impulse, and he glances up in surprise. "Saying Bjarni was turning domesticated and acting like a housewife?"

He shrugs. "He's so easy to taunt, I can't help it."

I look at my hands, then back at him, not sure if I want to broach the subject, but unable to leave it alone. "Don't you think that was kind of… sexist, maybe? Or homophobic?" I bite my lip. "Because it kind of sounded that way, and I don't… it didn't feel very nice to hear."

He stares at me, towel half raised to his face, water dripping off his chin. "No," he says. "Fuck. No. I didn't mean it that way."

I take a deep breath. "Okay," I say. "But do you think… do you think Bjarni took it that way? That he's… ashamed? Of me? Of us?" I have to look away again, can't keep my eyes on his face, and when I turn away, Thorstein is there.

"*I* don't think that," Thorstein says. "I've seen these two sparring for decades. They could say anything to each other, and they'd end up fighting."

He squeezes my shoulder. "Come with me," he says, and I follow him to the back of the house, where there's a closed door to one side. "I don't let many people in here," he says.

"I've never been in here," says Magne, following behind me. "And for what it's worth, Justin, I don't think Bjarni's ashamed to be with you. I think he's proud of you and wants to show you off. You do look great together."

Thorstein opens the door and steps aside to let us in. The room is big, taking up at least half the width of the house, and has windows looking out over the back garden. The whole back wall has a work bench against it, and there's a huge weaving loom in one corner and a big spinning wheel in another. The doors have been taken off the closet to show shelves full of labeled baskets.

"Wow," I say, turning to look at everything. The walls have framed embroideries in rich colors, and woven art pieces in all shades of fiber.

"Shit, Thors," Magne says. "I didn't know you had a whole studio in your house."

"If anyone in this family is going to be accused of doing girly things," Thorstein says, "You might as well start with me."

I look at him and he's smiling down at me. "I spin, weave, and embroider. Fuck," he says. "I've even been known to attempt knitting, though I'm crap at it."

"Thank you," I say, softly. I touch some wool in a basket on the table. It's soft and I try to imagine what it's like to spin it into yarn.

"I also," Thorstein says, "Follow a spiritual practice that lets me control my *berserkr* nature, using meditation based on spinning with a drop spindle. It was known as a female-only practice in the Viking era."

He smiles a lopsided grin that makes him look more like his brothers.

"Listen," Magne says. "I'm an idiot, and I should think before I speak. Bjarni's really trying to be a better man, and so should I."

"Okay," I say.

"Anyway," he says. "It was the idea that I think he'd fuck someone without consent that really set him off."

"No wonder he hit you," Thorstein says.

"You don't think *that* do you?" I say.

"Of course not." He squeezes my shoulder as we file out of the room. "Even at his worst, he's never been that much of an asshole." He looks up at we come back into the kitchen. "I think we've just been angry at each other for so long it spills out sometimes."

"Why are you so angry?"

He sighs. "It's a long story. He… ratted me out to Dad once, and it ended up…" He shakes his head and turns away.

Thorstein steps over to the fridge, extracts a bottle of beer, and hands it to him. "He couldn't have known what Dad would do," he says. "That he would force the Elders to take it so far."

Magne looks back at me, twists the cap off his beer, and takes a swig. "A friend of mine ended up dead, I nearly died, and I *did* spend the next twenty-five years thinking both of my brothers hated me."

"It was the beginning of our father's persecution of queer werewolves," Thorstein says.

Magne turns the bottle in his hands. "I know he didn't intend for any of it to happen, but it's hard to forgive."

"Oh," I say, taking the bottle Thorstein offers. I twist the cap off and take a sip. It's rich, a little bitter, and very tasty.

"So, what's our plan?" says Bjarni, finally back from the bathroom. His lip already looks better, and he doesn't even wince as he sips his beer, though I do notice him press the cold glass against a bruise on his cheekbone.

We find places to sit on the living room furniture that turns out to be as comfortable as it is attractive, and Bjarni pulls a sheet of paper out of his pocket, unfolds it, and hands it to Thorstein.

"I made two lists," he says. "Five names in order of most likely to be our culprit. The first is based on what Justin can remember about him, and the second is based on who's most likely to be pissed that things are changing, becoming more inclusive." He leans back into the sofa cushion and puts his hand on my knee.

Thorstein glances at the list and passes it to Magne. "Jens Harkett is second on one list and not on the other, while Ryan Maclean is first on that list but not on the other. Otherwise, the names are all the same?"

"Yeah. Harkett fits the physical description, but he lost his wife and son to Dad's anti-gay policies. Maclean only fits the description if you have a really good imagination, but he's pissed that you're trying to drag us into the twenty-first century."

"Harkett might miss his wife," Magne says. "And who wouldn't, looking like she does?" He swigs from his bottle and examines it like he's surprised it's almost empty. "But he turned Tyler in to Dad and the Elders himself." He frowns. "I wasn't there, but I wouldn't be surprised if he even led the hunt, after the Elders decreed the poor kid was guilty." He finishes the beer and clunks the bottle down onto the coffee table – very carefully aiming for a coaster.

"Tyler got away," says Thorstein. "He's safe because of you."

"He almost died."

I must look confused because Bjarni says gently, "Tyler was gay. I told you how Dad treated wolves he thought were deviant."

"Oh," I say, resisting the urge to move closer to him. He squeezes my leg.

"So, you think Harkett should be on the second list?" Thorstein says.

"I do," Magne answers. "I definitely wouldn't rule him out."

"What about these new wolves?" says Bjarni. "Are you sure there were only two?"

"No," admits Magne. "But I only saw two, and everyone I talked to saw the same two. If there are more, they're laying low."

"And there have been no signs of them since Sunday night?" says Thorstein.

"Not a trace."

Thorstein looks thoughtful. "Okay. I've informed the Elders we'll have a very small number of suspects for them to question at Freysblöt. That'll speed through the whole pack before long. Someone will either make a run for it or try to bluff through."

"I hope you're right," says Magne.

"I might be able to tell who it was," I say, and all three of them look at me. "My nose is getting better. I think I could tell if I got close enough."

Bjarni moves his hand to the back of my neck. "I don't want you to have to do that."

"I don't, either, but it's better than letting him keep making unwilling people into werewolves, and maybe accidentally killing them."

"In the meantime," says Magne, "we'll keep a close watch over Justin, in case this guy or his lackeys tries to get to him."

"Maybe he should just stay here until Freysblöt," Bjarni says. "I'm pretty sure Katie would be okay giving him the time off, even if he can't exactly tell her why he needs it."

Thorstein looks at me. "What do you want to do, Justin?"

I want to crawl into Bjarni's lap and let him take care of me. But I also want to be stronger.

I stare at the beer bottle in my hands for a few seconds, then I say, "I don't want him to think I'm afraid." I look up, meet Thorstein's eyes, then Magne's, and finally Bjarni's. His fingers tighten slightly on the back of my neck.

"I like my job in the gallery," I say. "And I like staying in the city for a few days each week. I don't want to disrupt the life I'm finally putting back together. Not even for a couple of weeks." Then I look back at my hands. "As long as it isn't too much trouble. I mean, having to keep watch over me." Because I'm not quite ready to throw aside all protection. I'm not *that* self-destructive.

All three of them smile.

"You're no trouble," Magne says.

"Not at all," says Thorstein.

Bjarni leans close to growl in my ear. "I think you're the *best* kind of trouble."

Chapter Sixteen

WHEN WE GET BACK to the farmhouse, Bjarni disappears into the upstairs bathroom and when he comes to my room, he's wearing sweatpants and a t-shirt.

"Not sleeping naked?" I say, teasing.

"One, not in someone else's house," he says. "And two, I don't want to be too tempting for you."

"But you're still going to torment me by lying next to me in a bed that's not really big enough for two people?" I gesture at the bed in question – the one in my room here in the farmhouse is bigger than the one I had at Bjarni's, but it's still only a double. It's spacious enough when it's just me, but it will be close quarters for both of us.

"I can watch over you from this chair across the room if you'd prefer," he says, pulling the hard wooden chair away from the desk under the window and putting it as far as possible from the bed.

"That's okay," I say. "I can cope."

In bed, he spoons me against him and kisses my neck. "You want me to read to you for a while?"

"Do you want to read to me?"

"I'll do anything you want me to," he says, and interrupts when I start to talk. "Except fuck you. Not tonight. Not until the full moon's passed."

I reach for the book on the bedside table, one of Raine's that was the only one I could find in her apartment that wasn't paranormal romance. I mean, I brought some of those, too, but I usually prefer fantasy or historicals.

Bjarni takes it from me, rolls onto his back, and reads the cover. "Dragons?" he says.

"I like dragons." I wriggle closer to curl up against his side and rest my head on his shoulder.

"I have nothing against dragons. Dragons are cool." He flips to the first chapter. "If you like dragons and fantasy and stuff, you should ask Magne for recommendations."

"How do you know what he reads if you've hardly spoken in years?" I say, trying to find a comfortable position for my arm that won't seem like I'm trying to grope him.

"We shop at the same bookstore. We have the same last name. I'm sure he knows what I read, too." He cranes his neck to kiss the top of my head, and then he starts to read.

I realize I've drifted off when there's a sudden jump in the narrative that makes no sense. I don't say anything, though; I just listen to Bjarni's voice and slip away into sleep again. The next time I wake the light is out, the book is on the table, and I'm curled up against Bjarni's back.

I smile, wriggle closer, and I'm asleep again.

And I dream of running on all fours, wolf paws flashing, carrying me into the forest. And it's wonderful until I'm knocked off my feet, and there's pain, and *him*, and he's hurting me.

I wake thrashing, fighting, Bjarni's arms tight around me, his voice gentle. "I'm here, Justin. You're safe. It's only a nightmare."

"Let go," I say. "Bjarni, please." And he does, reluctantly. I make it to the garbage can before I throw up.

"You're okay, *kjaereste*." Bjarni's voice again. His hand is on my back, stroking gently, calming me.

I puke until there's nothing left and then I let him pull me close, lift me back up to sit next to him on the edge of the bed.

"Was it the same dream?"

I nod.

He kisses the top of my head, breathes warm breath into my hair.

"I can still smell him," I say. I look up at him, feeling utterly miserable, soiled and wretched. "I can… I can still *taste* him." I can't keep my voice from shaking.

"You want me to get you a glass of water?"

"No." I slide to the floor, glance at the garbage can like maybe I'm going to need it again and lay my head on his knee.

"I'm so sorry, Justin. I promise he won't ever hurt you again." He rests his hand on my head, strokes my hair.

I shift position, creep between his knees. "Bjarni."

"I'm here."

"I need… I need to get his smell out of my nose. I need to get his taste out of my mouth." I look up at him again and he cups his hand around the side of my face, strokes his thumb along my cheekbone.

"Please," I say. "I need to…" I don't want to beg but I don't know how else to ask. I move my head along his thigh.

"Justin," he says softly. "No. I told you." He holds my head firmly on his leg, not letting me move closer.

"I'm not moon-mad," I say. "Or even moon-drunk." I press my face into his thigh. "Please."

I hear him breathing, just a touch of raggedness to his usual quiet, steady inhales and exhales.

"Fuck, Justin," he says, but his hand relaxes, and he doesn't try to stop me when I bury my face in his crotch, breathe deep to fill my nose with the scent of him. I might whimper when I feel him harden against my face.

He doesn't stop me, either, when I shift onto my knees and pull the waistband of his sweatpants out of my way, wrap my fingers around him, and take him in my mouth. Only his fingers tighten a little in my hair and his breath hitches.

I'm not subtle, or clever, or slow. I want only one thing, and I stroke him, suck him, doggedly, desperately, listen to him struggling to keep from making any noise. He gasps in time to the bobbing of my head, and I swear I hear his teeth grind together as his semen fills my mouth and I'm overwhelmed by the taste of him. And I can relax.

I lay my head on his thigh again and he strokes my hair.

"Thank you," I whisper.

"Justin, come here," he says, and pulls me gently back onto the bed to sit next to him, and tucks himself back into his pants. "Do you want me to…?" He slides his hand up my leg and cups me, and my body responds.

But I shake my head. "Just hold me, please," I say.

He tucks me back in bed beside him and just before I fall asleep again, he says, so quietly I might be imagining it, "Everything I have is yours, *kjaereste*. Everything I *am* is yours." And he wraps his arms tightly around me and I fall asleep that way, the scent and taste of him filling my senses and making me believe everything will be okay.

The moon-drunkenness doesn't hit until late the next night, and at first it strikes me as uncontrollable giggles.

Bjarni just smiles and shakes his head and takes me by the hand. "Time to get you out to the woodlot before you start howling and chasing rabbits."

We leave the house barefoot, dressed in sweats and t-shirts, but he makes me put on a hoodie.

"Come on, *kjaereste*," he says, trying to stuff my arms into the sleeves. I start laughing again and have to sit on the stairs. "It's getting chilly out at night, and I can only do so much to keep you from getting cold."

I try to sit up straight and help him by holding my arm out, but I get my hand in the wrong armhole, which seems like the funniest thing I've ever seen. Eventually, he gets both my arms into the sleeves and the zipper done up – it's probably a good thing it's not a pullover.

When I can't manage to navigate the doorway or the front steps, he sighs, scoops me up, and tosses me over his shoulder which makes me laugh so hard tears come. And that makes me cry.

"I'm such a fuck up," I wail.

"No, you're not," he says, setting me back on my feet in the long grass somewhere far past the lawn. "But remind me not to get you really drunk on booze, if this is what you're like." But he's smiling when he says it. He leads me through a gate into a pasture full of small brown cows that watch us curiously, but don't seem very concerned.

"Even those cows know," I say.

"What do the cows know?"

"How stupid I am," I say, and then one of them, with long fur over its eyes like bangs, moos, and it's so funny I almost fall over laughing.

And then I guess I go full moon-mad, because I don't remember how we get to the wood lot. It's like a forest, but tamer, with less undergrowth and bristly brown and white pigs rootling around the trees. I re-gain something of my senses when Bjarni parks me under a tree and orders me to stay put.

I slide down the rough bark, not caring that my shirt catches and a branch scrapes my back. Crouching, I watch him. I'm a wolf, I'm sure of it, except of course I'm not. He pulls his shirt over his head and hangs it on a tree. His sweatpants follow and I stare at him, naked, bathed in moonlight.

His dark gold hair looks paler, almost silver, in the light that dapples him, his fair skin shining, his tattoos blending with the shadows cast by tree branches, so he looks like something that grew out of the forest, something wild and elemental. His eyes catch the light and gleam and I want him so badly I can hardly think, but I can't move, can only stare.

And he changes. His face pushes out to make room for his big teeth descending. His fingers and toes sprout claws. He gains a tail, and his body hair lengthens and thickens until it could almost pass for fur.

The joints in his arms and legs shift, bend differently, bones re-aligning until he's no longer a beautiful man standing naked in the moonlit forest. He drops to all fours and becomes something primal, not really a wolf, but something that could pass for a wolf – a very very large wolf – in the dark of night or the uncertain shadows of the forest. He's no longer the same kind of beautiful; he's magnificent. And I still have a boner for him so hard it aches.

He makes me feel tiny, like I should be worshipping at his feet, and when he tips back his head and howls, I can't help but join in. My voice is tinny in comparison, and not very wolf-like, but it sings out of my anyway, and he doesn't tell me to stop, only weaves his voice in and around mine, making me feel stronger. Like maybe I can someday be as glorious as he is.

From not far off, there's an answering howl and I crouch low, wanting to creep closer to him to hide, but not wanting him to think me weak.

"It's just Granddad," he says, his human voice sounding wrong coming from his werewolf body. The traces of his childhood accent have grown more pronounced. "He's keeping watch, making sure we're alone while you learn to be a wolf."

Then I look at him, and he grins, and I take off running. On two legs, on four legs, I can no longer tell. The moon sings so loudly in my ears, in my blood, that I can't hear anything else, and I run. For a moment, I'm afraid, remembering something like this happening before, something bad. But he's here and I'm safe, so I run, and chase shadows, and howl.

I come to my senses sometime later. It's full day, but which day I don't know. We're at the edge of a field, curled in the grass. There are dirt stains on the knees of my pants, and my hands and feet are filthy. Every muscle aches, but it feels strangely good.

Bjarni is heat at my back and I roll over to look at him. He's still in wolf shape, but he forms his face into a smile.

I touch his cheek, feel the way the bones have altered, shifted to push outwards into a muzzle. He looks like a werewolf, but he also still looks like Bjarni. I stroke his hair, his neck, his chest. He growls softly when I slide my hand lower.

His wolf paw changes into a human hand, grasps my wrist gently, and moves my hand away. "You're not done yet," he says, low and rumbly. "That was only day one. You've two more days at least to get through."

"I'm not mad," I say. "Or drunk." I roll onto my back so he can see the tent I'm making of my loose sweatpants. He keeps me rolling, all the way over onto my other side, and he pulls me against him, my back to his chest.

"You will be," he says and holds me firmly still. "Now rest while you can."

I try to obey, to rest, but I fidget until the sun creeps across the grass to find us, and then its warmth lulls me, and I bask in it until I sleep again.

And then there's more running, and howling, and chasing shadows, chasing rabbits, chasing the big werewolf who watches patiently over me. The whole time the moon sings to me, like a ringing in my ears but musical, almost words but not in any language I understand. And she sings in my blood like a faint crackle of electricity, an almost-burning on my skin, restless energy in my muscles.

I run as a wolf, or so it seems, in and out of patches of moonlight, between trees, startling pigs that snort but don't flee because they're too large to be bothered by the likes of me. I find a stream and drink its ice-cold water, and it's the best thing I've ever tasted. And I run again, and the whole time I have a huge golden shadow, a warm, strong presence letting me know I'm not alone, I don't have to be alone ever again.

The next time I return to my human self, it's mid-run and so sudden I stumble and sprawl on my face in the deep moss under a grove of maples so lush they block the moonlight entirely. Bjarni's there to help me up, to make sure I'm not hurt, and I hold onto him as I climb unsteadily to my feet. Two feet.

I'm panting this time, exhausted, exhilarated. He doesn't try to move away, even though it can't be comfortable, having me cling to his fur. After a moment, I decide to sit down.

The moss is thick and cushiony, if cold, and I sprawl on it. I pat the springy green growth next to me.

"Sit with me," I say, and he does. I put an arm around him, lean against him, breathe in the smell of him.

It's important, for some reason, to fill my nose with the smell of him, the sweetness of forest, of damp earth, of dew on trees, the musk of werewolf, the tang of sweat, and still the faint cedar-soap that is Bjarni.

It's deep night, and my body aches and the moss is deep and soft and even though I'm cold I curl up to rest. And soon I'm not really even cold, because he's curled his body around mine, lending me his warmth.

And I sleep. And my dreams are running and running and silver in my blood and howling and there's a fear lurking like something bad will happen, has already happened. But instead of darkness knocking me over and hurting me, there's gold shining almost silver-pale in moonlight, the wolf I love always next to me, making me stronger, lending me his strength so I can learn to protect myself.

When I wake, I want to crawl back into that dream, where I'm loved, and cared for, and supported. I don't want to be awake here where I'm alone, and poor, and have fucked up my life over and over.

I curl miserably into myself, trying to regain sleep and that beautiful golden dream, but the sun finds a gap between the leaves and stabs through my eyelids, so I sigh, and roll over, and open my eyes… and his pale blue gaze looks back.

"I thought you were a dream," I say, and touch his face, run a fingertip over his big teeth. "Are you a dream?"

"I'm here, *kjaereste*," he says. "I'm real."

"Do you love me?" I say, head spinning like I've downed three glasses of cheap wine, one after the other. "Or was that part of the dream, too?"

He looks at me for a long time, letting me stroke his face, and I watch – I feel – the bones shift as he changes back to human shape. I feel a smile tug at my mouth, blink slowly as the sun shifts and makes my eyes water.

"That wasn't just part of your dream," he says. He pushes himself up on one elbow to lean over me, brushes a kiss gently on my lips. "You're still drunk, though."

"Tell me anyway," I say. "If I forget, you can just tell me again."

"Tell you what?" he says, voice gently teasing.

"Tell me you love me." I close my eyes, trace the line of his eyebrows with my fingertips. His lips brush mine again, then withdraw. "Unless this is a dream, too."

"What if it was a dream?" His voice is breathy. I open my eyes and he's watching my face.

"Then I don't want to wake up."

Another soft kiss. "It's not a dream," he says. "I'm here, I'm real, and I do love you."

"I *knew* it," I say, and can't keep the drunk giggles in.

"Did you?" Gentle teasing in his voice again.

"No," I say. "But I wanted it to be true."

He tucks me close again. "Try to sleep a bit more," he says. "You're not quite through this."

"But there's something I need to tell you," I say.

"What's that?"

"I forget." I breathe in the smell of him, the smell of moss and trees and the stream, cold and delicious, not far away.

"That's okay, *kjaereste*," he says.

"No, it was important."

"You'll remember later."

I frown, bury my face in his chest, and try to make my brain focus, just for a moment.

"What did you say?"

"Nothing, *kjaereste*."

"Not now, before, When I woke up."

"I said I'm here."

"After that."

I can almost feel his smile, but I refuse to open my eyes until I remember what I needed to tell him. Not yet. Not when I feel safe and warm and… something important.

"I said you're drunk." He's laughing softly, still teasing me. I poke his chest.

"After that."

"I said I love you." His voice is deep and smooth and smoky, and I feel it in my chest, in my bones. In my rapidly hardening cock.

I feel safe and warm and wanted. And loved.

"That was it," I say. "And I needed to tell you…" I tilt my head back, open my eyes, look at him, his ridiculously handsome face, his pale blue eyes. "I love you, too."

He doesn't answer. He just smiles. And then I sleep again, and it's night, and I run and the moon sings to me, but her voice is softer, and I'm slower, tired. I stumble more, but he always catches me.

My howls are quieter, less wild-sounding, from a throat that feels less wolf-like, more human. But he still howls with me, telling me it doesn't matter how weak my voice is, I'm still a wolf, still a werewolf even if I look mostly human.

Now when I drink from the stream it's so cold it makes my teeth ache, makes my paws – my hands and feet – go numb where I crouch up to my wrists and ankles in the iciness of it.

And the aching tiredness feels less pleasant and more like I'm trying to carry something too heavy, only that burden is my own body and I'm not sure I can lift my feet anymore, even to get me out of the icy water.

Bjarni, who's been running next to me wolf-shaped again, returns to human form to lift me out of the stream, to hold my shivering form to his body.

"I think we better get you to Granddad's cabin before you get hypothermia," he says.

"Is it over?" I ask. "The full moon?"

"It is," he says.

"Am I done being drunk?"

"Maybe," he says. "But if you're not, you're too tired to run anymore."

I let him carry me. I want to be strong, but I'm just too weary.

"How come you're not tired?" I say, resting my cold face on his warm chest.

"I am," he says. "I'm exhausted. But I've got a lot more werewolf endurance than you do." He kisses my face. "I'll get us to Granddad's, and he'll give us whiskey and bacon and eggs, and we can sleep in front of his woodstove until we feel strong enough to walk home."

"You're naked," I say.

He snorts. "I'll go get my clothes once you're safe with Granddad."

"You might as well just hand him over to me, now," says a voice. I've heard that voice before. Not in a dream or a nightmare, but in real life. In the club, telling me to get out of the way so he could bother Katie.

I open my eyes and two very large men – not Thorstein-big, but maybe just about Magne-big – are blocking our way.

Chapter Seventeen

BJARNI SETS ME ON MY FEET, keeps his hand on my elbow to help me stand, and steps between me and the two men.

"Don't give us any trouble," says the bigger, tougher-looking man. "And we won't give you any trouble."

"You're already in more trouble than you can imagine," Bjarni says. "Your only hope is to walk away, now, and then go show your throats to my brother, your pack leader."

"Our master is not your pack leader," says the other man, but he sounds uncertain.

"The idiot who turned you two into werewolves is in plenty of trouble of his own. You want to escape what's going to come down on him, you better walk away." Bjarni squeezes my arm gently, like he's trying to tell me something without saying it. Too bad I haven't learned much werewolf body language yet.

"Did you know your 'master'," and Bjarni sneers the word, "Is a murderer?" I can tell he's not afraid of the other men, who might be big, but are newer wolves even than me, and won't have much of their werewolf strength yet. I wonder why they don't seem to be tired, so soon after the full moon. Surely, they must have been running and howling for three days straight, too?

"That was an accident," the bigger man says.

"He disemboweled her by accident?" Bjarni lets heavy skepticism into his voice. "You really have no idea what you've gotten yourselves into the middle of. You want to get out unscathed, walk away now."

"Give us the pretty little fairy, and we'll go." The big man turns his head and spits off to one side.

"He's our pack, not yours," the smaller man says. He still doesn't sound like he quite believes his own words and the bigger man scowls at him.

"Walk away," Bjarni says, and even I can feel the compulsion in his voice, and it's not directed at me. I half expect it not to work, but if they were made by the same man who made me, and Thorstein could use compulsion on me, then it stands to reason Bjarni could compel these two.

They both turn at the same time and start walking. I breathe a little easier.

"But you can't…" protests the shorter man. "He said…"

"He obviously didn't tell you everything," Bjarni says.

I feel another hand on my other elbow and realize that in my weariness, I didn't hear another werewolf come up behind me. And it says something about how tired Bjarni is, after all, that he didn't either.

"I told them enough," the other werewolf says. "To get them to do what I needed them to do." It's a voice from my nightmares and for one very long moment, I can't move, my body frozen in place. Memories of fear, pain, weakness overwhelm me.

Then Bjarni whips around but has to drop his hand from my arm to do it. He meets my eyes, and suddenly I *can* move. I jerk away from the grip on my arm, the claws digging into my skin, and fling myself towards Bjarni, twisting to meet my tormentor as I do. Bjarni catches me, sets me behind him, and tackles the other wolf without a word.

They go down in a flurry of snarls and snapping jaws, changing shape as they fight.

For a moment, Bjarni separates himself from his opponent. "Go, Justin," he says. "Get Thorstein."

I hesitate. I don't want to leave him to face three werewolves by himself.

"Stay where you are," says the other werewolf, the man who changed me, and I can't move.

More snarling, tearing. They're so similar in coloring I can hardly tell them apart when they're moving so quickly, dodging and lunging, striking and grappling.

"Get him out of here," says my attacker, and the two big men stop walking away, and come for me.

"Go, Justin, now!" And Bjarni lunges for the other man's throat with teeth and claws, keeping him occupied so he can't compel me again.

I run. And I run. I don't know the way back to the farmhouse from the woodlot; I don't remember following the path there. But my werewolf senses know the general direction, so I run, and hope I come through the trees and fields close enough to one of the houses.

I run, and the moon is silent. Every shadow that seemed like a friend and playmate before now seems sinister, like it could be hiding an enemy. And I hear crashing behind me, so I know the other new werewolves are following me. But even though they don't seem tired, they're awkward in the woods. Much more awkward than I am, and that makes me less afraid.

If I can just keep running, I might make it. I might get to Thorstein's and safety, find help for Bjarni. Because I don't know how old or experienced that other werewolf is, the one who changed me, but he seemed rested and unafraid, and that can't be good.

So I push my fear aside and concentrate on my footsteps. Even before I was made a werewolf, running was one of the few things I was good at. My human body knows how to move quickly on two legs, even in the woods, even tired, and my werewolf nature, even undeveloped, knows the forest. So I stop thinking and let my muscles and my instincts carry me.

And I start to hope.

Until the bigger man tackles me from behind.

He almost misses, I almost get away, but his hand catches the hem of my sweatpants and my feet tangle together, and I fall. The impact with the ground stuns me, knocks the breath out of me, and all I can do for way too long is curl up on the forest floor and try not to scream, or throw up.

And then he's on me, grappling me, trying to pick me up and throw me over his shoulder.

"No!" I yell. "Fuck off!" I kick out and there's a crunch, a grunt, the smell of blood, and then, impossibly, he's dragged off me. For a breathtaking moment, I think it's Bjarni come to my rescue.

But it isn't. This werewolf has more grey fur than gold, has deep lines on his face, has bigger ears and moves much more stiffly, though there is definitely still power in his limbs. He looks like Bjarni will probably look when he gets much, much older.

"Granddad?" I say. Of course, he's not *my* grandfather, but no one's told me his name, so I don't know how to address him.

"You're fast. Almost couldn't catch up," he says, and laughs. "Go on, now." His voice is thick and slurred around his teeth and he has the same accent as his grandsons, but much stronger. "Go get Thorstein. I'll keep this one off your ass."

He turns back to face the big man and I run again. I can see the thin trickle of smoke above the trees that tells me Thorstein and Raine have lit their fireplace against the evening chill. I can smell the sharpness of burning hardwood.

I run, but now I have a real direction, can aim directly for Thorstein's house instead of trying to find the farmhouse first and finding my way from there. My muscles burn like they're consuming themselves to keep me on my feet and moving, but I'm almost there. I can smell the grass of the lawn, the dungy scent of sheep, the musty musky odor of the marigolds that grow all along the front of the house that Thorstein will use to dye his white sheep wool yellow.

And I'm almost there when the other werewolf, the slightly smaller one, tackles me, and he does a better job of it that his larger companion.

We tumble out onto the lawn and as he tries to hold onto me, I can feel how wasted his muscles are, like he's spent too long without proper food or exercise. The stench of him, of unwashed male and stale beer and worse, makes my nose sting. He's unhealthy, and I think if I hadn't already been so exhausted, he never would have caught up with me.

And I remember that I have claws and teeth, and I use them to put distance between us.

"Thorstein!" I yell, trying to force my voice louder when I have no breath left. I stumble backwards towards the porch as the other werewolf lunges for me again.

"Don't fight me, kid, and I won't hurt you."

I slash at him with my claws, feel the fabric of his shirt catch and tear, feel his skin catch and tear. Then footsteps behind me, passing me, and Thorstein is knocking the other werewolf to the ground.

He drops to one knee beside the other wolf, grabs his neck in one huge hand and forces the man's head back, exposing his throat. I smell the sharp scent of urine and terror. Thorstein growls, flings the man down onto his belly on the grass and says, "Don't fucking move until I get back. Do you understand?"

The other werewolf nods, chokes out a "yes" and Thorstein is gone, dropping his clothes on the grass, changing shape as he runs.

I start to follow, but Raine's hand on my arm stops me. "Sweetheart," she says. "You're in no shape to do any good."

I look at her, try to stand up straight, to show her I'm fully capable of helping, but then I almost fall over.

"I have to go back," I say. "He was there. My attacker. He was… Bjarni…"

She smiles gently. "Don't you think I know exactly how you feel?" she says. "But I don't even have claws yet, and I'd only get in the way. But at least I can keep myself upright." She touches my face. "I don't think he sent you here just to get help," she says. "He sent you to keep you safe because he can't. Not while he's trying to fight the bad guys."

I try again to take a step, and again I almost fall, and I have to admit defeat. "I hate being so weak," I say.

"Fuck, sweetie," she says. "You just spent three days and nights running your ass off, and then sprinted flat out across several very large fields. *And* you gave that guy – who is much bigger than you are, I might add – some new scars to think about. You did more than anyone could expect of you." She puts her arm across my shoulders and turns me towards the door. "You did good."

"But –"

"He'll be okay. Bjarni's one of the strongest werewolves in our pack, and now Thorstein's on his way to help."

"He was exhausted," I say. "From watching over my dumb ass for three days and nights."

"Come inside," she says. "You're freezing."

And I realize I'm shivering, my teeth chattering. "What about him?" I gesture at the other werewolf, still face down on the lawn and watching us warily.

"He's not going anywhere."

"Please don't let him kill me," the other werewolf says. "Please."

Raine looks at him, pitiless, but then her face softens. "He's not going to kill you."

"I might," I say, but there's no real anger in it anymore, and even though I don't mean it, I still feel bad when he whimpers and presses his face into the grass.

I let Raine lead me inside and even let her help me into the shower, but I draw the line at letting her wash or dry me, even though I know she has zero interest in my naked body. I mean who would, if they got to sleep with Thorstein every night?

When I'm as clean as I'm going to get in the scant time I'm willing to waste on showering, and once my shivering has stopped under the onslaught of hot water, I dry off and wrap a towel around myself and sit meekly on a kitchen stool while Raine bandages my cuts and scrapes, all of which are superficial. I drink the glass of whiskey she gives me and sip the cup of tea. I eat a granola bar, and then an immense sandwich, and pull on the sweatpants and t-shirt she gives me, which must be hers because they're snug, and Thorstein's would be huge on me.

"What's taking them so long?" I say, halfway through my ham and cheese on homemade rye. It's probably delicious, but I'm so worried I can hardly taste it.

"The woodlot's not exactly the closest part of the farm," she says. "And maybe the bad guys are leading them on a merry chase." She doesn't seem worried, which should calm me down. At least her ease helps me get through my food without throwing up. I'm ravenous and need to eat and rest and heal. At least I can do the first one while we wait.

"Maybe they're –" I don't let myself finish the thought, let alone the sentence.

"They're fine," Raine says, and as if to underline her statement, there are footsteps on the porch.

Thorstein comes in, pulling his shirt over his head. He's breathing hard but doesn't look hurt.

"How is he?" he asks Raine.

"Superficial cuts, already healing," she answers. "Miraculously avoided hypothermia. Pushed completely beyond his limits and hardly able to stand, but he'll be okay."

"I'm right here," I say. "Where's Bjarni?"

"Granddad took him to the farmhouse." He tilts his head toward the door and we both follow, though it takes me a couple of tries to stand up and make my legs work.

"The other werewolves?" Raine asks.

"They ran when I showed up. Granddad and I decided it was more important to get Bjarni home than to catch them."

"But you know who they are?"

"I know who the ringleader is, yes."

My brain catches on the part where it was more important to get Bjarni home. "Is he okay?" I say, grabbing Thorstein's arm so he'll look at me. "Is he –"

He stops, puts his hands on my shoulders. "He's hurt," he says, gently. "But he'll live."

I gasp out a breath that sounds like a sob and try to hurry after him when he continues out onto the porch but I can hardly make my feet move one in front of the other.

Raine takes my arm and drapes it over her shoulders to help me along, to support some of my weight so my legs can do the rest. "Come on," she says.

Thorstein has stopped next to the werewolf still face down on the grass. "Are you going to come along quietly?" he asks.

"Yes, sir," the other man says.

"Then get up."

The man gets up. He seemed much scarier in the club, in the forest, but here in the bright glare of the porch floodlight I can see he's weary, malnourished, and older than I had thought. He smells of fear, piss, and B.O.

"Come on."

The man follows meekly behind Thorstein as we walk the path to the farmhouse. I want to run ahead, to make sure Bjarni really is okay, but it's all I can do to move at all, even with Raine's help, so I trail along behind, and soon the two men have vanished behind the trees.

When we reach the steps up to the farmhouse front door, Thorstein is waiting. "You did good, Justin," he says.

I just sigh, too tired to argue. "I wish I was stronger."

He shakes his head. "You did exactly what Bjarni needed you to do." Then he leads the way inside.

The other werewolf turns to follow then stops, flicks his glance to me, and says, "You're stronger than you look. Broke that guy's nose and cut me good." He ducks his head, like he's afraid he shouldn't have spoken, then moves tentatively through the door after Thorstein.

Everyone is gathered in the kitchen, where Bjarni sits on a chair, looking like he was recently hosed off in the shower, holding himself upright apparently by sheer force of will. Colleen and Hilde fuss over him, cleaning cuts, applying butterfly bandages and steri-strips, and wrapping him in gauze. Even from the door, where I stop to prop myself upright on the wall, I can smell blood and peroxide, and the distinct whiff of the bergamot-scented soap I bought myself when Raine took me shopping, that I forgot to take with me to the city.

His jaw is tense, and his eyes are closed, and he looks utterly done in. There are claw marks on his chest and arms, some of them scabbing over and others frighteningly deep. But despite his exhaustion and his injuries, he doesn't look defeated. He looks magnificent.

I watch until Colleen tapes down the last bandage and turns to stir something on the stove. And I realize I smell pasta cooking, and meaty tomato sauce.

My stomach rumbles, loud, and Bjarni's eyes open and a smile tugs at his mouth. "I recognize that belly growl," he says, and turns to look at me.

And I can't move, caught in the shine of his eyes like a cow in the headlight of an oncoming train. And it might as well be that everyone else in the room vanishes because all I see is him.

He holds out his hand and I move like I'm in a trance, step towards him, not noticing my sore feet or my overtaxed muscles. His fingers are warm and strong on mine.

"*Kjaereste*," he says.

I have a sudden mortifying memory of begging him to tell me he loved me. How did he answer? I can't remember. I hope that was a dream.

I prod a few brain cells into alertness and say, "You look like I feel."

He laughs. "Same to you." He brings my hand to his lips, kisses the backs of my fingers, and I'm suddenly aware of people all around us in the kitchen, watching. Are they watching? A flush starts somewhere below my belly button and spreads through my limbs and up my neck until I must resemble a tomato. If tomatoes glow in the dark.

"I'm okay," I say, trying and failing to reclaim my hand. He keeps my fingers tangled with his.

"I'm not," he says, grimacing. "But I will be. Eventually." He tugs on my hand, making me step closer, and points at the chair next to his. "You look like you need to sit down." He squeezes my fingers. "I think Thorstein's going to have to drive you into Riverbend tomorrow."

Riverbend. I forgot. Tomorrow must be Wednesday. I have to try on clothes and then spend two days working at the gallery. Right now, just staying awake seems like too much to accomplish.

"I promise to be sufficiently recovered for our date on Friday," he says. "Though I'm glad I'm taking you to dinner and not hiking in the mountains." He grins and I resist the urge to glance around, to see who's listening, watching us talk about dates. I mean, it's not like they don't *know*, it's just that we haven't – he hasn't – been very open in front of anyone else.

"Okay," I say. It's all I can manage, but he smiles and moves his hand to rest on my leg and I realize he's still naked, just wrapped in a damp towel for modesty.

And I realize everyone else in the kitchen has been talking to each other the whole time and probably not even noticing us at all.

At the other end of the table, Granddad is sipping something hot from a huge mug. I smell apples and cinnamon. He sees me looking and winks and I realize he's still half in wolf shape and hunched over not because he's tired, but because that's the shape his spine is.

"So I finally meet the young man who's claimed my most wayward grandson's heart." He grins and he really does look like an older version of Bjarni.

"Hi," I say, suddenly feeling desperately shy. "I'm Justin."

"Thorleif," he says. "But you can call me Granddad. Everyone else does."

"Hi," I say again, feeling so tired I've gone stupid.

"And yes, this is what your sweetheart is going to look like in another century or so."

"Granddad," says Bjarni, his voice full of affection.

"It's true," Granddad says. "Get as old as me, and you start to lose the ability to change *out* of wolf shape. One day, I'll be all wolf and will never come in from the woods." He turns back to me and grins wider. "I don't fear it," he says. "I look forward to it."

Colleen puts huge plates of spaghetti in front of Bjarni and me and then serves one up for Granddad, too.

"Everyone else can dish up their own," she says. Then she turns to the werewolf standing awkwardly in the corner, looking like he's hoping not to be noticed.

"I suppose you're hungry," she says.

"Yes, ma'am."

"I imagine he'd probably like to clean up," says Raine. He jerks his eyes up to hers then quickly looks away.

Thorstein moves to stand next to her. "You were living on the street?" he says. "Before he found you? Made you an offer you couldn't refuse?"

"Yes, sir."

"How long?"

"Five months," the man mumbles. "Wife left me, lost my job. The usual sob story." The tone of self-deprecation in his voice is so familiar I stop shoveling pasta into my mouth to stare at him.

"What was your job?"

"Finishing carpenter," the man says. "Was damn good at it." He stares at his hands, then looks up at Thorstein as if daring the bigger man to judge him. "Wife left me, and I started drinking. A lot. I really fucked up my life. That guy… the werewolf… he said he'd give me a new life, only he'd be my master. Food, shelter, women if I wanted, I just had to do what he said." He looks at his hands again. "Didn't know he'd want me to hurt anyone."

"I'll show you where you can wash up," Thorstein says. "We'll find you something to wear, give you dinner. If you're as good a carpenter as you say, I can find you work."

The other man looks up then away. "But he said…"

"He lied. We're all werewolves in this room, and we help our own. But I am afraid we're going to have to keep you locked up for now, until we sort this out."

The man's shoulders slump. "He put me in a fucking dog crate. Said he couldn't let me run loose 'cause of the full moon."

"Our basement is a lot more comfortable than a dog crate. I've had to spend time there myself, from time to time." A shadow passes over Thorstein's face, but he doesn't elaborate.

The man looks up again, something that might be hope in his eyes.

"I'll show you the way," Thorstein says. "There's a shower, a bed. I think there's even a tv down there now." He starts towards the basement door, then pauses. "But first, tell me, the werewolf who changed you… Was he the same one giving orders tonight?"

"Yes, sir."

"And how many others are there?"

"Him, the big ugly guy, and this kid here." He points at me, then looks at me more closely. "But I guess you're not a kid, are you? Just small. Sorry." He looks back at Thorstein. "He says he tried to change a woman, but she was too weak, and she died."

"And that's all?"

"All I ever saw."

"You know any of their names?"

"I heard him –" and he nods at Bjarni "– call the pretty one Justin. Never heard any other names."

"And your name?"

"Steve," the man says, looking surprised anyone would want to know. "Steven Chambers."

"I'm Thorstein." He holds out his hand and the other werewolf, Steve, shakes it tentatively. Then Thorstein shifts his grip so they're grasping forearms instead. "And I'm your new pack leader."

Chapter Eighteen

I WANT VERY BADLY to go home with Bjarni, to lie next to him in his big bed, so I can make sure he's safe, and alive. But when Thorstein lifts his brother right out of the chair and I get up to follow, he shakes his head.

"You both need your own beds, alone," he says. "You need rest."

"I'm too tired to anything besides sleep," I say.

"Right now, yes. But I've been where you are, and I know what I did with Raine as soon as I had the slightest bit of energy." He grins. "It turned out to be a bad idea when I needed that energy later, no matter how important it seemed at the time."

I try to protest again, but he doesn't even let me get the words out. At the foot of the stairs, he turns and says, "Say goodnight and go get some sleep. And for fuck's sake, have a lie-in tomorrow morning. I'll come get you around noon to drive you to Riverbend."

I sigh. "Fine." I lift Bjarni's hand from where it rests on his chest and squeeze his fingers. He opens his eyes halfway.

"Sorry, *kjaereste.* Was I supposed to be arguing to let you sleep with me?" He squeezes my fingers back. "I'm so tired I can't even keep my head up, let alone… get my other head up." His grin is a shadow of its usual curve.

"Too much information, Little Bear," Thorstein says. "And you're heavy, by the way. Hurry up and say goodnight."

Bjarni ignores him and reaches up to touch my face. "Sleep well, Justin." Something of his old energy creeps back into his smile and hits his eyes. "My fierce grizzly."

"Shut up," I say. "I ran, that's all."

"You clawed that guy good. I saw." He brushes his thumb across my lips.

I just shake my head and let him pull me closer so I can kiss him. It's brief and awkward, seeing as he's held in his brother's arms, but there's the promise of more in it. Much more.

"All right, enough," says Thorstein and makes us stop by simply walking out the door.

I drag myself upstairs and sleep, and for once I don't dream at all.

The rest of the week passes quickly and the whole time I have to force myself to focus because I'm so nervous about Friday and my dinner date with Bjarni. Which is really dumb, because it's not like we haven't been on a date before. Or seen each other naked and panting.

But suddenly it's Friday afternoon and my new clothes are hanging in the back room of the gallery – already paid for in full when I arrived to try them on and pick them up. And Mrs Walker has asked for me, specifically, to help her decide on framing for her newest masterpiece.

Finally, after dropping a frame sample for the third time, she fixes me with her fierce little old lady glare and says, "What has you so jumpy today, young man?"

"He's got a date," calls Katie from across the room, where she's dusting the tops of framed art.

"Ah, that explains it," Mrs Walker says. "Perhaps I should come back next week, then." I can see she's trying very hard not to smile, but her eyes are crinkling so much at the corners it's cracking her foundation.

"That's okay," I say, summoning a smile. "I promise I'll pay more attention to what I'm doing."

"I can finish up," says Katie. "You're almost done, it looks like, and anyway, you need to go change."

I check my smart watch and it says it's 4:37 then immediately informs me my heart rate has suddenly become elevated.

"Why am I so nervous?" I say, and Mrs Walker finally lets her laughter out.

"Is she pretty?" she asks, and I look frantically at Katie, who has wandered over to lean against the design table.

"*He* is very handsome," she says.

For a fleeting moment, Mrs Walker looks confused, but then she smiles warmly. "Good for you, Justin," she says, patting my hand. "Just be sure he treats you right."

"Shoo," Katie tells me, flapping her feather duster at me. "Go get changed."

So I do, awkwardly getting undressed and re-dressed in the gallery's tiny bathroom and rubbing a bit of product through my expensive new haircut to make it lie right. I'm just walking back out to the front, buttoning up my jacket, when the door chimes and I look up. And freeze.

He's dressed in blue so dark it almost looks black, with a lighter blue shirt that makes his pale eyes look insanely bright. The top layer of his hair is pulled back from his face, emphasizing his cheekbones, which in turn draw attention to the width and curve of his lips.

Everything fits him so perfectly I can see exactly how broad his shoulders are, how trim his hips, how muscular his thighs. I can't breathe.

As if he can feel me watching, he looks up from closing the door and meets my eyes. And *he* freezes, his gaze dragging up and down my form, inspecting me. I force myself to be still, to not try to stand straighter or suck in my skinny gut.

There's no expression on his face, but his look feels hot as he takes me in. When he reaches my eyes again, he walks forward past Katie and Mrs Walker as if they don't exist. He stops in front of me and takes my hand, brushing his fingers across my knuckles.

I force sound out of my throat. "Hey," I say, feeling lightheaded.

"Justin." His voice is hardly above a whisper. "You look… perfect." He brings my hand up to his lips and kisses it, turns it over to kiss the inside of my wrist and I can't stop the shiver that seems to start in my toes. "Fucking hell, you look good."

"You, too," I say. I'm saved from having to say anything else when Katie wanders over, faux casual.

"Oh, hello Katie. How nice to see you," she says. The sarcasm in her voice is echoed by her raised eyebrows.

"Oh, hello Katie," Bjarni says, turning to her but keeping hold of my hand. "How nice to see you." He bends to kiss her cheek.

"And I'm Mrs Walker," the old lady says, holding out her hand for Bjarni. Instead of shaking it, which would mean letting go of my hand, he takes it and plants a kiss on her swollen arthritic knuckles.

"Pleased to meet you," he says.

She pulls her hand back and frowns at him, then pokes him on the chest with a bony finger. "You better treat him like a prince," she says. "We're very fond of Justin."

I feel an intense flush creep up my neck.

"I intend to treat him like a king," Bjarni says. "*My* king."

"Good," says Mrs Walker, fixing him with her glare. Then, she suddenly says, "Are you a doctor? He deserves a doctor. Or a lawyer, maybe?"

"No, Ma'am," he says. "I'm an accountant."

"Hm," she replies. "Do you make good money?"

I cover my face with one hand and pray to disappear into the floor.

"Very good money," says Bjarni.

"I suppose that will do, then. I hope you're taking him somewhere nice."

"Is Chez Louise nice enough?"

"That will do," she says again. But she smiles more warmly. Meanwhile, I'm finding it difficult to breathe again. Chez Louise has a months-long waiting list just for the chance to make a reservation. And it's supposed to be the best – and most expensive – restaurant in Autumn County.

"Shall we?" says Bjarni, turning to me. I pull myself together enough to nod and follow him to the door.

"Have fun, kids," calls Katie. "Don't do anything I wouldn't do."

As soon as the door shuts, Bjarni mutters, "I know what she does on dates, but I couldn't really say anything in front of that nice little old lady who has apparently decided you're under her protection." He grins down at me and twines his fingers more securely around mine.

"So you're an accountant," I say, bumping my shoulder against his arm as he leads me down the sidewalk.

He looks at me, grin still firmly in place. "Yeah, I am," he says. "I even have all the official bits of paper to prove it." He swings our joined hands a couple of times. "And it sounds more glamorous than 'farm manager'."

"Yes," I say, grinning back. "Glamour is the first thing I think of when someone says 'accountant'."

He laughs.

"So where are you really taking me for dinner?" I ask, trying to match my steps to his and noticing that he slows down so I don't have to trot to keep up with his longer stride.

"I'm *really*," he says, "Really, really, *actually* taking you to Chez Louise, which happens to be conveniently located a few short blocks from your very glamorous place of employment."

I almost stop right there on the sidewalk, but manage to only stumble, making him glance at me.

"You really are?" I manage to say.

"I really am."

"How?"

He shrugs. "My charming personality, obviously."

I can't resist a grin. "Obviously *not*," I say, bumping his arm with my shoulder again.

"I'm terribly insulted," he says, but he's still wearing the shit-eating grin. Then the side of his mouth twists. "Thorstein got me the reservation. Both the owner and the executive chef are family friends, but for some reason they're more willing to do favors for him."

I hide my smile this time and resist saying, "I can't imagine why."

"The chef agreed to squeeze us in as long as we let him decide what we eat and drink. And if I don't behave, we'll never be allowed in again. And Thorstein will no doubt get royal shit, too." He bends and brushes a kiss on my cheek without breaking stride. "I think he really just wants to see who's turned me into a one-man man."

"Do you get banned from restaurants frequently?" I'm teasing, but also half-serious. I have to remind myself that, however he makes me feel, I really don't know Bjarni Thorvaldson that well.

"I do not. Unfortunately, Sven's been to pack gatherings, and may have witnessed me in an advanced state of inebriation." He grimaces. "He may also have had to stop me from inflicting bodily harm on a cousin or two. And my little brother."

"Oh," I say, sorting through the information and trying to decide how I should feel about it.

He pulls me to a stop, and we step off the sidewalk, out of the way. I see the sign for Chez Louise just ahead. "I don't get shitfaced like that anymore," he says. "Or pick fights with my cousins. Not since Dad… died."

"It's okay," I say.

He tilts my face up with his free hand, making me look into his eyes. "I'm trying to be better, *kjaereste*. I want to be someone my brothers can be proud to know, to be good enough for you."

I can't keep my eyes on his after he's said something like that. I look over his shoulder, seeing people notice us standing so close together, holding hands. Most of them look away, uninterested. A few of them sneer, and one or two smile openly when they meet my eyes. I smile back.

Then what he's said sinks in. "You think… you're not good enough for me?" Disbelief makes my voice higher pitched than usual.

"I know I'm not," he answers.

"That's… that's just dumb."

He raises his eyebrows, smirks a little. "Are you calling me stupid?" His lips twitch and the corners of his eyes crinkle.

"No, I mean…" I scowl, realizing he's trying not to laugh at me. "I'm the fuck-up, remember?"

He shrugs. "And you're smart, and kind, and fucking adorable." He kisses my cheek. "And everyone likes you." He kisses my other cheek. "Now, are you ready to eat some of the best things you've ever put in your mouth?" He can't stop the wide grin or the dimples. "Besides my huge –"

"Bjarni!"

He laughs.

The restaurant is even more lush inside than I'd even imagined. Not that I've spent much time thinking about what fancy restaurant decor looks like. It's somehow extremely rich-looking, but not over the top.

We're seated at a corner table with a glimpse of window and more privacy than a spot in an open dining room ought to have.

Bjarni holds my chair for me and tucks it under me as I sit, managing to get me the exact right distance from the table. He sits in the other chair and takes my hand, lacing our fingers together again.

"How are you?" I say. "Your injuries, I mean."

"Could be worse," he says. "A couple gashes are still giving me trouble, but I'll live."

A waiter stops by with a bottle of wine, and I watch Bjarni taste the offered sample and nod. Our glasses are filled, and the waiter vanishes again, murmuring that the first course will arrive shortly.

I trace designs in the condensation on my glass. "You paid for my clothes," I blurt out, and it sounds accusatory. "You didn't have to do that."

"Consider it an early birthday present," he says. "And anyway, I'm the one getting the most enjoyment out of them."

"What?"

"I get to look at you wearing them," he says. "You look so fucking good." His nostrils flare and he adds, "And maybe later you'll let me take them off of you, one piece at a time."

My chest feels tight. My *pants* feel tight, and I have no comeback.

"You look really good too," I finally say, which is nothing like the witty retort I wish I had.

The waiter appears with appetizers, and I don't have to try to think of something more clever to say, at least for a little while. I don't think I've ever been so tongue-tied on a date. Especially not with someone I've already slept with. But this date, for some reason, feels important, like I have to get it right.

It helps that he doesn't seem anxious at all, and between bites he tells me about what's been happening at the farm over the last couple of days and fills me in on what exactly happens at a Freysblöt, so I'll be prepared.

"It's like an early harvest festival," he says. "First fruits, you could call it." He gestures with his fork as he talks and I'm mesmerized by the way his jaw and throat move as he chews, swallows, talks, chews some more.

"And"– here he points at me with his fork –"Thorstein and Raine have decided to plight their troth."

"To what their what?" The phrase sounds familiar, vaguely medieval. I chew slowly, because the food is so delicious, I can't rush through it even though I forgot to eat lunch in my nervousness and I'm ravenous.

"Plight their troth," he says. "It's an extremely old-fashioned way of saying they're declaring their intention to marry. For werewolves, though, it's as good as getting married when it's witnessed by the pack at a gathering."

He grins. "Big Bear is over the fucking moon. Symbiont bond, getting married, kid on the way. He never dared dream he could have any of that."

"He deserves it," I say, finishing off an amazing fillet of crispy salmon and setting my fork aside.

"Yeah, he really does." He sets his fork aside and the waiter materializes out of nowhere to refill our wine glasses and whisk away our empty plates.

"So, I was thinking," he says.

"You think?" I say, pretending surprise, and then regretting saying something mean. I look up from the new plate that has appeared in front of me. I'm glad, now, that I *did* forget lunch, because I intend to eat everything the waiter delivers.

"Sometimes, yes, more than one brain cell fires at the same time," he replies placidly, then flashes me his grin. "Why don't we stay in the city tonight?"

I could swear there's something uncertain in the way he looks at me. "Magne sent me a list of the best bookstores," he says. "I thought we could go book shopping tomorrow before we head back."

I feel my mouth stretch in a smile so wide it's got to look idiotic. "You want to take me book shopping?" I tap the back of his hand with one finger. "I think that's the most romantic thing anyone's ever said to me."

He smiles back, and the uncertainty is gone, if it was ever there in the first place. "Does it count as –"

"As courting?" I laugh. "Yes, I think it counts a lot as courting me. I might not even make you sleep on the couch tonight."

Eventually, we reach the end of a long and spectacular meal and sit sipping fancy coffees while waiting for the bill. But instead of the bill, a large man in chef's whites strides over to our table and glowers down at Bjarni.

Bjarni grins a slow grin, then gets to his feet, looking lazy as fuck, and holds out his hand. For a moment, I think the chef is going to smack it away, his scowl is so deep. Instead, he suddenly grins and grips Bjarni's arm.

"Thorvaldson. You little shit. How are you?"

"Sven." Bjarni smacks the other's shoulder. "I'm good. You?"

"Can't complain." He slants an inquiring look at me.

"This is Justin," Bjarni says. His grin tempers down to a soft smile and he looks at me with just the slightest hesitation. "My boyfriend."

I want to stare at him, but I make myself get to my feet and grip the chef's arm werewolf-style. "Hi," I say. "The meal was amazing."

His smile is very wide, and full of big teeth, but he seems pleased that I mentioned it. He looks like he could be a cousin of the Thorvaldson brothers, though I don't think Sven is a Norwegian name. Not that they couldn't still be cousins.

"Good to meet you," he says. "Make sure this dumbass doesn't push you around."

"Why does everyone say that?" Bjarni says.

Sven just shakes his head. "You two need anything else?"

"I'm good," I say. "So full."

"That was fucking amazing," Bjarni says.

"I'll be sure to tell Gregory to use that in his next advertising campaign," says Sven. "Chez Louise is fucking amazing."

Bjarni snorts. "Can you get them to send over the bill?"

Sven smirks. "Didn't Thorstein tell you? Dinner's on him."

"He what?" Bjarni looks almost irritated.

Sven just waves and leaves.

"Now you know what it feels like," I say. "To have someone pay for stuff for you."

He shakes his head and gets out his wallet to leave a generous tip tucked under the edge of one of the plates. "Dammit. This was supposed to be my treat for you."

I slip my hand into his, trying not to be too obvious. I mean, I'm sure everyone in the restaurant has already figured out we're on a date, but I still feel uncomfortable being too visible.

"It *was* a treat, thank you," I say.

Outside, it's getting dark, and the air is fresh, with an edge that tells of coming autumn.

We walk slowly, too full to do more than stroll, and when we reach Bjarni's Mitsubishi, he opens the passenger door for me, but stops me before I get in.

"Did you have a good time?" he asks, freeing his hand from mine to lean both arms on the roof of the car, caging me in and leaning close.

I glance around, but there aren't many people – the shops are all closed now – and those who are around don't pay us any mind, except one group of women who slow as they pass and seem to be checking out Bjarni's ass. They look up at us and smile, and one of them says, "Nice catch," and I don't know if she's talking to me or him. Bjarni looks up at the women and smiles his cocky smile.

My blush burns against the cool breeze. "That was amazing," I say, trying to put the woman's comment out of my head. "You –" I don't quite feel bold enough to say what I was going to say. "You look really good."

"So do you," he says, leaning against me so I feel his body heat seep through our jackets and shirts. "But that's not what you were going to say."

I look over his shoulder, study the texture of the wall of the shop across the sidewalk.

"Go on," he says gently. "I'm not going to make fun of you, whatever it is."

I bite my lip and look quickly at his eyes, then focus on his collarbone. "You made me feel special," I mumble, realizing it sounds even dumber out loud.

He shifts a hand from the roof of the car to my face, strokes his thumb over my cheekbone. "Look at me, Justin."

I meet his eyes and almost look away again. They're intense with something I'm not brave enough to try to read.

"You *are* special," he says.

"You spoil me," I retort. "New clothes, fancy food, book shopping."

But I can't keep the smile off my face.

"I'm going to spoil you for the rest of your damn life," he says, suddenly fierce. "If you'll let me."

I can only stare at him until he kisses me, mouth hot and demanding, tongue probing. I only just manage to keep in the moan that threatens to slip out of me.

"Now," he says, moving a hand to my hip then sliding it around to my ass and pressing me closer so I can feel him getting hard. "Are you really going to make me sleep on the couch?"

Chapter Nineteen

I'M SO JITTERY I DROP my keys trying to unlock my apartment door. Bjarni scoops them up and does it for me.

"Am I making you nervous?" he says into my neck as he follows me in, and I jump. "I *am* making you nervous. What's wrong?"

I turn around and he steps back to give me space. He closes and locks the apartment door and hands me my keys.

"I don't know," I say. "I've been nervous all day." I walk into the kitchen and drop my keys on the counter, slide my jacket off and hang it up.

Bjarni takes his jacket off, too, and drapes it over a chair, the movement drawing my attention to the width of his shoulders and the bulge of his biceps under the fabric of his shirt. He looks around.

"It sure looks like someone moved out and left most of their stuff behind. Is any of this yours?"

I look around, too, trying to see it as he does. Raine took anything that might give the place a personal touch, and I haven't had the money to add any of my own touches.

"Not really," I say. Even the books and DVDs on the shelf are hers, ones she wasn't attached to enough to take with her to Thorstein's.

"Because you're a guy and can't be bothered decorating, or you just haven't had a chance?"

"You should talk," I say. "Except for your bedroom and the living room, your house looks like it's been emptied and staged for a realtor to photograph." Then I sigh and say, "I haven't had a chance." Which is at least sort of true.

He touches my arm and I jump again. It's not a flinch away like I used to do, at least. "What's wrong?" He steps closer and I make myself breathe normally. "You can't still be afraid of me? Not after the full moon. Are you?"

"I don't know what's wrong." I fiddle with my keys on the counter, pull my wallet and phone out of my pockets to join them. "I just… It feels like…" I bite my lip.

He rubs his hand up and down my arm but doesn't try to get closer or to touch me anywhere else.

I shrug. "It's dumb."

"I bet it's not." He cocks his head, studying me, then walks past me into the living room where he studies the shelf of DVDs. "Want to watch a movie?" He holds up one with a dragon on the cover.

"Okay." I let him turn on the tv and set up the movie while I open the fridge. "Drink?"

"Beer?" he asks, hopefully.

"Sorry. Juice, milk, or water. And I think Raine left a few open bottles behind." I duck down and open the cupboard next to the fridge. "Um… vodka, gin, and… yeah, that's it."

He straightens up from the tv. "Uh… juice, I guess. With vodka."

I get glasses and start pouring. "I should have bought some beer," I say. "Sorry. I wasn't thinking. I thought we were going back to the farm after dinner."

"We still can." When I look up, he's sprawled on one end of the couch, feet on the coffee table, remote in hand. He looks so sexy I could die.

"No," I say. "I'm not letting you get out of taking me book shopping so easily." I hand him one of the drinks, then settle on the other end of the couch.

"You're kind of far away," he says.

"I know. Just… give me a minute."

"What were you about to say? Before?" He takes a sip of his drink and leans forward to set it on the coffee table. "You said 'it feels like.' It feels like what?"

I open my mouth and he says, "And don't tell me it sounds dumb."

I close my mouth again, sip my drink, and say, "Something feels… important. Like tonight is important and I can't mess it up. So I feel like anything I say or do is going to be the wrong thing." Like sitting way over here on the opposite end of the couch instead of next to him.

He studies my face. "Yeah," he says. "I feel it, too."

"How can you be so calm, so… self-assured?"

He lets his smile widen. "Advantages of being an asshole, I guess. I'm used to pretending nothing matters even when it does."

"Does… does this matter?" I'm suddenly worried that I've already done or said something that really does make him not care, that will make him decide to leave if I say or do something else wrong. Should I move closer to him, or would that be too needy? And why the fuck does it make my stomach hurt to think I might screw up this date when it's already gone so well?

His mouth quirks up a little more. "Yes," he says. "It matters. It matters that you're having a good time. With me. That you want me here. It matters so much I have butterflies in my stomach, and I don't think that's ever happened before." He picks up his drink, sips, puts it down, then shifts position to get his phone out of his pocket. He types something, then sets it down next to his glass, presses "play" on the remote, and the DVD starts.

The movie turns out to be an old 80s fantasy about a young wizard who has to face a dragon, and before I know it, I'm totally absorbed. About halfway through, I creep over on the couch until I'm sitting right next to Bjarni.

He puts his arm over my shoulders but doesn't try to pull me closer, like he's not sure how comfortable I am, like he doesn't want me to feel pressured. I lean against him and feel his breath, then his lips, against the top of my head. I sigh, and all my nervousness vanishes like it was never there and I feel him relax next to me. Everything feels right and perfect and when the credits roll, I dare to look up at Bjarni, to tilt my head and stretch my neck towards him. He brushes my forehead with his lips, and I make a noise of complaint so he kisses my mouth. I reach for him, grab his hair, and pull him closer.

Then his phone bleeps and he pulls away.

"Ignore it," I say, trying to pull him back. For a moment, he lets me, lets me try to devour his mouth, slides his tongue alongside mine, and shifts to pull me into his lap.

His phone bleeps again.

"Hold that thought," he says. "You might want to see that message, too." But he can't reach his phone with me on his lap.

I have to hand it to him, and before I relinquish it, I say, "First promise me you're going to kiss me again."

He grins. "I'm going to do a lot more than kiss you." He slides his hand up my thigh. I growl and he growls back, and I hand over his phone.

He looks at it, laughs, and shows it to me.

what does a symbiont bond feel like, he had texted Thorstein, *right before it happens?*

His brother's reply is, *If u hv 2 ask, u prob alrdy no. Dumbass.*

While I'm reading, another message arrives.

G-dad sez he sensed it in u. Prty sur i did 2.

I hand the phone back. "You'd think someone who learned to read and write in the dark ages would use fewer weird abbreviations," I say.

Bjarni snorts. "He learned to read when Magne did. I think he finds it freeing to not have to worry about making a spelling mistake."

I immediately feel bad for my comment, even if I didn't mean it to be shitty.

"Oh crap," I say.

"Dad didn't think Thorstein needed to be educated. Colleen was furious and insisted on teaching him." He tosses his phone onto the coffee table where it lands with a clunk. "He did it for Magne, mostly, but then he discovered how much he likes to read. He still doesn't write fluently, though."

"He spelled 'dumbass' correctly."

"Naturally." He grins and I grin back. Then his face goes serious. "Did you understand what I was really asking Thorstein?"

"You want to know if we have a symbiont bond," I say, something building in my guts that might be a terrible feeling or might be a good one. I can't tell yet. "But I thought it wasn't possible for…"

"The Elders… My dad mostly… always said symbiont bonds could only happen between a man and a woman. It's their main justification for persecuting queer werewolves."

"That sounds like my parents' thoughts on marriage in general."

"It comes from the same place, I bet." He rests his forehead on mine. "But the Elders can sense symbiont bonds, sometimes even before the people they're developing between. Thorstein can, too." He cups his hand around my face. "If he and Granddad think it's happening to us…" He straightens up and lifts me off his lap to sit next to him again.

"What?" I say.

He takes several deep breaths in a row, and the weird feeling in my belly intensifies but doesn't resolve into good or bad. When he meets my eyes, he looks so uncertain I want to put my arms around him, to hold him, to reassure him. And I want to hide before he can break my heart again.

"Do you want this, Justin?" he says.

"I barely even know what it means." My fingers keep twining themselves together, tighter and tighter, so I force my hands to be still.

"It means you'll never want anyone other than me, for as long as I'm alive. And –" He pauses, touches my clasped hands hesitantly. "It means I'll never want anyone but you, as long as you're alive."

"Will it make you love me?" I blurt out, then immediately flush hot, from my toes to my scalp. "I mean, I don't want to force you to feel something you don't want to feel."

He stares at me, brow furrowed, then snorts out a laugh. "Justin, I already love you."

"What?" My voice comes out as a squeak.

"I *did* tell you," he says, smile growing. "But then again, you were moon-drunk, and kept rolling onto your back to show me the giant circus tent you were making out of your sweatpants."

I wouldn't have thought I could blush *more*, but I do. I need a cold shower. An ice bath.

"Oh my God," I say. "I'm such an embarrassing drunk."

"You're cute as hell," he says. "And it was very hard to resist helping you with that particular problem."

"You didn't have to. To resist."

"Yes, I did." His smile turns gentle. "You weren't capable of consenting. Not really." He squeezes my hands. "But I should have said something when you *weren't* drunk. I just… didn't want you to feel pressured."

"You –" I'm having trouble breathing again, but the feeling in my gut is turning to a pleasant sort of excitement, and anticipation.

"I love you," he says, his voice going low and growly. "I'm so fucking in love with you, and I need to know if you want a symbiont bond with me, because if you don't, I need to get very far away, very soon, for a very long time, or it will happen anyway."

He's almost panting and all I can do is stare at him.

"Justin, please," he says. "Do you want me to leave, or do you want me to stay? Because if I stay, you're stuck with me for the rest of your life. Or mine. Whichever comes first."

"Bjarni –" I start then stop. "I –" I try again. Then I blurt out, "I think I've been in love with you since I opened my eyes in the woods to find some crazy naked guy watching me."

He laughs, but there's an edge to it, like he hasn't quite got the answer he needs yet. His fingers loosen on mine, then tighten again.

"Yes, I want this. I want you. I want… I want everything."

And all at once his breathing eases, and he moves his hand to my face, touching gently, tracing my eyebrows, my cheekbone, my lips.

"Fuck," he says.

"Yes, please," I say, and he looks puzzled. "I want you to fuck me."

"You want –" He pulls me closer, almost tentative.

"I want you," I say. "Inside me. Fucking me. Now. Please." And I pull away, get up, take his hand, and pull him up from the couch and towards the bedroom.

When we reach the door, it's like a spell has broken, like somehow that assurance that I'm not going to abandon him to sleep on the couch has returned him to his usual cocky self. He pins me in the doorway, pressing the length of his body against mine, possessing my mouth with his.

I push him away, but only far enough to reach the buttons on his shirt, and I think I tear a few free in my haste to get it off him. But he has a sleeveless undershirt on underneath, and I growl my frustration.

He doesn't even bother with the buttons on my shirt, except for the cuffs, and just pulls it over my head, undershirt and all. Then he pulls his own tank off and I see the bandages. I touch one, carefully.

"You're still hurt," I say.

"I'm fine," he says. "They're almost closed." He presses against me again, touching as much of his bare skin to mine as he can.

"Fuck." He trails kisses and gentle bites down my neck, my shoulder, my chest. He teases a nipple and laughs when I gasp, bury both hands in his hair, and arch my back.

"I fucking love how sensitive you are," he growls, and yanks open my belt, my fly, and slides a hand inside.

I have to push him away again to get his pants off, to find he's actually wearing boxer briefs. I laugh, and for a moment I can't stop. He takes a step back and looks at me, eyebrow quirked up.

"I didn't know you even *owned* underwear," I say.

"I find it best not to go commando in wool," he says, voice dry. "Even very expensive, very soft wool." He strips off his boxer briefs and takes another step away, letting me look at him.

And I stare. I drink in the sight of him, and even though I've seen him naked before I still can't comprehend how perfect he is. His tattoos emphasize the strength of the muscles in his forearms and hands. Every werewolf scar, every sun freckle, even each white bandage taped down with surgical tape, only adds to his masculine beauty of perfect tone, perfect proportion, of the way he moves, the way he simply exists so at home in his own physicality.

"Oh my God," I whisper. "I love you so fucking much." I meet his eyes, suddenly fearful again, because how could this perfect man, this deity, want *me*?

His answering look is intense, raw, and I realize that that thing, that vulnerable emotion I was so afraid to try to read, is obvious. It's passion, longing, *love*. And it's all for me. It makes me dizzy, euphoric, and I wonder if I can feel the symbiont bond growing stronger, solidifying because I'm not afraid anymore, because I welcome it and whatever it brings.

"I'm all yours, *kjaereste*," he says.

For a few more breaths we stand just looking at each other, then as one we both step closer, closer, until there's barely a molecule of space between us.

"If you want me, I'm yours," he says.

"If I want —" I snort in exasperation, take his hand, and put it on my erection.

His mouth twitches up on one side. "Well, it *feels* like you want me."

"Always," I say. "Constantly." I take a step towards the bed, and he follows, never allowing the space between us to grow, until the backs of my legs are pressed against the mattress and he's almost touching me.

"Come here," I say, and his arms are around me, and he's pressing me down onto the bed, kissing me, licking me, rubbing me, tucking his face between my thighs.

"Justin," he says, and nibbles the inside of my thigh, slides his tongue over my testicles and suddenly sucks one into his mouth.

"Holy fuck," I say.

He runs his tongue up the underside of my cock and laughs softly when I moan and clutch his hair. And grunts as I yank and pull him back up the bed to kiss my mouth again.

"Tell me what you want," he says into my neck.

"I told you," I say.

"Tell me again."

"Fuck me." I put my hands on his face, make him look at me. "There are condoms in the nightstand. Use lots of lube."

He strokes my face. "You're sure?"

I nod.

"I might hurt you."

"You probably will," I say. "But I'm a werewolf. I can take it. And I heal fast."

He frowns and I think he might refuse. He thinks I'm fragile, but I'm learning that I'm stronger than I look. He says, "You want me from behind?"

I shake my head. "I want to see your face."

He leans over me to reach the nightstand, puts a condom on my chest, and shifts position to get the bottle of lube open. He squirts some on his fingers and kisses me, hard, spreads my legs farther apart to slide his hand between, back between my ass cheeks, to massage my anus and push his fingers inside.

He doesn't bother with one at a time, just slowly slides three fingers into me, making me gasp. I moan when he pushes them all the way in.

"Okay?" he says, bends to flick his tongue across my nipple, slides his fingers out and back in, then presses them apart, opening me wider.

"Yes," I say, hoping sound is actually coming out of my mouth and that it actually forms the word. "Fuck yes."

"You ready for me?"

"Yes," I say again.

He shifts his weight, pulls his fingers out of me and says, "Put the condom on me." I tear the package open with my teeth, reach down to roll the latex onto his length, and realize he's the one taking charge even though I'm supposed to be the experienced gay in this relationship. And I'm so turned on by it I could explode.

He squirts more lube on his hand, levers himself off me to spread it on himself, and I watch. I watch him stroke himself to spread the clear gel around and then squirt more to rub between my legs.

He shifts again, bends my right knee until it's almost pressed against my chest and holds it in place under his arm. I wrap my other leg around the small of his back, dig my heel into his ass.

"Put me where you want me," he says, wrapping his free hand, the one that's not holding all his weight, around my hardness and stroking me.

I press him down between my legs and rub his tip against the circular muscle surrounding my asshole. I whisper, "Now," and he pushes closer, pushes slowly into me.

I grab his hips, pull him towards me, curve my back to a better angle, and feel him open me, split me, and it burns but it feels so fucking good. I must whimper because he stops moving.

"Justin? Am I hurting you?"

"Don't stop," I beg. "Please."

"Okay." He kisses me, strokes me, pushes deeper into me and I have to clench my teeth, turn my head away and bury it in his neck. He's so big. He's too big. But then he's inside me and it's like something eases and I imagine my werewolf symbiont racing through my bloodstream to my anal sphincter to heal me, to make it possible – pleasurable – for him to fuck me.

He thrusts slowly, stroking me with each push, careful not to be too rough.

"Still okay?" He nibbles my earlobe. I feel like I'm floating away, dissolving into nothing, all sensation and no thought. "Justin?"

"I'm so close," I whisper. "Bjarni. Oh fucking God." I don't care if I'm not making sense. He's filling me, *fulfilling* me, pushing me past my limit. And then I tumble over, clutching desperately at his back, his shoulders, his ass, trying to pull him farther into me. I might be screaming his name, and I'm definitely spurting hot semen up my belly and chest.

His breathing is ragged now, louder, and he keeps trying to hold back moans, and failing.

"Fuck, Justin," he breathes. "You're so tight."

"Don't stop," I say.

"I'm fucking coming," he growls, and the last word devolves into a guttural grunt that sounds like it's tearing out of him. He twitches, almost a convulsion, and again, and goes still.

He opens eyes that were squeezed shut and blinks to focus on me. "Holy fuck," he whispers. He shakes his head. "I feel the symbiont bond."

"Me, too."

He kisses me, gently. "I feel the fucking symbiont bond. You're mine now." He runs his hand up my sticky belly, my chest. "You're all fucking mine."

I tug a lock of his hair. The elastic he had it held back with at dinner is gone, pulled out by my clawing somewhere along the line. "And you're all fucking mine," I say.

"Yes," he says. "Yes I am."

Sometime during the night, I feel him get up, hear water running, and almost wake up all the way when he pulls the blankets away from me. I make a complaining noise and try to curl up in a ball, but he laughs softly and pushes me onto my back and cleans me off with a warm wet cloth.

It feels so nice I stretch out and let him take care of me. Until he pulls my legs apart and tucks the cloth between them.

I sit up. "You don't have to wipe my ass for me."

He laughs and lets me take the cloth. When I'm done, I fling it in the general direction of the laundry hamper, and he touches my face so lightly it feels like a breeze of air across my cheek.

"I love you," he says.

When I meet his eyes, there's no cheeky grin, only a soft look that makes my blood race.

"I love you," I say back.

"I also love *this*." And there's the grin, dimples flashing. But I only see it for a moment before he's bent over me and taking me in his mouth, sucking until I get hard, until I grab his hair, until I cry out and spurt into his mouth.

When I've caught my breath, I push him out of bed and when he laughs and gets up to climb back in, I swing my legs over the side and sit up, grab his hips so he has to stay on his feet.

"I bet you love *this,* too," I say, and slide my mouth over him, and suck, and stroke, and even bite just a little, until his hand finds that longer bit of hair at the top of my fancy new haircut and grips hard, and he thrusts between my lips, and cries out, and floods my mouth with spunk.

And *then* I let him get back in bed, tuck me close, and murmur, "I am the luckiest man alive." I feel the old urge to put myself down, to say he's not, that I'm not such a great catch, but it's easier to push aside this time.

"I texted Thorstein again," he says. "To tell him we're symbiont bonded."

"What did he say?"

"He said, 'Of course you are, you dumb fuck'." He laughs.

"And did he spell 'dumb fuck' correctly?"

"Naturally."

Chapter Twenty

THE PROMISE OF BOOK SHOPPING has me awake much earlier than I otherwise would be on a Saturday morning. I feel Bjarni already awake next to me and roll over to look at him.

"You still here?" I say, and I'm joking, but my words still have that edge of disbelief I can't seem to get rid of.

"Did you think I was going to change my mind and disappear in the night?" he says, smiling back at me.

Something twists in my chest, some lingering bit of self-loathing, and my eyes slide away from his.

He touches my face, hesitation in the way his fingers rest on my cheek. "Justin?" Now there's self-deprecation in *his* voice. "Do you still think so little of me?" He doesn't sound hurt, exactly, just resigned, and that makes it somehow worse.

"It's not you I think less of," I admit.

"Even after last night?" he says, tracing the line of my jaw. "Even after feeling the symbiont bond? Your fucking parents really screwed you up." I wince and close my eyes, and he kisses my forehead. "I don't mean you're a screw-up," he says.

"Except I am."

"You're not." He sighs. "What I meant is they made you feel worthless.

They made you *believe* you're worthless. But they're dead fucking wrong."

I look at him again, try a smile. "Sometimes I almost believe that," I say. "Or at least I can forget what a fuck up I am for a while." I put my hand flat on his chest. *He* makes me feel like less of a fuck-up, but I can't quite make myself say it out loud.

"Do you think your parents were right about queer people going to hell?"

"No, of course not."

"Then why do you believe they're right about your value as a person?"

"I –"

"No matter how much you screw up your life – and your finances weren't even that bad – no matter how fucked up, you still matter." He sits up, tucks his knees up to his chest, and looks down at me. "And even if you can't see your own value, trust that *I* value you."

I move closer, butt my head against his hip, and he puts a hand on my arm, rubs up and down, and I sigh.

"Thank you."

"So do you want breakfast, or are you in too much of a hurry to get to the bookstore?"

My stomach growls, always my betrayer. "There's not much in my fridge. I didn't want anything to spoil while I was gone."

"So, breakfast sandwiches on the way, then," he says. "Coffee – or tea – to go?"

We get dressed – after Bjarni runs out to the car in just his dress pants to fetch a duffle bag he brought with a change of clothes – and I throw my stuff into the trunk. Getting dressed up felt like a fairytale, but I'm glad we're both back in familiar jeans and t-shirts. I couldn't ever really relax with either of us dressed like we were for dinner.

The first store we stop in has a decent paperback selection with a very large science fiction and fantasy shelf, so I can see why Magne likes it. Bjarni finds a few thrillers and I point out a couple of British supernatural mystery series he might like – and am stupidly pleased when he buys the first book of each to try. I find a pristine hardcover of a recent literary folk horror fantasy that I've heard good things about.

When we get to the checkout, he takes my book to pay for it and I bite back a protest. He sees my look and smirks. "It's your birthday tomorrow," he says. "I'm paying for all your books today, so buy whatever you want."

"Oh, happy birthday!" says the older man behind the counter, looking at me over the tops of his half-moon spectacles like someone from a children's story. "Twenty-five, right?"

I laugh. "Sure, why not?"

He smiles back. "I'll give you our birthday discount, even though you're a day early." I notice he applies the ten percent off to the whole pile of books, and not just mine.

On the way back to the car, Bjarni detours into a big, brightly lit pharmacy and when I realize he's heading for the "family planning" section, I almost duck away to pretend to look at magazines. But the store is nearly empty, and he doesn't seem to care who notices us together. And why should I care, anyway? This is what I wanted.

When I stop next to him, he says, "Which condoms do you prefer, *kjaereste?*" and I almost slink away again. The teenager stocking the shelf farther along glances over and then back to what he's doing. I bite the inside of my cheek and take a box from the display and hand it to Bjarni. He drops it into the basket he's holding, and adds another box, looking at me from the corners of his eyes, which are crinkling with the effort of not smiling.

I raise my eyebrows, and he laughs. "The farm is not exactly convenient to a drugstore," he says. "But if you'd rather buy condoms and lube from Mrs Freely at the post office in Crossroads…" He leaves the sentence hanging.

The teenage employee glances up again, and I resist the urge to hide behind Bjarni. "You two need any help?" he asks.

"I think we're okay." Bjarni selects a bottle from the lube display and is about to add it to the basket when the employee moves closer.

"Here," he says. "If you like that kind, get this one." He grabs a large bottle from the bottom shelf. "You'll save some money, and you don't have to worry about running out."

Bjarni puts the bottle he was holding back and takes the offered one. "That's one huge fucking bottle of lube," he says.

The teen snickers. "You have a boyfriend looks like *that*," and he nods in my direction, "you're gonna want the big bottle."

Bjarni looks at the employee, then at me, then back to the teenager, and I swear I'm just going to expire on the spot.

"Good point," Bjarni says. "Thank you." His smile grows from amused to shit-eating.

Back in the car, he says, "See."

"See what?"

"Even a random drugstore employee thinks you're fuckable."

"So my value is in the tightness of my ass?" I say, aiming for lighthearted but landing on sulky.

He sighs and shakes his head. "That's not what I meant." He pulls the car out into traffic and in a few minutes we're on the highway. He hands me his phone. "You're going to have to navigate. Our next stop is already up on Maps."

I look at the screen, and the phone lights up to my fingerprint. "This bookstore is in Great Valley," I say.

"Thus, why we are currently on the highway," he says.

"I thought we were hitting all the shops in Riverbend today." I look at the screen again. "Great Valley's almost an hour's drive."

"Can't sit still that long?" he teases. "You can turn the radio on." A smile tugs at his mouth. "Magne says Hawthorne Books is the best used bookstore in Autumn County." He pokes my leg. "And they apparently have a good poetry section."

"It sounds familiar," I say, studying the map as though it will tell me something about the store we're headed for aside from where it is. "Maybe I've been there. If they have textbooks, I probably went while I was at GVU."

"There," he says. "You're educated. That has value."

"I didn't finish my degree." I look away from the phone, watch his eyes checking traffic, his strong hands holding the wheel. "Are you going to point out everything about me that somebody might think has value?"

"Yes," he says. "You like to learn. You're curious and interested in lots of things."

"Some people would say that means I lack focus or am easily distracted."

"You're smart."

"Maybe I should just keep hating myself, so you'll keep complimenting me." Again, I aim for joking, and miss. I lean back in my seat and close my eyes.

"I don't like you hating yourself," he says. "But I'm happy to compliment you as long as I live."

He accelerates around a slower car in the driving lane, hands sure on the wheel. "You're beautiful," he says. "You're sexy. You're kind."

"Stop it."

"I thought you liked it?" he teases. "And before you say, 'only if you mean it,' I *do* mean it. Every fucking word." He puts his hand on my leg and squeezes. "And the way you look at me…" He trails off, checks his side mirror, then the rearview.

"How do I look at you?" I say.

He shakes his head. "Like *I* mean something. Like I'm something delicious you want to devour. Something… something precious you want to possess."

"Bjarni," I say. "You have poetry in your soul." I put my hand over his where it still rests on my leg. "Not just money and field rotations."

He snorts. "Fuck off, Leyendecker." But he smiles and the way he says it, he might as well be telling me he loves me. "If you think I'm worthwhile, then I guess I better try to be… well, better."

"You're perfect," I say.

"No, you're perfect." And we both laugh, and for a moment, I feel so good I could burst.

But the closer we get to Great Valley, the more nerves clench in my belly. I sit up straighter in my seat and clench my hands in my lap, feeling the edges of Bjarni's phone bite into my fingers. I haven't been back since the day I tried to run away from my life and got turned into a werewolf. It's a bigger city than Riverbend, but what if I run into someone I know? What if I run into my parents?

"You okay?" Bjarni says, glancing at me, then back at the road to make sure he's in the right exit lane for the part of town we're aiming for.

"Just really anxious all of a sudden," I say.

"Do you want me to take you home instead?"

"No." I clench and unclench my hands in my lap, and just remember to point out the next turn we need to take. "No, we're here now, and I really do want to see this amazing bookstore of Magne's." I shove aside the feelings of worthlessness that fill me at the thought of running into my parents or their evangelical missionary friends. Like Bjarni said, they're wrong. I *do* have value. And I refuse to let them make me return to the weak little fuck-up I was a month ago. I can stand up for myself. I stood up to Bjarni Thorvaldson, notorious womanizer, and made him fucking *woo* me to get me back. I can stand up to my terrible father and mother and tell them to leave me alone, that thirty-four years of bullying is enough.

Even after that internal pep talk, I still can't take Bjarni's hand when we get out of the car and sidestep like I didn't see him reach for me. In Riverbend, I'd have been happy to be seen walking down the street hand-in-hand with another guy, especially one as hot as Bjarni, but here in Great Valley I feel vulnerable. It's a bigger city, which should make it more anonymous, but it's always felt less tolerant, and I find myself growing afraid again.

Once we're inside the bookstore, though, every thought vanishes at once and I stare around me. Shelves and shelves of books, each with a subject posted on the end. There's a staircase leading up directly ahead, and another to one side, leading down.

Bjarni laughs softly. "You should see your face."

"I have always imagined that paradise would be a sort of bookstore," I say, unable to keep the reverence out of my voice. Of course, Borges said "library" not "bookstore," but close enough.

"That sounds like a quote."

"Mmm." I nod, absently, scanning the shelf labels and trying to decide which way to go first. It feels like when Raine took me to the bookstore near the gallery, but better, because this one is three times the size and I'll be able to afford more than one book.

Bjarni's hand on the small of my back startles me and I take a step away.

"Justin?" He sounds concerned, confused by my reaction. "Did I say something wrong?"

I look at him, glance away. "No," I say. "It's just…"

"You're afraid of something," he says. "Do you… not want to be seen with me? It's okay in Riverbend where no one knows you, but in Great Valley you're, what, ashamed?" His voice is soft. He touches my face and I jerk away, and I see something harden in his eyes before I have to look away again.

"Bjarni…"

"Forget it," he says. "I'll be in the fiction section when you're ready to go." He's always so cocky I forgot he can be vulnerable, too. I grab his hand as he starts to walk away.

"Don't," I say. "It's not you. I just… I don't feel comfortable in Great Valley." I make a frustrated motion. I really don't want to taint this bookstore, this *day* with my insecurities. "It's not like Riverbend here. I got the shit kicked out of me here, more than once. I'm not ashamed." I move closer, hold his hand tighter and try not to be nervous about it. "I'm proud to be with you. I *want* everyone to know we're together. I'm just…"

The hardness in his face eases and disappears, and he squeezes my hand. "You're afraid," he says, gently. "It's okay. We'll just be drinking buddies while we're here." He *sounds* okay, but there's a twist to his smile. "And if anyone tries to hurt you, I'll be the one doing the shit-kicking."

"I'm sorry," I whisper.

"No," he says. "Don't be. I can live without putting my hands all over you for a few hours. Just know that I'm going to make up for it later. Now, go spend all your money."

I smile, feeling a little better, at least. "I don't have any money, remember?"

"Go spend all *my* money, then." He grins. "I'm going to go find some pulpy spy novels."

I wander until I find a sign pointing to a back corner, promising poetry, and smile when I see the shelves and shelves of slender volumes. I've got half a dozen in my hand before I even get through the first shelf and I make myself slow down and consider each book more carefully, think about which of the ones I've already read that I really want to read again, and which of the unfamiliar names look the most promising.

When I finally straighten up, an hour has gone by, and I've managed to restrain myself to eight books. I can't keep the dumb grin off my face, and I wish I hadn't been so touchy with Bjarni. While Great Valley might feel unsafe, this bookstore is like a haven.

That thought is confirmed when, in the midst of wandering and trailing my fingers over book spines, I find a shelf of LGBTQ+ books with a huge queer pride flag over it, and a sign declaring "This is a safe space" in big block letters. I pull out a book of essays on intersectionality and gay and trans rights and add it to my hoard of poetry books.

More wandering, and I end up in the romance section, looking for something with werewolves and smut, because why not? I find another two books by the author of *The Wolf's Best Mate* and tuck them into my pile.

When I find Bjarni, he's not even in the fiction section. He's in science, frowning at a shelf labelled "Theoretical Mathematics."

"Good with numbers, hunh?" I say, and he looks up. I want to kiss him, but then I notice his empty hands. "Didn't you find anything?"

"I have a stack up at the front counter." He looks at my armful. "Is that it?

I laugh. "Eleven isn't enough?"

He starts to reach for my face but stops himself, making it into a gesture at the shelf of math books. "I wanted to go to university, you know?" he says. "My grades mostly sucked, but math I was good at. I worked my ass off in high school to get my grades up enough that I could get into the program I wanted." He breathes a long breath out his nose. "Dad thought theoretical maths was a waste of time. I mean, why would a farmer need to know how the universe works? I guess I should be glad I at least got to study something. I'm a really fucking good accountant."

"You should get a couple of those," I say, and glance over the titles. I have no idea what most of them even mean.

"I wouldn't even know where to start anymore," he says, touching one finger to the spine of a book called *The Language of the Universe.*

"Why not just try that one?" I say.

"You mean pick a random book that might or might not be good, based on a title that sounds interesting?"

"Yes, that's exactly what I mean. Where's your sense of adventure?"

He sighs and looks away. "I came over this way to look for farming books. Next aisle, I think." He slips past me, and I watch his back for a moment, then pull *The Language of the Universe* off the shelf and tuck it into my pile. I saw the wistful look on his face, and I can't resist.

By the time we leave, I've added more books to my pile after swinging by the poetry section for one more look, then several more when I discover they have a local authors section that includes a shelf jammed with poetry chapbooks, many of them published by Hawthorne Books itself.

Bjarni doesn't comment on the math book I snuck in with my purchases, or maybe he doesn't notice. He takes the bags after we've paid – after *he's* paid – reminding me that this trip is my birthday present.

"What do you want for lunch, almost-birthday boy?" he says, as we stroll down the sidewalk. I don't have to feel guilty now about not holding his hand because his hands are occupied by our bags of books.

"Sushi," I say.

"You know a good place?"

I look around, studying the street names. This isn't too far from when I hung out in university. "Yeah," I say. "I'm pretty sure there's a good place up a couple of blocks and around the corner."

I can't help sneaking glances at him as we walk, wondering if he's as hurt as I would be, if he didn't want me to touch him anymore.

Finally, he sighs and says, "I'm not mad at you, *kjaereste,*" and I dare to meet his eyes.

"I'm –"

"Don't be sorry. There's nothing to be sorry for. And anyway, even if I *am* hurt, it's nothing like how badly I hurt you."

"Is it a contest?" I say, and he laughs.

"Gods, I hope not. I really don't like hurting you."

I look away again, feeling better, and glance up the sidewalk to see how close we are to the street we need to turn down, and almost trip. I stumble to a stop. "Oh, fuck," I say.

Bjarni stops beside me, looks at me, concerned, then looks up to see what stopped me.

A man and a woman, my parents' age, are standing beside a display of pamphlets on the corner. The woman smiles beatifically at everyone who passes while the man darts out like a used car salesman, offering booklets and waving a Bible. I can hear their voices and wonder why I didn't notice them sooner.

"Do you know those people?" Bjarni says. "Are they – ?"

"My parents' missionary friends," I say. In a way, they bullied me worse than my parents did, and shored up my mother's and father's beliefs in my sinfulness when they might have eventually accepted me. "They're the ones who used to show up wherever I worked, who got me fired three times, and made me quit out of pure embarrassment more than once. They even showed up to some of my classes so my professors had to call campus security. It was fucking mortifying." I realize I'm shaking, my hands trembling so hard they won't stop.

"Do you want to go around the block the other way?" Bjarni says. "Or find somewhere else to eat? I can take you home and make you a nice grilled cheese and ham." He smiles gently, like he's hoping to lighten the mood. "Or do you want me to play big bad wolf and chase them away?"

I force myself to breathe, to remember the times I panicked, and Bjarni would say over and over, "Breathe, Justin. Just breathe," and he would rub my back, or hold my hand, and it helped. And it helps now, even though it's just a memory I'm evoking. Because he's here, beside me, asking me what I want. Supporting me.

I can do this. I *can*. "No," I say. "I won't let them intimidate me." I see warmth in his eyes. Love. "I won't give them that power over me. Not anymore." I straighten up, stop trying to hide behind the sign for a vegan cafe. "Come on." And I continue down the sidewalk as if I didn't even see the Fields.

And I keep walking, looking straight ahead, until I see them notice me, realize who I am, until Mrs Field turns her saintly smile on me and Mr Field steps towards me.

And I stop, and shove aside my fear, my self-loathing, and turn to Bjarni, who's right there for me, and I smile at him, put every bit of love and want for him onto my face where anyone can see it. And just as Mr Field opens his mouth to speak to me, I put my arms around Bjarni's neck, pull him down to my level, and kiss him.

I pretend we're at home, on the farm, safe and private in his bedroom, and open my lips to his, slide my tongue into his mouth and feel him respond just as fiercely. And when I finally pull away, I let my tongue linger so our tongue-tips stretch and touch for a moment. Then I smile again, and he smiles back.

Mr Field makes a strangled noise, and I turn my smile on him, but let my teeth show. "Oh," I say, making my voice bright and cheerful. "Mr and Mrs Field! How nice to see you."

"Oh, child," says Mrs Field, clutching her hand to her throat. "Your parents would weep to see how you've let this deviant lead you back into sin. After all they did for you!"

Bjarni grins his wickedest smile but doesn't say anything.

I laugh, making it as merry a sound as I can manage. "Oh no," I say. "Bjarni hasn't led me into sin." I lean over like I'm about to tell them a secret, and they both unconsciously lean closer. I whisper loudly, "I led *him* into sin." I move away and smile up at Bjarni.

"It's true," he says. "I used to be straight."

I manage – barely – not to burst out laughing. I tuck my arm under his elbow, since his hands are full of shopping bags, and turn to walk past them.

"Give my regards to my parents," I say. "And let them know that if they, or you, ever contact me again, there *will* be a restraining order."

"Also true," says Bjarni over his shoulder as I lead him away. "My uncle's a cop."

Chapter Twenty-One

Once again, I wake too early, but this time Bjarni whispers for me to go back to sleep and tucks the blankets around me.

"Come back," I say, groggy.

"I have to go help Thorstein wrestle a pig onto a spit," he says. "I'll be back soon." Then he kisses my cheek and I'm asleep again before I hear him reach the bottom of the stairs.

I wake for real when I smell fried ham and hear Bjarni swearing under his breath as he tries to maneuver a tray though the door without dropping anything.

I sit up, blinking, as he climbs up onto the bed and sits next to me, putting the tray across both our laps. It's one of those bed-trays with legs and a rim around the edge to keep your breakfast in bed from sliding into your lap.

"Hah!" he says. "I didn't even spill your tea." He grins at me, the expression making his face boyish, and I blink some more, trying to make my brain work.

"Tea?" I say and he laughs and hands me a big mug off the tray. I sip, and the hot steam soothes my eyes. "Oh! This is really good!" I can't keep the surprise out of my voice, and he snorts at my response. The tea tastes like it has something a little sweet and floral in it, and it's brewed perfectly.

"Happy birthday, *kjaereste*," Bjarni says.

"I forgot," I say and laugh. I feel a bit stupid, but it *is* first thing in the morning.

"You'll get better with waking up as your werewolf nature develops," he says, nipping my bare shoulder.

I take another sip of the delicious tea then notice the mug it's in: handmade and glazed in a Craftsman-inspired design of blue morning glories. "When did you get this?" I ask.

"That's part of your birthday present from Thorstein and Raine. The rest is downstairs."

"But he paid for our dinner. I thought that was my gift?"

"I told you you were going to be spoiled. Now eat, and you can open the rest of your presents." He picks up a fork and stabs a slice of fried ham and stuffs it into his mouth without cutting it then washes it down with a swallow of coffee out of an ordinary black mug just like the others in his kitchen cupboard.

"The tray is from Granddad, but the way," he says once he's swallowed. "I asked him not to wrap it so I could use it this morning."

I look more closely at the wooden object holding our breakfast. The wood is smooth and polished, stained a medium brown, and all the joints are cleverly hand-worked to fit without nails.

"It's beautiful."

"He made it for you." He taps the wood with an index finger. "Quartersawn oak from one of our own trees that came down in a storm a few years ago."

"He hardly knows me," I say, covering my dismay with another sip of tea. Rose petals: that's what makes the black tea sweet and floral.

"He likes you," Bjarni says, and my dismay is replaced with something else, something warm.

"Shouldn't I wait to open my gifts until everyone can be here?"

He shakes his head. "It's going to be busy around here all day, prepping for Freysblöt. The Elders will arrive in the late afternoon, and everyone else sometime in the morning." He squeezes my knee. "The Elders are going to want to talk to you." He sounds apologetic. "To get your version of events before they question Jens Harkett."

"My attacker."

"I'll probably have to talk to them, too. But by the end of the night tomorrow, it will all be over."

Suddenly I don't feel so happy. I set down the piece of toast I was eating and press my hand to my stomach. I feel sick.

His hand on the back of my neck is warm and reassuring. "It'll be okay. I promise."

"Are you sure he'll even show up?"

"He'll be here. He knows the Elders have called for him, and he doesn't think he's done anything wrong, but not showing up would be as good as admitting guilt."

"What if the Elders side with him?"

"Not gonna happen. He can't lie to them, and if he does, they'll be able to smell it. He's a murderer and a rapist, either one of which would condemn him on its own. But he's too self-righteous to run. He believes the Elders supported my father because they agreed with him, not because they were controlled by him."

He leans over and kisses my cheek. "I'm so sorry this had to happen on your birthday, *kjaereste*. But it will be over soon, and we can get on with being stupid and in love."

I have to smile at that. "Am I stupid or am I in love?"

He snorts. "You're beautiful, is what you are." He takes the tray and leans over the side of the bed to set it on the floor. Then he turns back to pull me against him, finding my skin with his hands and claiming my mouth with his own. He kisses me long and slow, letting his tongue linger, until I'm lying flat in bed, breathless, lips swollen.

He looks down at me and traces the side of my face. "Happy birthday," he says, and his grin turns wicked as he slides his hand across my chest and down my belly to curl his fingers around my cock to stroke me.

"You have too many clothes on," I say, tugging at his t-shirt and trying not to be too obvious about how his touch is dissolving my brain.

"This is *your* day, Justin," he says, following the path his hand took with his mouth, pausing to tease my nipples before moving lower and lower, letting me feel his teeth and his tongue as he goes. By the time I feel his breath on the insides of my thighs, I'm panting, gasping, and when he slides his lips over my hardness I moan. Loud.

"Bjarni, fuck," I say.

He responds by digging his fingers into my hip and sucking harder. Then he lifts his head to say, "I promise tonight I'll take more time with you. After tomorrow we'll have all the time in the world, and I'll do whatever you want me to do to you." And he puts his mouth on me again and I'm pretty sure there are fireworks – or at least birthday sparklers – behind my eyes when I climax.

There are packages with my name on them waiting on the kitchen table, and I examine them while Bjarni sets about making a fresh pot of tea. He uses a brand-new teapot that matches the mug, only it has a pattern of creamy white roses. And one of the brightly wrapped packages has three more mugs, each with a different flower.

I turn each one carefully in my hands, delighting in the tactile beauty of them, and drinking in the lovely designs. "These are... fuck, these are gorgeous."

Bjarni hands me a cup of tea. "Raine was so excited when she and Thorstein found them in a gallery in Great Valley. She was worried you might not like the flowers, but I told her you like pretty things."

I poke him with my bare foot. "They're perfect."

From Magne and his girlfriend there's a couple of books with a bookstore gift certificate made out for a generous amount tucked between them. One of the books is a signed poetry chapbook by Cara Stillwater.

"I heard her read once, in Great Valley. Before I stopped trying to write." I flip pages carefully. "She was really good. Not just the poems, but the way she recited them, too."

Bjarni says, "She's Magne's ex," and I look up, startled. He grins. "I didn't think they were speaking anymore." He looks like he wants to say more but isn't sure he should.

"I can practically see gossip leaking out your eyes," I say.

"He got her pregnant," he says. "And don't tell him I told you; he doesn't even know *I* know."

I make a zipping-my-lips motion and stare at him, eyes so wide it almost hurts. When he doesn't say anything else, I ask, "Didn't Magne want kids?" I mean, I can totally imagine him as a dad. He'd be good at it.

"*He* did," Bjarni says.

"Oh," I reply, then realize what he isn't saying. "*Oh.* Oh no."

"Yeah. I mean they weren't in love or planning to get married or anything. No symbiont bond. But still…"

"Fuck." I look at the book and wonder how hard it was for Magne to ask his ex for it, or if he maybe found a copy at a bookshop. Maybe Elias was able to get him a copy.

The second book has a sticky note on the cover in sprawling but readable writing that says, *Had to get this one used because it's out of print, so it's signed but personalized to someone named Nikki.* That makes me smile. It's a copy of *The Practice of Poetry* by Robin Skelton, and if I was going to buy myself a how-to-write poetry book, it would be that one.

"How does Magne know I like poetry?" I say. "That I even attempt to write it?"

"I may have let it slip," Bjarni says. "And no, I didn't read your notebook. You left it open in the kitchen in your apartment and the words looked poem shaped. And I already know you like reading poetry, so I made an educated guess."

Then there's a box from Colleen that contains a hand-stitched quilt in a Celtic knotwork pattern of deep greens with touches of purple and blue. I hold it up and it's enormous.

"That'll look great on our bed," Bjarni says. *Our* bed.

From Hilde there's a t-shirt that says *World's Best Uncle* with a note to the effect that I'll be the first in the family to have one, even beating Magne to it. The fact that she thinks of me as her brother's future kid's uncle makes my grin way wider than it should.

The last gift is from Bjarni, and I try to protest. "You already –"

He cuts me off. "I *already* told you I intend to spoil you." He raises his eyebrow, so I just take another sip of tea and carefully remove the paper from the box he hands me. It once held bottles of rum, according to the printing on the side, but it smells like…

"It smells like tea!" I say and pry open the flaps. On the very top is a leather-bound book with the initials JCL embossed on the bottom right corner. I flip it open to find it filled with creamy blank pages. Next to it is a small thin box that holds a fountain pen. A Namiki Falcon. And there's a bottle of forest green ink.

"Bjarni…" I say. I can feel tears pricking the backs of my eyes.

"There's more," he says, hiding his grin behind the rim of his coffee cup.

I set the writing implements aside and look into the box. All I can see is glass jar tops filling each of the cardboard partitions that once held booze. I pull one out and there's another under it. When I've got them all lined up on the table, there are two dozen antique glass-topped canning jars, each filled with a different kind of tea and labelled in handwriting that almost looks like calligraphy.

I read "Extra Choice Keemun," "Tippy Golden Assam," and "Jasmine Green Dragon," before I can't read any more because my eyes have filled with tears. I'm glad I'm already sitting down.

I blink hard and look over at where Bjarni's leaning against the counter.

"I thought you might be tired of those ancient tea bags Colleen dug out of her pantry," he says.

A hot tear escapes my eye and runs down my cheek, and he sets his coffee aside to kneel beside me and wipe away the tear with his thumb. I sniff and press my face against his palm.

"I feel so…" I grope for the right word. "Accepted," I say. "Loved."

"You are loved, Justin," he says, and pulls me close. "So fucking much."

He doesn't tell me not to cry, he just holds me as I sniffle into his shoulder and hands me a tissue when I'm done.

I look at the array of jars cluttering the table. "How did you know what to buy?"

"I had help. Su – Magne's girlfriend – is a tea connoisseur. She told me which shop to go to and sent me a list of her top picks. Then she told me I had, in her opinion, chosen the best possible gift for a tea drinker with an empty tea cupboard."

I sniff and blow my nose. "She likes you."

"She really doesn't." He laughs. "But she loves Magne, and *he* likes you. I'm the asshole brother who hurt him." He taps the side of one of the jars. "I think I might be slowly redeeming myself, though."

"You redeemed yourself with me," I say. "So, I guess there's hope."

"Have you forgiven me, then?" he teases.

I pretend to consider. "We'll see how you perform tomorrow tonight, after everyone has gone home."

"How I *perform*?" he says, mock indignant. "Is that all I am? A burlesque show? A sex toy?"

"You're *my* sex toy," I say.

"Yes, I am," he replies.

There are six Elders – seven if you count Granddad, but I don't think he's officially part of the council – and they start showing up just after five.

Two of them – one man and one woman – are still straight and tall, while the rest are in various stages of becoming permanently wolf-like. Granddad isn't even the most changed; one man isn't able to stand on two legs at all and wears very loose clothing so he can move freely on all fours.

Each Elder is dropped off by relatives who pause to consult with Colleen, who has set up the living room with tables for tomorrow's potluck, before driving away.

When all the Elders are in the farmhouse kitchen, Thorstein comes to get me where I'm waiting with Bjarni on the front porch. Bjarni gets up, too, but Thorstein puts a hand on his shoulder. "Only Justin," he says. "They'll call for you after, Little Bear." Bjarni scowls but squeezes my hand and sits back down.

The Elders have not saved me a chair, and I'm left to stand at the empty place at the head of the table. I'm grateful for Thorstein standing next to me, or I might be overcome by the desperate urge to flee.

Granddad gives me an encouraging smile from the other end of the table, and I'm reminded of how like Bjarni he looks. Even his cheeky grin is the same. I try to relax. I haven't done anything wrong.

"You are Justin Leyendecker?" says one of the Elders, a woman with very long silver hair and grey eyes.

"Yes," I say.

"How long have you been a werewolf?" asks a man with grey-streaked dark hair. He sits hunched at the table, like he can no longer sit upright.

"About a month," I say, telling them when I think it must have happened.

"And were you asked if you wanted to be changed?" asks a man who looks like he was a redhead when he was younger. "Were the details explained to you?"

The questions go on like that, and I answer each one. Thorstein has already told them everything he knows, everything I told him, and everything he and Bjarni were able to figure out about the circumstances of me being made a werewolf and assaulted and everything that came after. Now, they ask me about each detail, to make certain for themselves that I've been truthful.

At first, it's easy to answer, just "yes" or "no" or the occasional "I don't remember." It gets harder when they begin to ask about my assault, not because I don't know the answers, but because I don't want to think about it.

"It's okay, son," says one man, the one who's so far stuck in wolf shape he walks on four legs. "Take your time."

I realize there are tears streaming down my face when Thorstein steps away to reach the box of tissues on the counter and holds it out to me.

But finally, they ask and I answer the final question.

One man stirs in his chair and says to Thorstein, "Under your father's leadership, this one would be just as guilty of a crime as Jens Harkett is."

"My father was wrong," Thorstein says.

"Same sex unions are against the natural order," says one of the women, a greying blonde with intense dark eyes.

Thorstein snorts. "So my father said. Again, he was wrong."

"There can be no symbiont bond between two men or two women," says the ex-redhead.

Thorstein draws breath to speak, but Granddad beats him to it. "Again," he says, "Wrong. Utterly. Fucking. Wrong."

"You are not part of the Elder Moot, Thorleif," says the silver-haired woman, and I think there is regret in her voice. "By your own choice."

"Because I didn't like how my son controlled you lot," Granddad says.

"And it doesn't matter because this isn't a matter of opinion. It's a matter of fact."

"And can you demonstrate this assertion of yours?" The woman sounds amused, and I can't tell if it's because she thinks he can't or because she knows he can.

"Bjarni!" Granddad suddenly bellows, making everyone except Thorstein and the silver-haired woman jump. "Get your ass in here!"

Bjarni swaggers through the door like he doesn't care what anyone in the room thinks, but I can feel his tension when he stops beside me.

"Hey Granddad," he says. "Respected Elders." The way he inclines his head is barely respectful at all, bordering on insolence, and more than one of them shoots him a dirty look.

"Little Bear," says Granddad. "Is your Grizzly here –"

"Proper names, please, Thorleif," says the silver-haired woman. "Let's make sure we all know exactly who is involved here." She really does seem amused.

"Bjarni, son of my son Thorgrim," Granddad says in an only slightly mocking voice, "Are you and Justin symbiont-bonded?" He grins, showing a lot of big teeth, and Bjarni echoes the expression.

"Yes, we are," Bjarni answers.

Every one of the Elders stares at us, except the silver-haired woman, who's looking at Granddad with bright eyes.

"Not possible!" says the blonde woman, and Thorstein snorts.

"All of you, as Elders, can sense symbiont bonds, can you not?" he asks.

"Of course we can," says the ex-redhead.

"Well…" Thorstein gestures at me and Bjarni.

I feel the looks of six Elders bore into me, like they can read my mind, like I can sense them sensing me. And one by one, they nod, even though some of them don't look happy about it. The silver-haired woman laughs, and it's a reassuring sound.

"There goes your last argument, Haakon," she says and the ex-redhead scowls.

The Elders look at each other.

"Justin and Bjarni have committed no crime for loving each other," says the silver-haired woman, her mouth quirking up in deep amusement when she says Bjarni's name. "I hereby witness their symbiont bond to be true and valid." And one by one, the others agree, though the ex-redhead looks like he's been made to suck a lemon, and the blonde woman doesn't look much happier.

"Now when are you two getting married?" says Granddad, and Bjarni laughs.

"Don't rush us, old man," he says, but his smile is affectionate.

"While I hate to, as you say, rush you," the silver-haired woman says, "It might do the pack some good to be made to witness your union." She looks at Bjarni. "And since both your brothers are plighting their troth tomorrow evening, you might consider it."

"*Both* my brothers?" He looks at Thorstein, who shrugs.

"Magne texted this morning."

"Well, there's no pressure *now*."

"There *is* no pressure," Thorstein says. "It's enough for the pack to know same-sex symbiont bonds are possible, and that you two are together."

The silver-haired woman, who seems to be the unofficial head of the Elders, nods to us. "You two may go. You'll be called back after we've questioned the accused, when we're ready to decree punishment." She doesn't say when they've determined guilt or innocence. But I guess if werewolves can't lie to each other, my testimony is enough to determine the truth. Questioning my attacker is only a formality, and maybe a last chance for him to try to justify his actions.

Back outside, I can finally breathe. I grope for Bjarni's hand, and he laces his fingers with mine. "Let's go home for a little bit," he says. "You look like you need a drink."

When we reach the house, I sit on the porch swing while he fetches two glasses of smoky whiskey. Then he sits next to me and pulls me close.

I lean against him, sipping my drink and listening to the sounds of the farm as night slowly creeps in.

Finally, Bjarni says, "I guess we should find something to eat while we wait."

"Do you think he's here yet?"

"I haven't heard his truck. I haven't heard anyone since the last of the Elders got here." He takes my empty glass and tucks it under the swing.

"I'm hungry, but I'm too nervous to eat," I say.

"Me, too." He pushes against the porch railing with his foot, gently rocking the swing, and I slide down until my head is in his lap. My eyes drift closed, and I feel safe.

Until the voice from my nightmares comes out of nowhere and I think I really have fallen asleep, only to dream that terrible dream again.

"How fucking cozy. The Thorvaldson black sheep and his pet fairy. Shouldn't you be begging the Elders for your lives right about now?"

I pry my eyes open, and the nightmare doesn't vanish with my waking. He's standing at the bottom of the steps, and he's holding a shotgun.

<h1 style="text-align:center">Chapter Twenty-Two</h1>

I SIT UP AND SCRAMBLE desperately backwards, like I can claw my way through the back of the porch swing and the wall of the house and escape.

My breathing is so panicked and loud I don't hear Bjarni at first, when he speaks. He stands slowly and steps deliberately between me and Harkett. He reaches behind him, finds my hand, and squeezes. "Breathe, *kjaereste*," he says, voice low and calm. "Panic isn't going to help us right now."

And for some reason, the simple fact that he says "us"– not "you" or even "me", but "us" together – helps me focus. I slide off the swing and wedge myself between it and him, on my feet, still if not calm.

"What do you want, Jens?" he says, tone reasonable and measured.

"Don't be all buddy-buddy with me, you little shit. I want what's mine." Harkett is just as I remember him, somewhere around six feet, hair that was probably once blond, muscles that were probably once as ripped and sculpted as Bjarni's, pot belly that probably used to be firm. He looks middle-aged, but is probably much older, and therefore more powerful.

"And what's that?"

I'm trembling so I stuff my hands under my armpits to stop it, rest my forehead between Bjarni's shoulder blades, and try to concentrate on breathing, on not freaking out. I faced the terrible people from my past; I can face my more recent attacker.

"I made him," says Harkett. "I gave him the gift of the werewolf. He's mine now."

"That's not how it works, and you know it. He belongs to himself, and he belongs in the pack. It's not like licking a cookie to make it yours. You don't get to own him because you bled all over him."

That makes me laugh. It's a hysterical sound, but it's better than crying. I edge sideways to see around Bjarni, but he keeps me mostly behind him with one hand on my hip.

"You used to be the cousin I liked best. The most interesting of Thorgrim's kids," Harkett says. "The one most like him, who shared his values. I thought for sure he'd lock your brainless do-gooder brother away for good and you'd take over one day."

He turns his head and spits, weighs his shotgun in one hand, and shifts his grip to hold it with both hands. I don't know much about guns, but it looks like he's making sure it's ready to fire.

"I'm nothing like my father, and I sure as hell don't share his values," Bjarni says through gritted teeth. "My father was a piece of shit, and so are you, Harkett. Now get the fuck off my lawn and present yourself to the Elders. They're waiting for you at Colleen's house."

"I'll go when you give me the kid. I need him to bear witness for me. Him and that other one. The homeless dude."

"He's not a kid, you thick shit, and he has a name. And so does your other forced conversion."

"And I won't speak for you," I say. "The Elders have already asked me all the questions they care to."

"I don't give a shit what their names are. And you'll say what I tell you to say. Or I'll blow your sugar daddy's brains out right here."

I try to step around Bjarni, to do what, I don't know. Maybe just to get between him and a shotgun blast to the head. He tightens his fingers on my hip and all I can do is edge out beside him a little more.

"Sure, killing me would definitely bolster your case," Bjarni says, all traces of reasonable gone and replaced by contempt. "What you should be doing is admitting your guilt and arguing that the death penalty is barbaric. That's the only way you're walking away from this."

Someone else steps out of the shadows behind Harkett. "Truck coming, boss."

Bjarni cocks his head. "Magne. Coming up the farmhouse driveway."

The hope I felt at the news of someone coming fizzles into nothing. Unless we make a lot of noise, Magne won't know we need help.

"The fuck's he doing here?" says Harkett. "He was banished."

"Thorstein's undoing a lot of the crap Dad pulled," Bjarni says.

"Go keep an eye on the house," Harkett says, and his big biker-looking minion lopes off into the trees, ignoring the path in favor of skulking through the bush. He's quieter than he was last time we met, I'll give him that.

"What do you think you're going to accomplish?" Bjarni asks.

"I'm going to prove *you're* the criminal. That you've been fucking this waste of symbiont. That you're a sexual deviant and I've just been trying to save this pack from corruption. And if it gets your brother removed as pack leader, so much the better."

"That makes no fucking sense."

"Look," I say, somehow managing to make my voice come out clear and even. "If you just want me to go with you to see the Elders, that's fine, I'll go."

I pull free of Bjarni's hand and step around him. My hands are shaking, so I stuff them in my pockets.

"Justin…"

"It's okay, love," I say, adding the last word so quietly I don't think Harkett can hear it. It's for Bjarni alone. "We already know what the Elders have decided about you and me," I say louder.

Harkett moves startlingly fast, darting forward to drag me down the steps and across the lawn. He levels the shotgun at Bjarni.

"I almost liked you, you utter waste of spunk," he says to Bjarni, and I'm standing just close enough I can see him move his finger from the trigger guard, tuck it in around the trigger, and tighten it.

And maybe I've gotten faster, too, because I grab his arm and yank and the gun goes off and it's so loud I'm deafened, my ears are ringing, and I can't tell if Bjarni is okay.

There's movement behind the porch rails and then a golden shadow knocking Harkett backwards and growling. And then I'm surrounded by werewolves and movement, and I'm confused and disoriented until a gentle grip on my arm pulls me out of the fray and back to the porch.

"Hi," says my rescuer. She smiles at me and brushes a lock of improbably long black hair out of her face. "I'm Su, Magne's girlfriend. You must be Justin."

"Um, yeah," I say, and turn back to the lawn. Where is Bjarni?

I spot him, finally, because I see Thorstein, so huge he's hard to miss, and he's holding Bjarni back as he tries to pull free, to get at Harkett.

Magne is holding Harkett's arms behind his back, and Granddad has the big thug, who looks angry and confused, by the throat. The Elders have made a ring around all of them and are watching.

When I see how Bjarni is fighting Thorstein's hold, I relax. He can't be hurt that bad. But then I see the blood.

"Oh, God," I say, and almost fling myself down the stairs. But Su catches me, and she's impossibly strong.

"He's okay," she says. "Just wait and let Thorstein do his pack leader schtick."

Something makes me trust her, and I let her pull me away from the stairs. "You don't even like Bjarni," I say, and she laughs.

"I have good reason not to," she says. "But I also know the real culprit was their asshole father."

Bjarni finally stops fighting his brother, and Thorstein leads him over to the porch, to me. They're both scowling, but when Bjarni sees me, his expression softens. "Are you okay?" he says.

I nod. "You're not," I say. "He shot you."

"Thanks to you, he mostly missed," Bjarni says.

Thorstein snorts. "He also had his gun loaded with bird shot. You'll be picking pellets out of his chest for days, but he'll be fine."

He looks back at where the Elders surround Harkett and his henchman. The big new werewolf sits sullenly on the grass.

"I have no idea what the fuck we're going to do with that one," Thorstein says. "He didn't know what Harkett told him was wrong, but he's real fucking piece of work."

Magne comes over to join us, leaving the Elders to do whatever they need to do. Whatever is happening is quiet enough I only catch the odd word, until Harkett yells and we all look at him.

"Fuck you!" he says. "You're all wrong. All of you."

The Elders just wait until he's done ranting, then the silver-haired woman – Leah – says, "Justin, come here please."

This time, Thorstein lets Bjarni take my hand and come with me and follows us himself.

I stop in front of Leah and wait. "It is werewolf custom that the injured party may execute the guilty party's punishment personally. Do you wish to do so?"

"What's his punishment?" I say, even though I already know. It feels wrong, but I also can't feel bad about it.

"Death," Bjarni says gently.

"I – No. I… I don't want to do that. I –" I look at Bjarni, at Thorstein, at Leah. They all look grave, serious, but none of them is judging me for not wanting to kill my attacker with my own hands.

"Fucking pussy," Harkett says. "At least have the guts to do it yourself."

"Even if I wanted to," I say. "He'd just order me not to, then he'd kill me. And even if he didn't order me, he'd kill me anyway, because he's stronger than me."

"You would be given assistance," Leah says.

I shake my head, grip Bjarni's hand so tight I can feel his bones grind together. He doesn't complain.

"Will you choose someone to act on your behalf?"

"I –" But Bjarni speaks up before I can finish the sentence, which is okay, because I didn't know how to finish it, anyway.

"As Justin's bonded partner, I claim the right to act on his behalf." I look at him in horror – not that he'd do this for me, but at the thought of how it might affect him to *have* to do it.

"Are you sure, Little Bear?" Thorstein says. "As pack leader, I can take that responsibility myself."

"I'm sure."

"You don't need this on your conscience," says Magne, there so suddenly and so quietly I jump.

"Neither does he," snarls Bjarni, jerking his head at Thorstein.

Magne makes a face, but nods. "You're right. Let me."

"You don't need this, either."

"I've already done it once," Magne says, eyes flicking towards the porch where Su, now joined by Raine, waits. "What's one more?"

"No," says Bjarni.

Leah interjects, calm and reasonable. "It is Bjarni's right to act for his partner." She looks at me. Everyone looks at me. I look only at Bjarni.

"Please, *kjaereste*. Let me do this for you." Does he know I can't resist him when he says, "please"?

"I don't want… I don't want this to change you. To… hurt you."

He turns me to face him directly, puts a hand on each side of my face and rests his forehead on mine. I can smell his blood, his cedar-soap scent.

I rest my palms on his chest.

"Let me do this for you," he says. "It fucking kills me that I couldn't protect you. Let me make sure he'll never hurt you, or anyone else, ever again. Please."

I shake my head and press myself against him. "Oh, God," I say. "Please be safe." Then I step back, and nod.

"Okay?" he says.

"Okay," I whisper.

He squeezes my shoulder and steps around me. "You better start running, you utter shite," he snarls at Harkett. "And start praying to whichever god you think might give a rat's ass what happens to you."

Harkett sneers back. "Fuck you. Fuck all of you Thorvaldson faggot-lovers. I'll see you in Hell." Then the Elders step aside.

"Jens Harkett, you have been sentenced to be hunted to death," says Leah. "For the crimes of rape, murder, and changing three humans to werewolves without properly informing them of the consequences."

He spits at her feet, and she snorts.

"Run. Now," she says, and he snarls, strips off his clothes, and runs, changing shape as he goes, heading farther into the farm.

When he's gone, she says, "How long of a head start did we agree on?"

"We didn't," says the very wolfish Elder.

"Hmm." She turns to Bjarni. "Off you go then."

He undresses, hands me his jeans and t-shirt and is gone so fast I hardly see him move.

"Thorstein," she says. "Magne." The brothers step forward. "Will you oversee?" They both nod and head more slowly for the trees, remaining in human shape.

"I suggest we all wait at the farmhouse," says Leah. "I believe Colleen mentioned a vat of chicken stew and endless loaves of fresh-baked bread."

I try to force down some stew while I wait, but I only manage a few bites, and only when Raine practically forces the spoon to my lips. Finally, I pretend to be going to the bathroom and slip out the front door to pace back and forth on the porch.

The moon rises, past full, but I can just feel it singing in my veins. I watch the stars come out, and the moon get higher and begin to descend.

When I hear the door open, I turn, trying to think of some way to convince Raine or Colleen or whoever it is that I don't need to wait inside. But it's Magne's girlfriend, Su.

"Hey," she says.

"Hi," I say.

She leans on the railing next to where I've been pacing and stares out into the dark. She's not a werewolf, but I can't tell what she is. She smells human, but also not human, and I already know she's way stronger than she should be. She's tall and a little curvy and very beautiful, and if I was attracted to women, I'd probably find her overwhelming.

"I've been where you are," she says, quietly. She seems kind of introverted, and didn't talk much over stew, though there were lots of other people to fill the void.

I lean on the rail and try to appear calm. "Oh?"

"Mm." She looks down at her hands, then back out at the night. "I mean, Magne and I weren't together yet. But he… he did for me what Bjarni's doing for you. Hunted down my rapist."

"You? But you're so strong."

"Not when the prick attacked me, I wasn't."

"That's what Magne meant when he said, 'What's one more?' When he offered to do this so Bjarni wouldn't have to?"

"Did he say that? Yes, I imagine that's what he meant." She sighs and turns to look at me. "It sucks, because you know putting the responsibility for the violent death of a thinking being on him is going to change him, somehow. Hurt him maybe. But *not* letting him do it would torment him just as much. Maybe more, in some ways. Especially for someone like Bjarni."

"What do you mean, for someone like Bjarni?"

"He's tough, he's strong, and he's had to stand by while his father tried to destroy both of his brothers."

"Yeah," I say, wondering how she can know him so well, when she doesn't actually know him at all.

"He's used to being the strong one, but…" She pauses and straightens up from the railing. "He's going to need you to be strong. But you can't let him know you're doing it." She laughs.

"I…" What do I say to that? "Thank you."

"No problem." She goes back in and doesn't even try to convince me to go with her. And having someone understand exactly what I'm feeling eases the desperate ache in my guts, even as it makes me want to cry. Again.

Inside the house, the murmur of half-heard conversation goes on, and maybe I should go back in, but I couldn't bear to sit there and make polite small talk while the man I love is putting himself at risk to deal with my problem. I can't bear this.

But I have no choice, do I? So I pace and worry, and it gets darker. And finally I notice the crickets in the grass along the side of the house have gone quiet. I hear soft footsteps.

Out of the shadows come the shapes of three large men, the shortest in the middle.

I run down the stairs to meet them. Thorstein and Magne walk on each side of Bjarni, holding his arms at the elbow. He's covered in blood.

"Oh, my God," I say, and cover my mouth with both hands. I feel sick. I feel terrified. And I push those feelings aside.

"Most of the blood isn't his," Magne says.

"I'm okay, *kjaereste*," Bjarni says. His voice is raw. "It's over."

I reach out hesitantly, take his hand, and his fingers are strong on mine.

"Take him home, Justin," Thorstein says, so gently I very nearly do cry. "Clean him up and put him to bed."

"I'm fine," Bjarni says. "Though I admit I could use a hot shower and a stiff drink."

"You're in shock," Magne says. "I've been there, remember?"

"Okay," I say. "Come on, sweetheart." I don't try to make the endearment only for his ears this time. I don't care if his brothers hear. I tug on Bjarni's hand.

He lets me lead him home, lets me undress him and sit him in the tub. I wash him gently, hosing away the blood with the detachable shower head, scrub his hair, and carefully rinse where the bird shot hit him. It's already healing and as I watch, several steel pellets fall out and hit the bottom of the tub with a plink.

I try not to be freaked out at how docile he suddenly is, or when he abruptly leans forward, retching, and vomits into the tub. I just rise it down the drain and get him a glass of water, force myself to be calm, to be the strong one for once.

Then I dry him off and lead him to bed, tuck him in, and crawl under the blankets next to him. He curls away from me, and I curl around him as much as I can, since he's so much bigger than me.

For while we just lie together. I can feel from his breathing, from the tension in his muscles, that he's not asleep.

"He's dead," he finally says.

"I know." I stroke his hair.

"I think…" he says. "Maybe I should have left. The other night. Gone far away so you could find someone else to be happy with."

"What?" My whole body feels cold, my fingers and toes tingling like I've been out in the snow. I feel like I've been punched in the throat, kicked in the solar plexus.

"I ripped his fucking entrails out," Bjarni says.

I make myself stay calm when I want to scream. When I want to demand to know what he meant about leaving me. Instead, I stroke his arm, kiss the back of his neck and say, "You don't have to tell me."

"I wanted to make him suffer for what he did to you," he says. "And I'm not fucking sorry. I... I'm not a good man, Justin. I'm violent, cruel. You deserve so much better than me. If I'd left, if I'd refused the symbiont bond, you could have that someday." He curls up tighter, pulling away from me. "Instead, you're stuck with me. I'm sorry."

I try to think carefully, rationally. I need to be the strong one, to soothe him. But I'm suddenly furious at him.

"Fuck you, Bjarni Thorvaldson," I say, like I'm stating a simple fact. He jerks like I've hit him.

"I'm sorry."

"Fuck what I deserve, what you deserve, what anyone deserves. What about what I *want*?"

"Justin," he says, anguish in his voice. "You should have only good things. You –"

I cut him off, viciously. "No. Fuck that. I fucking want *you*, you asshole." I wrap my arms around him, press myself into his back. "You're fucking mine," I say. "And I'm yours. And you can fuck right off if you regret symbiont-bonding with me."

"No, I didn't – That's not what I meant." He twists in my arms, like he's trying to look at me, but I bury my face between his shoulder blades.

"We're a team, Bjarni. And I love you." I take a deep breath. "Unless you're trying to tell me you don't want me."

"No. Gods, no. I love you. I want you. I'm just fucking stupid."

"Yes," I say. "You are."

"I don't regret anything. Not loving you, or bonding with you, or killing that asswipe who hurt you. I promise, *kjaereste*. I'm still yours. Only yours."

"Good."

And maybe he actually needed someone to get mad at him, because after that, he sleeps. But I can't. I lie next to him, watch over him, stroke his hair when he gets restless. And slowly, the night passes.

Very early, the birds begin to sing, and he stirs. It's still dark, dawn still a ways off despite the cacophony of birdsong, but I don't need daylight to see him with my werewolf eyes.

While he was sleeping, I rummaged in the bathroom and found the bottle of massage oil he'd used on my legs, what seems like a very long time ago now. It's on the nightstand, and when he stretches, I nudge him until he rolls over, onto his belly.

"Let me rub your back," I say. "You've been tense all night. I don't know how you can sleep so tense."

"Mmm," he says, groggy when he's usually awake instantly. I push the blankets back and sit astride his thighs, rub oil on my hands and run them over his back. I don't really know how to give a proper massage, but I know what feels good to me, so I follow the shape of the long muscles along his spine, press and rub and knead, and he makes appreciative sounds.

Even though I've seen him naked and put my mouth on most of his body, I've never really spent a lot of time looking at him from behind, except maybe to check out his ass. He has fewer werewolf scars on his back, but plenty of smooth, sculpted muscle, that bull tattoo, skin freckled where the sun hits him the most.

I trace the shape of every muscle, and when I've explored his back, I rub his shoulders, his neck, down one leg and up the other. Then I bite my lip, add more oil to my hands, and stroke the big muscles of his perfect ass.

He groans and twists his head to look at me from half-closed eyes. "That feels good," he says, and pushes his butt against my hands. I dig my fingers in and try to ignore the fact that touching his superb ass is giving me a raging hard-on.

When I rub my hands up from the dip of his thigh over the round of his butt, my thumbs slip between his cheeks and he grunts.

"Sorry," I say. "This oil is slippery."

He snorts. "No," he says. "Do it again." So I slide my fingers into his butt crack and he gasps when I find his anus. "Is this okay?' I say, doing it again, lingering, rubbing the circular muscle firmly.

"Fuck yes." His hands tighten on the sheets and his breathing goes uneven.

"Do you want my fingers in you?" I say, surprised at my own boldness, but refusing to stop now. I'm enjoying it. *He's* enjoying it.

"Yes," he says, so I press two fingers inside him and he pushes back against them, a soft moan escaping his throat. Then he says, "No," and I stop, pull my fingers away.

"I want *you* in me," he says, and I freeze with my fingertips just touching him.

"You mean…?"

"Fuck me, Justin," he says, tilting his head to rest his brow on the pillow.

I massage him some more, wondering where my boldness suddenly went.

"Gods, Justin, I want you," he says and twists to look at me again. He rummages in the nightstand, finds a condom, and hands it to me. "I need you."

"Okay," I say. "Okay." And I tear open the package, roll on the condom, and smear lube on myself. I press the head of my cock to his anus and hesitate. I mean, it's not like I've never topped before, it's just… he's always been the dominant one. But he's sprawled there, legs open, wanting me. My erection throbs in my hand and I press harder against him.

"Yes," he says, so I push harder, slowly, feel him open to me, push in more and watch myself disappear into his beautiful ass.

"Oh, my God," I say. I grip his hip, nudge his left leg straighter and his right more bent so he's half-rolled onto his side, and lay myself along his back, reach around him and find his cock with my lube-slippery hand, stroke him and listen to his breathing lurch.

I match my thrusts to my strokes, feel him arch his head back, clench his jaw, and try to hold in the noises of pleasure that want to escape him. I shift my position along his back so I can reach his hair with my free hand, slide my fingers through its silken strands, clench my hand into a fist, and yank.

He responds with a sound I can't interpret so I start to loosen my hold, but he growls, "Harder." I don't know if he means pull his hair harder, stroke him harder, or fuck him harder, so I do all three and he moans. His teeth flash, descending from a jaw that elongates to accommodate them.

I feel like I might lose control as my own werewolf teeth descend in response, and my claws extend. I let go of his hardness to run my hand over his chest, his belly, letting him feel my claws before wrapping my fingers around him again.

"Fuck, yes," he says, words almost lost in a panting moan, and he bucks under me, and roars, and there's the patter of semen hitting the mattress that goes on longer than it seems like it should.

I move my hand to his hip, watch my claws break the skin as I grip, hard, watch him heal almost immediately, and I can't hold back, can't stop, and I don't even know what kind of noise is coming out of me.

When I collapse onto his back, he sighs, reaches over to pull my thigh over him, and relaxes against the mattress.

I manage, somehow, to pull tissues from the box on the nightstand, clean myself up, and wipe up some of the mess on the sheets. He rolls over and looks at me, and I swear it's wonder I'm seeing on his face. He grins.

"My fierce, beautiful wolf," he says.

A flush creeps up my neck and I bury my face in his armpit. "Only sometimes," I say, and he chuckles.

Then he pulls the blankets up over us both and something feels settled between us, healed, and sleep claims me quickly.

At breakfast the next morning, he lures me out to the porch swing with a mug of tea and a bacon-and-egg sandwich. He sits and contemplates his own sandwich before taking a careful bite. I sense something in the tension of his shoulders. There's something he wants to say that he hasn't been able to say yet.

"That night," he finally begins, setting his plate aside. "The one… when you ended up at Thorstein's."

I swallow a bite of egg that suddenly feels dry and hard in my throat. Is he going to tell me he lied, that he had fucked someone else after all?

"I drove around most of the night." He stares at his hands, rubs a bit of bacon grease off. "After I called Katie and she told me to go home, I went to see Granddad." He looks up at me, bites his lip, looks away again.

"I was going to save this until after Freysblöt was over, but…" He hesitates, then digs into his pocket and pulls something out that clinks in his grip. "What Leah said made me think maybe I should just do it now."

He licks his lips and holds out his hand, and in his big palm are two silver rings, twined about by twisting Viking designs, not unlike the ones inked on his forearms.

He looks at the rings instead of at me. "Granddad and Grandma wore these when they were betrothed. He gave them to me that night." Now he does look up at me, eyes raw. "When I told him I thought I was falling in love with you." He takes a breath. "I told him before I said anything to anyone else. I didn't know yet… I hadn't been home, hadn't seen that you were gone."

I can't keep looking into his eyes, or at the rings, so I stare down at my own hands, fingers tangled in my lap. "Why didn't he give them to Thorstein? Or Magne?"

"Thorstein has our mother's ring to give Raine. And Magne's the youngest, and I don't think he was planning on getting married this soon."

I make myself look at the shining silver in his outstretched palm, but I don't dare touch it.

"Justin?"

"Yeah?"

"Please look at me."

I do. His eyes are soft, the raw look still there but tempered by something else, something gentler.

"Don't say yes if you don't want to. I really don't want you to feel pressured. But…" He takes a deep breath. "Marry me?"

My breath comes out in a rush, and I feel dizzy. I reach out and touch the smaller ring with the tip of one finger.

"Will you?" he says. "Will you let the pack witness us plighting our troth tonight?" He breathes carefully, like he's about to lose control and is desperate not to. "Or do you want to wait? I know we haven't really known each other that long…"

Maybe he doesn't want me to feel pressured, but how could I not?

"Tell me one thing," I say.

"Anything."

"Do you really want this? Do you really want me, or is it just the symbiont bond?"

"Yes. I want this. I want you. Fuck, Justin, how many times are you going to make me say it?"

"One more," I say, letting a smile curl my lips. Letting it turn into a stupid grin.

"I want you." He grins back at me.

I let my smile grow even more and pick up both rings. I slide one onto Bjarni's finger, and one onto my own. They fit perfectly, like they were always meant to be there.

About the Author

NICO SILVER LIVES like a hermit on the edge of the woods, but haunts used bookstores like a wraith. They fully expected to be found someday as a mummified old corpse crushed under a toppled to-be-read pile, but the rise of e-books has made that somewhat less likely, though the books will always outnumber even the dustbunnies. Nico will read just about anything, including the instructions on the back of medicine bottles, but has a particular fondness for good stories with a hint of magic. They write dark, sexy urban fantasy, and sometimes dream in black and white.

www.ingramcontent.com/pod-product-compliance
Lightning Source LLC
Chambersburg PA
CBHW022124310726
48972CB00007B/2179